JACK LOOKED AROUND THE ROOM. IT APPEARED COMPLETELY EMPTY.

"Seamus Muldoon," Jack called.

"Who?" Kathleen asked.

Jack peered into the corners for any sign of the leprechaun. "He and his family share this cottage with me."

Kathleen shook her head. "No one shares this cottage with you."

"He's a leprechaun," Jack explained.

Kathleen's voice was heavy with sarcasm. "Oh, *that* Seamus Muldoon. I look forward to meeting him."

Jack had a sudden doubt. He hadn't really prepared Kathleen for any of this. "You'll be all right, won't you?" he asked. "I mean, you won't do anything stupid if they show themselves, will you?"

"Of course not," she snapped. "I'll mind my manners."

Well, at least he'd warned her. He turned back to the middle of the room.

"Seamus, are you there? If you could make yourself visible, I'd appreciate it. It's a bit of an emergency."

Two leprechauns popped into existence in the middle of the room in all their green-plaid finery.

"Seamus and Mary Muldoon, at your service," Seamus announced with a little bow.

Kathleen fainted dead away.

Well, Jack thought, it could have gone worse.

He rushed off to get some water.

LEPRECHAUNS

Craig Shaw Gardner

Based on a screenplay
by Peter Barnes

HALLMARK ENTERTAINMENT BOOKS

HALLMARK ENTERTAINMENT BOOKS are published by

Kensington Publishing Corp.
850 Third Avenue
New York, NY 10022

First Hallmark Entertainment Books Paperback Printing:
November, 1999
10 9 8 7 6 5 4 3 2 1

Printed in the United States of America

Part One

Prologue

At first, all you see is color. A flash of brilliant yellow, perhaps, as bright as the first rays of morning, or a red so pure it might take your breath. You blink and realize the color comes from the single petal of a wildflower—one of a thousand such flowers filling the field before you and every one of them just now opening to the sunshine.

What is that?

It is something you might have seen just out of the corner of your eye, something almost hidden amid the riot of flowers, something that happened so quickly it might have sprung from your imagination.

It is something that you've never seen before.

Did the petals move all on their own? Or was there something that helped them along, tiny hands moving so quickly that you only got the merest glimpse before they are gone?

It has to be a trick of the light. Or something in the country air. And yet . . . and yet . . .

The morning breeze carries upon it the faintest of sounds, the tinkling of distant bells, perhaps, or the laughter of a hundred tiny voices. Or maybe it is only the wind after all.

You look at the panorama before you: the multicolored wildflowers on the hill surrounded by lush, living green and a sky of deepest blue. In the distance, you swear you can see the beginnings of a rainbow.

You've heard the phrase "picture perfect" many times. Until this moment, you realize you never understood what it meant.

The hundreds of flowers shake, although the breeze is gone. The disturbance is very specific, as if a small tremor is passing only through the field before you. A streak of gold flashes up from the flowers, rushing past in the blink of an eye.

It is gone in a heartbeat, if there was ever anything there in the first place.

Yet in that instant, you see it clearly. It is a flying creature, but not an insect. Small as it is, it is shaped like a person—a person with wings. And it looks very frightened indeed.

You blink again. A little person with wings. Have you seen a fairy—a very frightened fairy?

What could scare a fairy so?

You hear a rumble. The ground shakes beneath your feet.

The peace is shattered once and for all. You turn to watch the intruder approach.

The ancient iron engine rumbles down the track, steam belching from its smokestack. The engineer pulls a cord. A low, mournful whistle is heard throughout the valley.

The train is coming.

You shake your head. The train brings you back to reality. The countryside is playing tricks on you.

Who, even in a place like this, believes in fairies?

Chapter One

To Jack Woods, this was a whole different world.

He looked out the window of his train compartment. Although the space with its two facing benches might easily sit four, he had the little room all to himself. It gave him the sense that, for a change, he really had gotten away from it all. He gazed out the window at the rolling hills, glimpses of forests and farms, but mostly thousands upon thousands of wildflowers. Here, alone in this little rattling compartment, he felt as if this particular corner of Ireland was putting on a show just for him.

Jack sighed.

He didn't even want to look at the documents he had brought along or think about the work ahead of him. He'd spread them out before him, intending to review them before his arrival, but then he had taken one look at the scenery and everything else was forgotten.

His boss's voice echoed in his head.

"Remember this is not a vacation, okay? You're there to do a job."

Jack Woods was always on the job. He gazed out at the passing countryside, the rolling hills full of flowers. He had never seen anything quite so peaceful. It seemed as though time had stopped in this little corner of the world, and no one had ever heard of mergers and acquisitions and stock options. Jack sighed. He heard all too much about that sort of thing every day of the week. Now maybe, just maybe, for a few hours at least, he could pretend he was on vacation.

The train whistle interrupted his reverie. They would be coming into the station. He quickly gathered his papers together.

He was met at the station by Bert Bagnell, the estate agent who would show him to his rental cottage. They shook hands and exchanged pleasantries, Bagnell smiling all the while.

There was something about Mr. Bagnell that Jack did not precisely trust. Perhaps it was the way he would never quite look you in the face when he was talking to you, especially when he was reassuring you as to this or that fine point of their agreement. Still, Bagnell seemed quite open in his way. And he was certainly talkative. Surely, that shifty gaze was some odd local mannerism.

Jack forgot all about it when Bagnell ushered him from the platform and through the station, out to their transportation. It was an old-fashioned cart and horse. Jack remembered, from some cable documentary he'd seen, probably, that this particular rig was called a "trap." Not that he had ever expected to see one in real life.

Bagnell lifted the luggage into the cart bed, then waved for Jack to get up on the seat. The estate agent jumped up on the other side. Bagnell shook the reins, and the horse started off, slow but steady. They moved through an Irish village that looked as if it hadn't changed much in the last hundred years.

Jack was amazed by both his surroundings and mode of travel. He bounced back and forth as they clattered across the cobblestoned streets, a dozen small homes and shops to either side, the gray stone buildings brightened by dozens of window boxes overflowing with flowers.

At the edge of the village, the cobblestones were replaced by a rutted dirt road. Rutted and bumpy, with plenty of large rocks for the wheels to jar themselves on.

It might have been picturesque, but it wasn't smooth. Apparently, fine old carts like this did not include shock absorbers.

Still, the day was clear and sunny. A gentle breeze blew to cool the air. Over the intermittent clatter of the bouncing cart, Jack could hear the calls of a dozen different birds.

"So was it a good trip, Mr. Woods?"

Bagnell's voice brought Jack back to the here and now. He tried to nod. The cart hit another rock and his chin struck his chest.

"Fine, thank you. Yes," he managed.

"Not too much of the old turbulence, then? On the aeroplane?"

"No. It was okay."

"It was okay." Bagnell considered that for a moment. "That's good. Must be a terrible thing being bounced about like that."

As opposed to being bounced around like this? The cart clattered into and out of another rut, lifting Jack's backside six inches from the seat. All this up and down was making his teeth ache. Surely there had to be a better way of getting around the countryside.

"Don't you have a car?" he asked between bone-shaking bumps.

"Oh, yes, a fine one," the other man said. "But I don't use it too much since the Fitzpatrick brothers got their van fixed. The traffic's been too bad."

He drove the cart over a small stone bridge. The horse paused for an instant, and Jack got a good look at the meandering stream that had green hills to either side.

"It's very beautiful here," Jack said.

Bagnell's smile grew even broader as he looked over the countryside. " 'Very desirable,' as we say in the trade."

He shook the reins and told Jack that their destination was just over the next rise. The horse trotted on, the road a bit less treacherous on this side of the stream.

They reached the top of a small hill and started down the other side. Jack saw the cottage ahead. It was a small stone structure with a thatched roof and a flower garden. The same stream they had crossed a moment before ran directly behind it. Green grass rose to either side of the house, making the cottage look as if it was in its own little hollow.

The estate agent pulled the cart within a few feet of the front door.

Jack was quite taken with the place. "You weren't kidding, Mr. Bagnell. It's stunning."

"Did I not say so?" The estate agent jumped down from his seat.

Jack jumped down from the other side, his eyes still on the cottage. "Short of painting it shamrock green, it couldn't be more Irish."

Bagnell considered that.

"Well, as it happens, I do have a small decorating business on the side."

"No, it's okay—"

Jack blinked. Didn't the curtain just move? He pointed at the window.

"Is there someone living there?" he asked.

"No, no," Bagnell insisted. "That'll just be the wind."

Jack noticed the estate agent wasn't looking at him again.

Bagnell stomped upon the front step, bumped his shoulder against the door, then rattled the handle. He was making an awful lot of noise, almost as if he were warning someone—or something—to get out of the way.

Woods grabbed his luggage from the back of the trap. Two suitcases, his briefcase, and a set of golf clubs. Somehow, he managed to get all of them through the front door in one trip.

The front room was all built from natural wood, save for the large stone fireplace along one wall. The furnishings were simple but charming. The rough-hewn table, the high-backed chairs, the iron kettles and amber-colored bottles along the wall—this place could have come out of the nineteenth century.

Jack could only think of one thing to say. "Wow."

He let his bags fall to the floor and slowly strolled across the room.

"Wow, yes," Bagnell agreed. "You have a way there with words, Mr. Woods. You'll not see anything finer in the whole of Kerry—"

"Ow!"

"Mind the beam!" Bagnell called a second too late. No doubt he meant well.

Jack looked up at the low wooden brace that ran the length of the room. Apparently, this place was made for folks considerably shorter than himself. As he rubbed his head, Jack glanced back at the estate agent.

"It's a house for little people," Jack said.

Bagnell looked sharply up, straight at him.

"No. No, it's not. Not at all."

Odd that he should object to that. Probably another of those local eccentricities. Jack stopped rubbing his head and nodded. "It's exactly what I'm looking for."

"Good, good. You're here for a little of the old rest and recuperation, you were saying?"

Well, that was the official story. Jack nodded again. "That's right. Maybe do some fishing."

He looked around. He didn't see any switches on the wall.

"How do the lights work?"

"There are oil lamps in all the rooms." The agent waved to one on a table by Jack's side.

"No electricity?"

Well, Jack thought, that was sort of charming, too.

"No, it's too far to carry it."

Jack stepped through into the kitchen, careful to duck beneath the low beam.

"And the stove is oil, too?"

Bagnell followed him into the room, shaking his head.

"That burns peat. Straight from the bog, dried, and it makes a powerful fire."

Jack wondered if he had this right. "So to cook I set fire to . . . dirt."

"And you'll never want to use anything else. Will you be taking the let?"

Jack grinned. "Show me where to sign, Mr. Bagnell."

Bagnell nodded and led the way back out to the horse and trap. The papers were back at the estate office. Even here, Jack thought, he couldn't completely get away from contracts.

Jack looked back at the storybook cottage as Bagnell was about to climb on the cart. "I can't believe I'm getting it so cheaply. There's nothing you haven't told me about it, is there?''

"No, no. It's just that letting is a bit slow this time of year what with it being the"—Bagnell paused to clear his throat—"summer and all."

He spun about before Jack could say another word, then reached beneath the front seat of the trap and groped for a moment before he brought forth something the size and shape of a wine bottle, except that it was made of stone.

"And here to celebrate your new home," Bagnell said grandly, "a traditional housewarming gift for you."

"What is it?"

"Irish poteen," Bagnell said with a fair amount of pride. "The finest."

"Poteen?" Jack took the bottle in his hands. The stone was cool to the touch. "That's like whiskey?"

Bagnell frowned at the bottle. "A wee touch stronger maybe. Best not drunk close to a flame and try not to touch your gums on the way down."

Jack smiled. It was a nice gesture. Maybe he had Bagnell all wrong. "Well, thank you. I'll leave it in the cottage for later."

He turned and walked back to the front door. Bagnell started to say something behind him. He would talk to the agent as soon as he'd taken the bottle safely inside. This would only take a minute. He grabbed the door handle and pushed.

Jack grunted in surprise. The door wouldn't budge. Well, actually it would, just a bit, but then it would slam back into place, almost as though there were someone inside pushing back against it the other way.

Bagnell was at his side, frowning down at the knob.

"I think it's stuck," Jack admitted. He placed the poteen

on the ground by the door, then reached up to try with both hands.

"Ah," Bagnell said after a moment, "let me try. These old doors can sometimes be a bit sticky."

Jack stepped aside, and the estate agent took his place. Bagnell paused for a moment, then quite suddenly pushed his shoulder sharply against the door. Jack thought he heard someone cry out on the other side. He certainly heard a crash and a clatter, as if something had gone flying inside.

"What was that?" he demanded.

"Just mice," Bagnell replied, looking the other way. He grabbed the stone bottle and led the way back into the cottage.

Everything looked perfectly peaceful inside, with every chair, table, and knickknack still where Jack had last seen them. If something had gone flying, Jack couldn't see it now.

Bagnell marched into the kitchen and placed the poteen on the highest shelf in one of the cupboards. He nodded to Jack.

"It'll be safe there for your return."

Bagnell marched smartly out again. Jack hurried to follow. They climbed up on opposite sides of the trap.

"I'd like to move in today," Jack said.

"No problem"—Bagnell paused to urge the horse forward—"provided we have the four weeks' rent in advance."

"Done."

The horse was off at a trot. Jack turned around in his seat to get one final look at the cottage.

Maybe it was the breeze. Maybe it was some distortion in the old windowpane. But the curtains looked as if they were moving again.

Chapter Two

Jack Woods paused for perhaps the hundredth time that day just to look at the countryside. He was at the edge of a copse of trees, and the stream that wound its way all around the village appeared to widen into a small pool ahead.

The light was slowly fading. The sun had sunk toward the horizon, sending its rays streaming through the leaves. The light sparkled where it hit the water, bright white against the blue.

If this wasn't the most beautiful place upon the face of the Earth, Jack couldn't imagine what was. He and Bagnell had taken the bumpy ride back to the estate office and concluded their business in less than fifteen minutes. It was a far cry from the complicated contracts he usually saw at Sperry, Sperry, and McGurk.

He was in no hurry to return to the cottage. He had brought his shoulder pack along with his camera and a dozen rolls of film. He'd spent the entire afternoon strolling back in the general direction of his new rental and paused to take photos of many of the most scenic and charming corners along the way: rolling hills, quaint cottages, fields full of flowers. That was part of his job, after all.

At moments, the vistas through the camera's viewfinder would be so magnificent that Jack would actually feel a little guilty. He remembered stories about how, when certain primitive tribes first encountered cameras, the tribespeople were afraid they would steal their souls.

Could a camera steal the soul of a village? Jack was surprised at the thought as soon as it entered his mind. And yet, once he sent these shots back to the home office, this place was likely to change forever.

He'd worry about that later. Right now, he just wanted to enjoy the scenery. The sky was getting a bit dark for picture taking anyway. It was time at last to stroll toward home.

It felt good to walk, after the confines of the train and that less-than-comfortable ride in Bagnell's trap. Besides, the cottage was less than a mile from the center of the village.

Something rose from the pond's center with a whoosh of water. It was a woman. Since she had her back to Jack, she couldn't see him. She was rather like the Lady of the Lake rising to give Arthur Excaliber. You could believe that sort of thing in a place like this. While the lady did not have a sword, she also wasn't wearing any clothes.

She tossed her head. Her hair, because it was soaking wet, looked raven black, yet it shone with shades of red in the late-day sun.

It was a wondrously attractive back too, but, you know, perhaps he shouldn't be watching this. Some people might not think he had stumbled innocently upon this scene. Some might even take offense. It would be better if he quietly crept away.

She was a beautiful woman. Jack found it hard to pull his gaze away. Still, if he just quietly turned after a final glance . . .

Jack almost tripped and fell. He looked down at the ground.

His foot had gotten stuck in a mass of roots. Served him right for not looking where he was going. It was really wedged in there. Jack half wanted to swear, but he dared not say a thing. He had to get out of here before the lady of the lake looked his way.

The foot didn't want to come free no matter how he tugged. He'd have to untie his shoe, pull his foot free, then rescue the shoe too. It would just take a second. He sat down, putting his shoulder bag by his side.

He looked up. The woman was staring at him.

She looked straight at him. And he looked straight at her.

Jack realized he wasn't breathing. She truly was a beautiful woman. Red hair, green eyes, high cheekbones, full lips. And then, of course, there was the rest of her. He could sit and look in silence for a very long time, if he got to look at the likes of her.

She screamed.

The embarrassment came flooding back. Jack fumbled quickly with his shoe.

"Who are you?" the woman demanded.

Jack did his best not to look back at her naked—ahem. He turned and focused on the shoe, trying to stammer some sort of apology. "Er—sorry, but . . ."

Now she was getting properly angry. "Get out of here! I'll set the dogs on you!"

Jack could feel the sweat dripping down his forehead. Why couldn't he get his shoe untied?

"No—no—you don't understand," he tried again, still not quite looking at her.

"I understand well enough, you damned Peeping Tom!"

She turned and strode out of the pool. When she was mad, she looked magnificent. Jack reminded himself he was trying to get out of here. He glanced up again and saw she had a towel draped around her. And she was bending toward the ground, picking up rocks.

"I was just walking—" The foot pulled out of his shoe and jerked up into the air. He almost fell over. "I didn't realize—" He reached down and grabbed the shoe. It pulled free more easily than he'd expected. He almost fell over again. He looked up at the woman. "I'm very sorry."

He stood up, hopping on one foot. If he could get this shoe on quickly . . .

"You'll be sorrier when my brothers get you!" she cried, lifting one of the rocks in her hand. "I've seen your face!"

"I didn't mean any harm!" Jack called back. Now he couldn't get the shoe back on his foot. "I've only just got here and— Oww!"

The first rock she threw hit his shoulder.

That hurt. He grabbed his shoulder bag, his foot still not quite in his shoe, and stumbled away as best he could as the young woman tossed a few more rocks his way.

"I'll know you again when I see you!"

Jack ducked. He wished he could see her again. She looked magnificent.

Jack blew out another match before it burned his fingers. These oil lamps were solidly built, lovely to look at, and no doubt valuable antiques. What they weren't was convenient.

He had made it back to the cottage in one piece, if a bit sore in the shoulder. He thought, after all that adventure, he'd spend his evening reading. It was only now that he realized he'd really be spending it getting a trio of these antique things properly lit.

The theory here was simple enough. You took off the lamp's glass top, then held a flame to the top of the cloth wick, which descended into the lower part of the lamp, which held a reservoir of oil. It was a foolproof design. People had used these things for hundreds of years.

Then why was it taking Jack so long to light it?

Maybe the wicks had all dried out. He sloshed the base of the lamp. There certainly seemed to be plenty of oil down there. The two lamps in the other rooms had lit after three or four tries, but this one so far was impossible. Maybe if he really shook the darn thing. How hard could you shake one of these without spilling anything? He certainly didn't want to get a match too close to the oil. He could see the headlines now:

AMERICAN TOURIST KILLED
IN FREAK COTTAGE FIRE!

Jack sighed. This all seemed of a piece with that embarrassing incident with the woman in the pond. For something that had started as a beautiful day, it had certainly turned itself around.

He *would* get the wick to burn. Perhaps if he put the match on the edge of the metal brace that held it.

"Damn!"

The metal was searing hot from the last three matches. He pulled his hand away and sucked his burned fingers.

He strode back into the main room, where at least he'd managed to get the other lanterns lit. Maybe he'd carry one of the lamps from room to room. Maybe he'd just as soon sleep in the dark.

It was certainly time for him to take a break, before he did further damage. His gaze wandered to the kitchen, his thoughts to that high cupboard in the corner. Maybe it was time to sample a little of that poteen.

Careful this time to duck beneath the low beam, he strode over to the spot where the estate agent had left the stone bottle.

The cupboard door was wide open.

The bottle wasn't there.

What could possibly have happened now? Jack realized he was muttering under his breath. He looked around the room.

The bottle was lying on its side in a corner on the floor. "Strange."

Maybe the old wooden shelf it had been set upon was not quite straight. Lucky for him the bottle was made of stone. Jack retrieved the bottle, then took a glass from a lower shelf. He placed the glass upon the table, then pulled on the cork that closed the bottle. It was jammed in tight.

He'd had enough trouble today with stubborn oil lamps and rock-throwing women. A cork was not going to get the better of him. He reestablished his grip on both cork and bottle, then pulled.

The cork came free with a satisfying pop. Now that was more like it.

"Okay," he said to the bottle, "let's see what you got."

He poured himself a finger of the liquor, just to get a taste.

The liquid was pale and smoky and slightly sour smelling. But, hey, the estate agent wasn't about to poison him. This poteen was some sort of Irish tradition. The least he could do was sample it.

He took the slightest sip. Tasted okay so far. He drained the glass.

"Arrrh!"

It felt as if his throat was on fire. He choked. He gasped for breath. He slapped at his neck, hoping he could get some air.

What were you supposed to say at a time like this?

Oh, yeah. He remembered.

"Smooth!" he managed to croak.

He could have sworn he heard someone laughing. He looked around again. Nothing. It must be something about this old cottage. Curtains moved. Bottles relocated. And the noises the old cottage made sounded like laughter. Oh well. Some of the folks back at Sperry, Sperry, and McGurk would find those sort of things charming.

Back to the poteen. He thought a second drink would go down easier. He poured another modest libation and took a swig.

He was wrong. The flamethrower was right back inside his throat. He leaned on the table as he gasped for air.

"What *is* this stuff made of?" he called out, mostly to see if his voice still worked.

"Potatoes, you ignoramus!" another voice replied.

Jack whirled around.

"Who's there?"

He was all alone. At least he couldn't see anyone. He wondered if the poteen was playing tricks on him.

He turned back to the table.

The bottle had moved down to the other end.

Now, Jack thought, there had to be a reasonable explanation for this. Maybe he had jumped farther than he thought when he heard the voice. If he had heard a voice. This was all very confusing.

He leaned across the table to pick the bottle back up.

He lifted it an inch off the table when something yanked it back the other way.

Jack yelped. What was there? He couldn't see a thing.

He realized he was backing away. What was the matter with his feet? His foot hit the stool. Who had put the stool there?

Jack tripped. He was headed for the ground. No, not the ground.

He saw the stove rush up to hit his forehead.

It was a shame about the tourist. He seemed to have knocked himself out cold. Served him right though in a way, when he wasn't willing to share this fine poteen. Ah, well. He'd probably wake in the morning and think all of this was a dream.

In the meantime, what to do with all this fine poteen. Another drink, or maybe two. Ah, while you're at it, why not finish the bottle? Mr. Woods surely wouldn't mind. And better he sleeps than see the bottle levitate all by itself.

Down the hatch! Glug, glug, glug.

Ah. Smooth indeed.

Actually, that fellow asleep on the floor isn't at all bad for a tourist. Some have that reaction to poteen, they do. I'll just put the empty bottle back on the table, all polite and proper.

Hic. Oh, pardon me. *Hic.*

Not bad at all.

Chapter Three

Jack opened his eyes to the most intense and horrible light he had ever seen.

It must be morning.

He managed to sit up with only a couple of sledgehammers going off in his head. He was in the kitchen, over by the stove. He remembered something about falling after he'd done a certain amount of drinking.

Drinking. His mouth felt as if he'd swallowed twenty pounds of sawdust. And that on top of the pounding and the terrible bright light.

"Not another drop," he croaked. "Never ever."

Jack winced. It even hurt to hear himself talk.

But he heard another noise around here somewhere. Snoring? Yes, definitely snoring from the other side of the room, beyond the table and chairs.

He managed to stand, with some help from that same

table, and leaned forward to see who might be on the other side.

His hand hit the stone bottle. It went flying.

It crashed to the floor with the loudest and most penetrating noise Jack had ever heard.

That wasn't the end of it though. The snoring had stopped quite abruptly, followed by a cry of alarm and something tearing across the kitchen floor.

Were these the mice the estate agent had talked about? Jack had never seen anything move that fast. Whatever it was had already rushed completely out of the cottage.

Jack's curiosity got the better of the pain in his head. He staggered over to the front door.

Augggh! The sun was even worse out here. He staggered back, shielding his eyes against the glare.

Jack wouldn't swear to anything at the moment, but if there was a small human figure weaving away from the cottage, then he was dressed in green.

"Hey!" Jack managed.

But the fleeing figure took a turn in the path and was lost behind the high weeds. Exactly how small was this fellow, after all?

Jack decided he had to find out. He launched himself from the cottage with a groan. He heard the figure crashing through the brush ahead. At least, he thought he did. It was hard to hear anything over that pounding in his head.

The sun was still too bright, the colors blurring before him as he looked from side to side. Maybe none of this was real. Maybe it was still the poteen.

No, that was a definite crash up ahead, followed, Jack thought, by some faint but colorful cursing. He took a deep breath and walked onward. The pounding was getting a bit less pronounced. If nothing else, maybe the fresh air would do him some good. The path twisted back into the woods, then out again into sunlight.

He found himself back in the same forest glade with the same pond where he'd seen the woman the day before. The place appeared to be deserted. He was just as glad she wasn't swimming this morning. He didn't want anyone to see him just now.

He heard a noise ahead—a sharp crack, like a tree branch breaking, and a cry of alarm followed by a splash.

Someone had fallen into the water just up the way. Jack hurried to the far end of the pond. He was surprised to see that the stream widened here, turning into a bit more of a river. And there, right in the middle of the rushing stream, was the fallen branch, a bit of wood maybe four feet long. A decent current pulled the branch along. As Jack watched the branch pass, he saw two small arms, as if a child were clinging to the other side.

"Hang on!" Jack called. "Hang on!"

Whoever replied, his voice was hoarse and slurred. If there was a kid on the other side of the log, he sounded drunk.

Jack moved quickly along the riverbank, trying to keep up with the floating branch. But the current was getting stronger and swifter. In a minute or two, the branch would be beyond his reach. He would have to swim for it.

He'd been a pretty good swimmer once. He would just pretend he was in another one of his college swim meets and forget about the dozen years that had passed in between. He kicked off his shoes and dove in.

He moved forward with clean, hard strokes, swimming with the current, and easily overtook the speeding branch.

"Hang on!" he called again as he grabbed the broken wood with both hands. Kicking hard, he managed to direct the branch to the riverbank. The river bent about here,

and the current wasn't as strong in the shallows. Jack stood
and dragged the branch onto dry land.

That was it. His energy was gone. He slumped down
next to the wood.

He still hadn't seen who he had rescued.

"Are you all right?" He leaned forward to get a glimpse
of whoever was on the other side of the branch.

To Jack's surprise, that whoever was staring right back
at him.

It was a small man, maybe two feet high, with bright red
chin whiskers and a very wet suit and vest in various shades
of green, not to mention a three-cornered hat that was
somehow still atop his head. He looked every bit as startled
as Jack.

They stared at each other for a full second. Then the
small fellow seemed to remember something. He shut his
eyes tightly and disappeared.

"Oh, whoa!" Jack exclaimed. He saw the branches rustle
behind the place where the little man had stood a moment
before. Other branches moved farther away, heading back
toward the path.

The little fellow might be invisible, but he wasn't hard
to follow. Jack waded a few feet up the bank to fetch his
shoes, then went crashing after his quarry.

The little fellow's retreat grew much quieter as soon as
he regained the path. Jack reached the path mere seconds
later. But without the bending branches to guide him, how
could he tell which way the small man went?

Jack saw water glistening on the bushes at the side of
the path. The little fellow was dripping, leaving a trail. He
seemed to be headed back in the direction of the cottage.

Jack hurried to follow, watching the ground as he jogged
along. He saw water droplets shining on the tops of leaves
and bits of grass. The little man was still headed back

toward the clearing before the cottage, leaving both the woods and the path behind. Jack didn't want to lose the invisible creature's trail now.

He reached the end of the path and realized that he needn't have worried. The grass was trampled ahead in a line headed straight toward the cottage. He saw a small puddle of water just outside the front door; a trail of water spots led inside.

"Oh, that's just great," Jack muttered.

At the very least, he had to go in there and change his clothes. He was every bit as wet as the little man.

"Come out, whoever you are!" he called.

He waited a long moment. There was no response. Nothing at all.

"Or I'll have to come in," Jack added.

He took a deep breath and stepped inside the cottage.

The wet trail headed for the stove. There was a puddle in the far corner. Jack grabbed a handy ladle and stepped forward.

"I know you're there," he said to the spot above the puddle. "You're dripping."

Still nothing. It was time for sterner measures. He poked the ladle through the air above the growing puddle.

"Oof!" somebody cried. "Will you stop doing that!"

The small man in green popped into sight just above the puddle. He rubbed his stomach and frowned.

"I hate water. Water is for fishes!"

Jack knew exactly what was in front of him with a sudden and terrible certainty.

"You're—you're—" he tried to say.

The small man nodded.

"A leprechaun." He looked down at his sodden jacket. "A wet leprechaun." He took a deep breath and puffed out his chest as if he would rise above his current distress.

"Leader of the Kerry leprechauns. High Marshal of the Green Order, Chief Poteen Taster to the Great Fergus." He gave the slightest of bows. "Seamus Muldoon, at your service."

"What in the Grand Banshee's name do you think you are doing?" another voice called. From the pitch and tenor of the demand, this one seemed to be a female.

Seamus frowned. "You blind? I'm talking to your man here. I have no choice. He pulled me out of the river."

"Are you mad as well as stupid?" the voice demanded.

"I have to," Seamus said a bit sheepishly. "He—saved me."

"He *saved* you?"

"He did. Gallantly, I have to say, without a thought for himself."

"You were drunk." With the flat certainty of her voice, the words were more a statement than a question.

"Of course I was drunk. There was a spare bottle handy, and the next thing you know I was up to my neck in water—" He shuddered. "I *hate* water!"

A small woman, also dressed in green, popped into existence right by Seamus's side. Even though she was only two feet high, she seemed to be the type not to be trifled with. "And you *let* him save you?" she demanded of the small man.

"I had no say in the matter, Mary. I didn't ask. He just did it!"

Jack was finding this all a bit overwhelming. He realized he was slowly backing away.

"That's no excuse," Mary pointed out. "You could have had the decency to drown."

"I could. I know. I'm sorry." Seamus hung his head, as if he were in total agreement.

"But now you're in his debt." She stabbed an accusing

finger in Jack's direction. "You know what that means?" She didn't wait for him to answer the question. "You're an idiot, Seamus Muldoon."

No matter what Jack did—blink, shake his head, rub his eyes—the scene didn't change. There were two little people having a flat-out argument right in front of his stove. Jack needed some air.

He stepped out the front door.

There, that was better. Warm sunlight, fresh country air, gentle breezes blowing.

And no little people arguing.

"Get a grip," he said aloud. If he said it aloud, it had to be true. There had to be some reason—no, *reasons*— behind all of this. "It's jet lag—it's that poisonous brew— hangover—bump on the head—I'm fine."

He took a few steps down the front path and turned to look at the cottage.

He jumped. Maybe he screamed.

The two little people were standing on the doorstep. Right next to the bootscrape. They were as high as the bootscrape, maybe two feet tall. And both of them were dressed in brightest green.

Jack blinked. The female half of the duo appeared to be talking to him now.

"I'm Mary Muldoon, Seamus's wife for my sins, of which there must have been hundreds to have such a terrible fate."

Seamus shook his head at that. "They say married men live longer than single ones. It only seems like it."

Mary shot him a withering look. "And you spend most of the time reading our marriage license, looking for a loophole."

They paused, as if they'd just remembered that Jack was still there.

"We're in your debt now, Mr. Woods," Mary said.

"You are?" Jack managed.

Mary nudged her husband.

Seamus nodded and began to explain. "If a mortal helps a leprechaun, that leprechaun is in his debt forever and a day. We're pretty much immortal, except when it comes to water. If we fall in, well—" He pulled himself up as if he could not bear to think of it. "And you saved me."

Oh, Jack thought. What could he say?

"I'm sorry."

"You weren't to know," Mary said.

"Forget about it," Jack offered.

Seamus shook his head. "Can't do that, much as I'd like to."

This was exhausting. The drink, his hangover, the rescue, his wet clothes. And the little people. It made his head spin.

"I've got to sit down," Jack announced.

Mary made a tsking sound. "You're soaking wet. I'll get you a towel."

"What about me?" Seamus protested.

"*You* can get pneumonia," Mary called as she hurried inside.

Seamus shook his head, then grinned. "You should meet my son Mickey. Mickey! Show yourself!"

A third leprechaun materialized just beside the door. This one seemed younger than the other two, maybe in his late teens. A rather handsome young fellow too, thinner than his parents, with a tight-fitting outfit of solid green and a shock of unruly red hair sticking out from beneath his cap.

Handsome, young . . . leprechaun? What was Jack thinking?

"Hello there," Mickey said.

What could he do? Well, Jack supposed he could introduce himself.

"My name's Woods. Jack Woods."

"Is this all a bit much for you, Jack?" Seamus asked. "Meeting us all together like this?"

Mickey grinned at that. "We're pretty overwhelming, aren't we, Da?"

"Are there—any more of you going to appear out of thin air?" Jack asked.

"No, no," Seamus said reassuringly. "There's just the Muldoon family in the cottage. Course there's thousands more leprechauns and solitaries around these parts. All fun-loving folk full of pep and vigor—"

"And booze, given half a chance," Mary cut in. "Here's your towel, Mr. Woods."

Jack blinked. He hadn't realized Mary had reappeared. Mostly, he saw the towel, with a little bit of Mary behind it.

Jack accepted the towel gladly.

"Thanks." Maybe, if his head were dry, he could think more clearly.

The younger leprechaun nodded pleasantly as Jack put the towel to his hair.

"Some say we're just a mischief-making, work-shy bunch of layabouts," Mickey ventured.

"That's just our friends though," Seamus added modestly.

Jack paused in using the towel long enough to ask another question.

"So what do you do?"

Mary spoke first. "The lep men drink and the lep women pick 'em up when they fall down."

"Don't listen to her, Jack," Seamus chided. "We leprechauns have work of global importance."

"Global!" Mickey agreed.

"We're in charge of changing the seasons," Seamus pointed out.

"Seasons?" Jack asked.

Seamus nodded. Sweat seemed to gather on his brow as he thought about it. "Four days a year, we're worked to the bone. We're a blur out there. Winter to spring, spring to summer, summer to—uh—er—"

"Autumn," Mickey added helpfully.

"Autumn!" Seamus agreed. "And then autumn to—the other one. It's a heavy responsibility." He paused, patting at his pockets, then looking up to Jack again. "You haven't got a drink about you, have you? My throat's so dry you could see a mirage on it."

"It was drink that got you into this trouble," Mary replied sharply. "You'd drink a nip in the air—and you were baptized with holy oil and a chaser!"

Seamus sighed.

"Never argue with a female leprechaun, Jack. You can't win."

Mickey waved to the others. "I'm off out, Ma."

"Where are you going?" Mary demanded.

The teen shrugged. "To do some mischief."

"That's all right then." She gave her son a motherly smile.

Mickey sauntered over to his father. "Can you lend us a couple of gold ones, Da?"

Seamus reached in his pocket and pulled forth a gold coin so large that Jack didn't think it would have fit in the pocket in the first place. Seamus tossed the coin to his son.

"Don't squander it," Seamus chided. "Promise you'll spend it on drink and women like any good leprechaun!"

"I promise, Da. G'day to you, Mr. Woods."

" 'Bye," Jack replied as Mickey disappeared. He noticed that both Mary and Seamus looked expectantly in his direction.

"Er—fine boy," he added quickly.

Both the little people grinned at that.

"Chip off the old block," Seamus agreed. "A credit to his father. He's going to grow up just like me."

Mary groaned at that. "Oh, Lord. So that would be two too many."

Jack kept on smiling. That seemed as safe as anything. No doubt he would wake up at any minute now.

Chapter Four

Ah, now, this was the life! Mickey Muldoon thought he could do no better. Strolling down the lane with gold in your pocket, a good friend at your side, and a jar of poteen between you. What more could a young leprechaun want?

Jericho O'Grady, a fine young leprechaun in his own right, was even thinner than Mickey himself and mostly wore a foolish grin. He took a long pull on the jug and handed it back to Mickey.

"And Mr. Woods's not from Kerry?" he asked.

"No, he has a strange accent," Mickey replied after he'd taken a pull of his own. "More like a Leinster lad."

"And he knows nothing about the trooping fairies?" From his tone, Jericho was quite astonished by this.

Everyone in Ireland knew of the animosity between the two great groups of fairies. First there were the trooping fairies and their like, fussy folk with their multicolored wings and fancy clothes, who liked nothing better than to sit around in their stuffy fairy castles all day. No knowledgeable soul would ever confuse them with those fine, sturdy individuals—the solitary fairies—who kept far more to themselves, perhaps taking an old cottage or a nice dry cave for their home. The leprechauns were proud to be solitaries, as were the dullahans, the grogochs, the pookas, and half a dozen other breeds who valued their independence.

"Best not to frighten the poor man," Mickey reasoned.

Jericho nodded at the wisdom of that. "I suppose he'll find out soon enough."

"Especially if he sees us crack a few of their smug blond fairy heads together." Now there was a thought to warm a leprechaun's heart.

Mickey and Jericho looked at each other and let out with a genuine leprechaun war whoop—the sort of cry to put a chill in the heart of a trooping fairy, not to mention doing a great deal to clear out the lungs besides.

Mickey placed a cautioning hand on Jericho's shoulder. He'd heard something above them. Were those fairies spying on them again? He pointed above as he heard a great rustling of leaves overhead.

"Whaw!" someone cried above. There was a great snap as if someone had broken a branch.

"Whoo!" came a second cry soon thereafter, and a second snap from a second broken branch. Whoever was up there was hitting them as he fell.

"Whoa!" The third cry, along with the third broken branch, clinched it. Mickey would recognize those cries of pain anywhere. It wasn't just any leprechaun falling out of that tree. It was Barney Devine, perhaps Mickey's closest friend since childhood. One thing about Barney: When you told him to drop in, he literally did.

A few more cries, a few more broken branches, and

Barney dropped just before them, landing smartly on his feet. He seemed to live to bounce about in trees. Mickey and Jericho both nodded to the new arrival.

Barney reached for the jug. "Quick, quick, give us a drink, Mickey lad. The fall's made me thirsty."

"You're always thirsty," Jericho pointed out.

"I'm always falling out of trees," Barney replied reasonably.

Well, you couldn't argue with that. Mickey gave him the jug.

"What were you doing up there, Barney?"

"Looking out for Count Grogan."

Just the mention of that trooping fairy was enough to put a cloud over the lot of them.

"May his fairy bones rot," Jericho said for all of them.

Barney grinned at that. "I thought I could drop in on him, quiet like, for a little clattering." He raised his fists by way of demonstration.

Not that Barney could be quiet about anything, but Grogan certainly deserved to be taught a lesson. Actually, Grogan and his bunch deserved whatever misfortune might come their way, with the way they looked down on leprechauns. And the way they carried themselves about, so hoity-toity, just because they had a set of wings . . . .

But enough of the trooping fairies. Someone else was on his way to visit.

The horse galloped toward them over the misty fields, truly visible one minute, lost within the mists the next. It was the figure on the horse, though, that was the most striking, what with his long black robes and the fact that his shoulders didn't sport a head. Not that he was headless, oh, no. He plainly carried his head in his right hand; it glowed with its own eerie, phosphorescent light. And in his left hand, he wielded a glowing human spine as his whip. Was it any wonder that his horse breathed sparks and flames from its nostrils?

He was just your average dullahan, after all. Mickey waved as he approached. The figure waved the human spine above his shoulders in reply; the rotted teeth curled up in a wry smile. Mickey would recognize that spectral head anywhere.

"It's Dunlang. How're things in Munster, Dunlang?"

The dullahan shook his head—with his hand, of course.

"Too peaceful," he replied.

"Stay around here," Barney offered. "We'll stir things up for you."

"I would, Barney, but the Grand Banshee herself's forbidden us from fighting."

Barney scuffed his shoes in the dirt. "Ah, we take no notice of that!"

"And today's the anniversary of myself meeting the executioner's ax," the dullahan continued, "and I'm riding up to Sligo to celebrate."

"Well, you're looking fine on it, Dunlang," Mickey agreed.

The dullahan threw his head high in the air.

"Thanks, Mickey!" he called down from overhead. "I can see from up here there's a few other dullahans already arrived! I'd best be off!"

He caught his head with the same right hand that threw it. "'Bye, lads. Do 'em mischief, whoever it is!"

They shouted good-bye as the dullahan rode away.

"Dunlang's a doomy sort," Barney said with the shake of his head. "He doesn't enjoy life."

"It's not easy with no head," Mickey agreed. It was another thing leprechauns could be thankful for: having heads and bodies attached. But they were getting behind on their mischief.

Jericho cried out in alarm, scampering back a half dozen paces. A five-bar gate that rose to three times their height had appeared to block their path. And behind it was a whole crowd of trooping fairies, hopping about, showing off their multicolored wings. A second later, who but Count Grogan, nephew to the fairy queen and eternal pain in the posterior, flew in and settled on the top-most bar.

"It's Count Grogan!" Mickey called. "The first of the fairy fools!"

"Mock on, Michael Muldoon," the count replied in his maddeningly superior tone. "You and that hairy mistake there, Barney Devine, make a fine raggedy-arsed pair." He waved his hand dismissively. "Clear the paths! You're polluting the grass!"

"And what if we don't?" Mickey demanded.

"Then I'll have to make you," Grogan sniffed.

Barney took a step forward. "You and which particular thousand trooping fairies would that be?" He pulled back his sleeves. "I'll flatten you without raising a sweat."

Grogan flew off his gate and landed right before them.

"Oooh," he moaned in mockery. "We're all trembling before Barney Devine, a powerful man with a powerful set of eyebrows!"

Well, a self-respecting leprechaun could only stand so much, couldn't he? There had to be a fight, didn't there?

And a fight there was. The leprechauns pulled out the wooden batons they reserved for this very purpose, while the trooping fairies did likewise with their weapons of glass. As usual, the bits of wood and glass magically transformed to quarterstaffs, and the fight was on.

Whack! Parry! Thrust! Mickey fought off a pair of trooping fairies, leapt high in the air, somersaulting about once, then once again, the fairies' staffs missing him by a mile. He noticed that Barney had taken Grogan on, personal like. Well, then it was up to Jericho and him to keep the other trooping fairies busy so that Barney could finish his little dispute.

Thrust! Parry! Whack! A couple of the trooping fairies lost their balance beneath Mickey's attack. That was what happened when you depended too much on those wings! Uh-oh, another pair of the winged wonders was in the way. Mickey planted his staff in the ground and vaulted above their heads, whacking both of the fairies with the pole as soon as he'd landed on the other side. Ah, these trooping fairies were no match for a leprechaun!

He heard cries of alarm from the edge of the battle. A human was coming! A farmer it was, riding a tractor and pulling a wagon behind.

Time for everyone to disappear.

The farmer's cart, full of hay and turnips, trundled past. The farmer was so tired, poor man, he wouldn't even notice if there was a fairy before his face, much less a battle going on in the field around him. Mickey and his mates waited for the cart to pass, then materialized quick as a wink, the better to jump on the wagon. All of them grabbed the turnips and started shooting the missiles at their opponents. A great hail of turnips, far too much for the likes of trooping fairies.

"Next time, Devine! Next time!" Count Grogan called, covering his head from the vegetable assault.

Mickey fell down laughing.

Could any victory be more glorious?

Chapter Five

Jack Woods would make sense out of all of this. A brisk walk was in order. Or if not a brisk walk, at least a quiet stroll, someplace where there weren't any leprechauns.

He walked down the path from his cottage until he came to a spot where the path joined a rutted road. In the distance, he saw a tractor approaching; a tractor being driven by an actual, full-size, human farmer.

"Great—a normal-size person," Jack murmured to himself. The fellow, slumped down in his seat, a battered hat on his head to keep away the sun, might be a farmer most anyplace. Maybe this would start things getting back to the real world. Jack leaned on a nearby fencepost and waved as the tractor drew near.

"Hi!" he called with a grin. "How you doing?"

The farmer nodded back, ever so slightly. Or maybe it was only his head bobbing up and down with the movement of the tractor.

Well, Jack would just have to start a conversation. He looked at the wagon that the tractor was hauling, piled high with produce.

"What you got there?" Jack called. "Turnips?"

The farmer's head bobbed just like before. What kind of an answer was that?

"Going to market?" Jack tried again.

The tractor drove on past without even a glance from the farmer.

"Speak English?" Jack called after the farmer.

Jack jumped. A turnip bounced off the fence at his side, as if someone had thrown it. But who, besides the farmer . . .

"Hello there, Mr. Woods! This here is Barney Devine and Jericho O'Grady. Two of the laziest leprechauns you'll ever meet!"

There, in the back of the wagon, atop the turnips, sat three leprechauns. He recognized young Mickey as the speaker.

"Hello, Mr. Woods!" the other two leprechauns chorused.

Jack realized his mouth was open. Nobody else would talk to him, but the leprechauns were everywhere.

"It's very good of you to let us stay in the cottage, Jack," a voice said at his side.

Jack jumped again. He felt as if someone had kicked him in the stomach.

Seamus Muldoon stood on the fencepost by his side.

He wished they wouldn't do that!

Seamus tipped his hat. "Sorry. Did I startle you?" He grinned. "I must stop doing that."

Jack nodded. He couldn't talk. Why should he even try? More leprechauns would show up. He waved at the departing tractor and wagon.

Seamus sighed. "A hundred years ago, I'd have been out on some mischief myself." He took a deep breath, shaking his head with regret. "Would you look at all this *nature* around here? Far too much of it, isn't there? Those trooping fairies have a lot to answer for."

Woods couldn't help himself. "Trooping fairies?" he asked.

Seamus nodded.

"They're responsible for all *this*." He waved dismissively at their surroundings. "I mean, what's the use of them making all these little leaves? Millions of tiny, weeny, mean things. Why not have a few huge, gigantic ones instead? You'd have somewhere to go if it was raining. And why's everything have to be green? A little imagination wouldn't go amiss there." He laughed sourly. "But oh, no, you try telling a trooping fairy such a thing. Not half a brain between them!"

So let's see if Jack had this right. "So you don't like them?"

Seamus nodded sharply. "They are the natural enemy of the leprechaun." His next laugh was sourer still. "If they were any further up themselves, they'd be inside out!"

Jack nodded. Leprechauns fighting trooping fairies. Well, why not?

He guessed he was starting to believe all of this.

It was a thankless job for the most part, being the chamberlain of a fairy palace. But someone had to make sure that everything was in order, that the palace glowed in just the right sort of magical way, that the watershees, bless their delicate fairy hearts, concentrated on keeping nature in order, that— Well, there were a thousand jobs to do every day!

But none of them was quite so trying as dealing with Count Grogan.

King Boric and Queen Morag led the way to the throne room, questioning the count at length. It was all the chamberlain could do to keep up. He wasn't as young as he used to be! But then, who was?

They all strode across the walkway that hung above the palace proper. Even now, in a time of strife like this, the chamberlain couldn't help but admire the magnificence of his surroundings. That many of the walls were made of cascading water was a particularly nice touch. And from this vantage point, one could not help but marvel at all the activity below. Look at all those fairies measuring leaves, carrying them from the "in" baskets to the "out" baskets, making sure that all those sunflowers and sheaves of wheat were the proper shade of gold, looking at every detail with magnifying glasses and microscopes. It did the chamberlain's heart proud to see all that activity. Not, of course, that anyone else upon the walkway took the slightest notice.

They were far too busy being outraged.

"The leprechaun riffraff pelted you with turnips?" the king demanded.

"Turnips?" the queen replied in horror. "That's worse than . . . cauliflowers!"

"Much worse!" the king agreed.

They were working themselves up into a proper snit. Once again, the chamberlain would have to be the voice of reason.

"It *could* have been overripe tomatoes," he suggested.

As usual, the others paid no attention.

"It just shows what they're capable of!" the queen fumed.

"Or avocados," the chamberlain suggested.

But they were already beyond reason.

"These bog fairies must be taught a lesson!" Count Grogan insisted.

Still, a chamberlain had to try. "Perhaps we could just talk to them and—"

"Too much talking!" the queen insisted.

"They show no respect!" the king added.

"No class!" the queen amplified.

"No work ethic!" the king appended.

"No dress sense!" the queen rejoined.

"Ghastly!" Count Grogan agreed. He would.

"To arms!" the king announced.

"To arms!" the queen repeated.

"Exactly." Grogan smiled. He'd gotten exactly what he wanted.

They approached the throne room. Two of the fairy guards pulled open the doors as they drew near. Grogan and the royals marched furiously through.

"Never a word of thanks, you know," one guard muttered to the other as the chamberlain hurried past.

The throne room was the most magnificent room in all of the palace, with lovely walls made of living and flowering vines. Too bad the chamberlain had so little time to admire it. He had a duty to perform.

"You can't call the fairies to arms, your majesty," he pointed out gently.

"I can do anything I want!" King Boric blustered.

The chamberlain shook his head. "The Grand Banshee decreed there must be no more fighting."

"Oh, *her*!" Queen Morag raged. Only a queen could place such a dismissive tone in two short words.

"I'm king here, Chamberlain!" Boric puffed out his chest. "I do all the decreeing from now to Michaelmas Tuesday!"

"Of course," the chamberlain replied most calmly. "When exactly is Michaelmas, sire?"

Boric paused, seemingly at a loss. He blinked and shook his head.

"Whenever I decide!"

"Jolly good," the chamberlain agreed. "I'll look forward to it." Oh, the things he put up with to keep the peace . . . .

"She's here!" The fairy guards had rushed into the room, and they did not look happy. "She's here! The Grand Banshee!"

Oh, dear.

With that, a great black crow, whose feathers held every color under the sun, flew in the window and landed on the throne. Not that it was really a crow, mind you. The bird form was merely the Grand Banshee's preferred mode of travel.

Once on the throne, she regained her true form, and a forbidding form it was. For the Grand Banshee had a terrible beauty, her skin the color of night, with fearsome light flashing in her eyes. She wore a gown that shone black and silver, and her mass of hair formed a great halo about her head.

She pointed to the king of the fairies, and the anger in her voice was enough to make the floors of the palace shake.

"Boric! I declared all fighting between trooping and solitary fairies must stop. But another brawl broke out only this evening."

"It wasn't our fault!" Boric said a bit too quickly.

"It never is," the Grand Banshee rumbled.

Count Grogan stepped forward.

"Barney Devine and Mickey Muldoon and the other

solitaries started the whole thing," he declared most authoritatively.

"They threw *turnips*!" Queen Morag declared in a voice that suggested there could be no greater sin.

The Grand Banshee sighed.

"I know they threw turnips. I'm all seeing, remember? And the way I see it, the count here and his hotheaded friends had just as much to do with the fight as Muldoon."

Count Grogan stiffened at the very thought of impropriety.

"It was a matter of honor."

The Banshee turned her glowering gaze to him.

"You deal with your honor, Count Grogan—such as it is—in a more peaceful manner from now on. While I deal with Muldoon and the others."

The chamberlain had never seen Count Grogan nod his head quite so quickly.

"I give you all fair warning. If this fighting continues, you will all pay the ultimate price! And you know what that is."

With that, the Banshee turned herself back into a crow and flew from the room.

Surely now the king and queen would rethink their rash judgments. For the Grand Banshee was the ruler of all things magical, both living and dead. It was with her permission that all fairies did their work. And should that permission be withdrawn?

As unthinkable as it sounded, it could mean the end of fairies—forever!

Chapter Six

Jack was overwhelmed by the beauty of this place. Sperry, Sperry, and McGurk had provided him with an instant camera to give them an assortment of picturesque shots. But *everything* was picturesque! Take that farmhouse over there, a little run-down perhaps, and in need of a coat of paint, but the way the ivy and moss covered the outside walls was stunning. And the broken-down barn behind it, the rusty tractor, the old car up on blocks—all of it seemed to add to the charm.

Jack took a photo. The camera whirred and ejected an instant print.

"That's an interesting camera you have there, Jack— sticking its tongue out like that."

Who? What?

Jack spun about. It was Seamus Muldoon.

"I did it again, didn't I?"

Jack nodded, leaning back against the fence.

"You did," he replied once he had caught his breath.

"Sorry about that." The way Seamus grinned, he didn't look sorry at all. "Perhaps you'll get used to it in time."

Jack shook his head. "I don't think so."

"Why? How long are you staying?"

Jack looked sharply at the leprechaun. "Just a few weeks. It depends."

"Depends on what?" Seamus prodded.

"Oh," Jack said. "Nothing special."

He realized he was being evasive. Why couldn't he tell Seamus the truth? Was it that he never expected the countryside to be this beautiful and unspoiled? Or was it that he was talking to a leprechaun?

He decided to change the subject.

He waved at the beauty around him. "And I don't think I could ever get used to this. Two days ago I was sitting at a desk in corporate America, and now I'm on a fence in the middle of Ireland talking to a leprechaun who doesn't exist."

"You're a lucky man," Seamus pointed out. "There's folks who'd pay a fortune to be in your shoes." He shook his head. "Mind you, if you told anyone they wouldn't believe you. They'd say you were mad."

Jack wondered about that last point himself.

"How many people *do* know about you?" he asked.

"You're the first round here for many a year. That's what you get for snatching me from a watery grave."

So there wasn't even anyone he could talk to about this. What if leprechauns were just a figment of his imagination?

Jack had a thought.

"Could I take your photo?"

Seamus grinned at that. "You could with the greatest of pleasure." He struck a classic pose, his hands on his lapels.

Jack snapped the photo. To actually have a picture of a leprechaun . . .

"You do realize," Seamus remarked as the camera spit out the photo, "I'll not come out on the fillum there."

Jack looked down at the developing image. Seamus was right. All the photo showed was the countryside.

"Probably for the best," Seamus continued. "It means no one can prove that we're here. But it means there's not a lot to put on your mantelpiece."

The leprechaun popped over to Jack's side, looking down at his photo of the farm. "Ah, the Fitzpatrick place." He sighed. "Home of the lovely Kathleen."

Lovely? Jack had a sudden thought. Could it be? That would be impossible—

Nothing was impossible when you were talking to a leprechaun.

"Kathleen?" Jack asked. "She's not a redhead, is she? Fabulous green eyes?"

Seamus nodded. "And a figure that would make a monk cry out, 'What the heck!' and hang up his sandals."

"I think it was her I saw swimming yesterday down at the rock pool." It was Jack's turn to smile, just at the thought of her.

"That'd be Kathleen, bathing like a goddess." Seamus got a faraway look in his eyes. "Sometimes there's a real advantage to being invisible."

He paused, holding his finger in the air as if he might test the wind direction.

"Ah, time for a quick one before the wind changes. See you later, Jack."

And he was gone.

Jack pushed himself away from the fence. He looked around, but he was alone.

He still couldn't get used to the way leprechauns came

and went. He looked down at the now developed shot that should have included Seamus. It showed nothing but rolling countryside, with not a hint of a leprechaun.

Well, as long as he was near the Fitzpatrick farm, maybe he'd pay a social call. He walked down the hill. Actually the place had two dilapidated barns and a pair of small shacks as well. Jack wondered if they were outhouses. The tractor, while rusty, looked perfectly functional. And the house itself, while it seemed even a bit more run-down when you got closer, was every bit as picturesque. It also looked deserted. Jack snapped a couple more shots as he walked around the nearer barn.

He stopped short. There, just around the corner, was Kathleen, hanging laundry on a line. She turned slightly, her shining dark hair suddenly in the late-afternoon sun. Gold shone about her head as if she had a halo.

The woman was even more stunning than Jack remembered.

A puppy came running across the yard, yapping happily at Kathleen. Jack wondered if he should leave. It was all well and good, wanting to see this beautiful woman again, but how could he even talk to her after what happened the other day? She had been quite angry at him then. Hadn't she threatened to send some brothers after him?

If only Kathleen weren't so beautiful. Jack hated to think he could never see her again.

The puppy jumped up, grabbed a sheet with its teeth, and pulled it off the line. But Kathleen didn't get angry. She laughed, a wonderful sound, and dove for the puppy, but the dog managed to pull the sheet just beyond her grasp. The dog growled loudly, proud of its prize, as Kathleen, laughing, chased it across the yard.

The game was so gentle, and so innocent, it set off an ache deep within Jack's chest. This was the woman he'd stumbled on the first day here, the most beautiful, joyous, and natural woman he'd ever seen. And this was the woman, because of that first day, who would probably never speak to him again.

"Give it back, boy! Here, boy!" she called to the dog. The puppy kept on running. Between the puppy's growling and Kathleen's laughter, they were causing quite a ruckus.

Jack had a sudden thought. If he could never see this vision of loveliness again, at least he could take her picture. She was so busy with her game, she would never even notice.

He raised the viewfinder to his eye and clicked the shutter.

But in that instant, the dog stopped growling. Kathleen stopped laughing.

The only noises in all the world were the click and whir of the camera.

Kathleen spun around to face him.

The photo poked out from the bottom of the camera, instant evidence of Jack's crime.

"You!" Kathleen called. She did not look happy. "Peeping Tom!"

Jack looked down at the camera in his hands. How could he explain? "No!" he began. "Listen! I didn't know— I was just—"

She pointed at the camera. "Now he's taking pictures!"

Jack heard a sound from the farmhouse. The front door opened, and four young men tumbled out. Three of them were very large and burly; the forth was merely burly. Jack bet any one of them could whomp him in a fair fight. But who said this was going to be fair? Jack also imagined these were the four brothers Kathleen was going to send after him to teach him a lesson.

It looked like lesson time was now.

"Thank you and good night!" Jack called.

He ran.

From the great crashing noises behind him, it sounded as if all five were chasing after him.

How long had Jack been running?

He wasn't used to this sort of exercise.

A nice, civilized round of golf. A half hour on some machine at the gym. Sure, he used to do some swimming back in college, but he'd never had anything like this cross-country chase.

Yet he managed to stay ahead of them. And even though every muscle in his body was screaming, he kept on running.

It was amazing what fear could do.

Every once in a while, he'd try to call back an explanation.

"I caught my foot and got stuck!"

"Get him!" one of the brothers screamed back.

"I didn't mean anything!" Jack yelled over his shoulder. "I was lost!"

"Leave him to me!" another of the brothers cried. "Don't you worry, Kathleen!"

Jack saw a group of houses ahead. He realized he'd run all the way to the village. He saw a church steeple rise above the other buildings. That was the answer! A church! Sanctuary! They wouldn't beat him up in a church, would they?

Well, maybe they would, but Jack couldn't run much farther. He turned and sprinted for the church.

"Why won't you listen to me?" he yelled.

The brothers were suddenly all around him.

"Head him off at the door, John!" one called.

"I'm trying!" another replied.

"I've got him—" the shortest of the four yelled as he rushed for the door.

Jack had dodged past him before he could even turn around.

"No, I don't!" the last admitted.

Jack slowed to a walk as soon as he entered the church. Apparently, the parishioners here were in the middle of a service. Oh, well. If the brothers killed him now, at least there would be witnesses.

Jack slid into an empty pew at the front of the church. He wished there was some way he could get rid of the Fitzpatrick brothers for good.

Maybe if he made himself as small as possible. Jack hunkered down a bit in his seat.

Where was Seamus Muldoon when he needed him?

Jack looked up at the pulpit. The priest was old—very old. He swayed back and forth as he spoke. He seemed to grip the sides of the pulpit to keep from falling over. His voice rose and fell as he droned on about something. Maybe he was giving a sermon. Or maybe he was just rambling.

"Remember this," the priest said. "You can always have the last word if you talk to yourself. That's why I do it. There've been mutterings in the parish about me, saying I'm too old. I'll never be too old, not till I'm six feet under!"

The priest stopped and glared at the back of the room. Jack took a peek around. All five Fitzpatricks were creeping down the center aisle.

"Kathleen Fitzpatrick—sit!" the priest ordered. "And that means your four muscle-bound brothers! I'm talking!"

"You're always talking, Father," Kathleen muttered, half

to herself. But she sat, a few pews back from Jack, where she could keep an eye on him.

She sat. And so did her brothers.

"Where was I?" the priest mused. "Oh, yes. Six feet under."

The priest went on.

And on.

And on.

At least Jack had a chance to catch his breath. And then some. He glanced behind himself after a half hour or so and noticed that most of the congregation was asleep, including all four Fitzpatrick brothers. Only Kathleen was wide awake. It must be very difficult to fall asleep, Jack reflected, when you looked that angry.

From his tone of voice, the priest appeared to be winding down at last.

"And so, in the words of the good book: 'Moab is my washpot!'"

The priest finished with a short prayer and an even shorter amen. As if on cue, the congregation awoke, including the brothers Fitzpatrick.

But while he had stayed awake, Jack had hatched a plan. He leapt to his feet and rushed over to the priest.

"An inspiring service, Father!"

The priest looked genuinely surprised. "You think so? Thank you, my son." He paused to think about it for a moment. "'Inspiring,' was it?"

Jack glanced over his shoulder and noticed the whole Fitzpatrick clan sidling forward. Still, they seemed not to want to get too close to the priest.

"It was," Jack told the priest.

"Good, good." The priest nodded. "Any particular bit? Only I forget sometimes what I said."

The Fitzpatricks shuffled a little closer.

"Pretty much all of it!" Jack said enthusiastically.

"All of it?" The priest grinned. "Ah, good! So, if my tired old ears are not telling me tales, you're not a local man."

"American," Jack explained. "I'm on vacation."

"American?" The priest considered that. "I met an American once. Tall man, with a droopy eyelid, and a fondness for Glenn Miller."

"I don't think I know him."

"No." The priest considered that too. "Well, it was a long time ago."

Jack decided it was time to change the subject. "This is a really charming church."

"Twelfth century." The priest nodded. "It has nothing of interest. Everything was stolen years ago. But I'll show you around. I get very few visitors."

He grabbed Jack's arm—mostly, Jack guessed, to keep from falling over—and steered his visitor toward a side door.

Jack looked back and saw the Fitzpatricks glowering at him. He tried to smile at Kathleen. She looked right through him.

He waved at the brothers as the door closed between them. Apparently, he would survive for at least another hour or two.

As soon as he thought it polite, he would ask the priest to show him another door—one leading out.

Chapter Seven

Now this was the nightlife!

Mickey Muldoon was hanging on to his charging ram for his dear leprechaun life, and he noticed that Barney and Jericho weren't doing much better on the ram that they shared. They were bounced and jostled and tossed and twisted, up and down and back and forth, shaking their teeth and mixing their innards, as the two rams raced across the fields. All in all, it was a grand time.

"Whoa!" the leprechauns called in unison, for the rams had suddenly stopped just before a rather large and forbidding hedge. Not that they were ever in any danger, for they all launched themselves into the air with double somersaults to land firmly on their feet. Just beyond the hedge they could see the cave with the half-hidden sign.

THE CROCK OF GOLD

A finer leprechaun tavern could not be had. They'd reached their destination at last.

"Sure," Barney said admiringly, "but animals have such good sense."

They waved farewell to the rams and marched on to the business of serious carousing.

It was not, however, one of the livelier nights in the Crock. A half dozen solitary drinkers all sat at separate tables. In a corner sat the fiddler, sound asleep. And the tavern keeper, one Myles O'Shea, glared as they walked in the room. Ah, well. Myles always glared. That was no different on the best of nights.

Mickey waved to his friends and laughed. "Is there anyone under the age of four hundred in here tonight?"

"The place smells like they're cremating toadstools," Barney agreed.

One of the older leprechauns rose from his table with a groan. All the rest of those in the room watched him as he slowly walked to the door. He disappeared from view for a moment, then reentered, shook his head, and sat back down before his drink.

"It's all right," he said solemnly. "It's still summer. Panic over."

Everybody in the room seemed greatly relieved. They all returned to their drinks.

Mickey and his friends stared at each other in disbelief. They found themselves a table in the dimly lit room. After all, this was as good a place as any to plan the night. But plan they must, lest they should find themselves asleep next to the fiddler.

Barney started the conversation.

"What mischief should we get up to tonight, lads? Turn the milk sour? Flatten the wheat fields?"

"Blossom shaking would be good," Jericho suggested. He was a simple lad with simple needs. "I hate blossoms. They have no right to be there!"

"Is that the best you can come up with?" Barney said, disgusted with all of them.

Then Mickey came up with a fine idea. "What about we sneak into the Grand Midsummer Ball up at the castle? It's the event of the year for all the trooping fairies."

Barney roared with laughter. "Good on yer, Mickey! Lot of beautiful young fairies up there who have yet to be introduced to the delights of a handsome, virile leprechaun!"

"We can cause a whole heap o' trouble," Mickey agreed with a grin.

Only Jericho didn't seem ready to join in the plan. "But the Grand Banshee has warned us to stay out of trouble, hasn't she?"

Barney glared at the lad. "Mickey, would you tell me who it is sitting opposite me? Because whoever it is is no leprechaun."

Jericho shifted uncomfortably in his seat. "I was only saying, it sounds like big trouble."

"Jericho, leprechauns are born for trouble," Barney pointed out. "The bigger the better!"

"You're right. I'm sorry, Barney. I was forgetting myself!" Jericho brightened at a further thought. "Will there be free drink?"

"Flowing like water," Mickey agreed.

"Count me in!" Jericho smiled. "And—er—would there be a little time for blossom shaking on the way?"

All three of them laughed at that.

Myles O'Shea leaned across the bar, the better to scowl in their direction.

"Quiet! I've customers concentrating on their drinking

here. This tavern has an Ireland-wide reputation for serious drinking! You're spoiling it! If you want to enjoy yourselves, then you should go down the road. Remember who you are!"

Barney, for one, was not impressed. "We're the true spirit of old Ireland!" He pounded his fist on the table. "We've got more 'get up and go' in us than a hatful of pookas!"

Well, now Barney had done it. For the moment you mentioned pookas, what could pookas do but appear?

Three of them showed up just like that, hideous troll-like things, with huge flat feet, short stringy beards, long stringy hair of every possible color, and the eyes of maniacs, tumbling and rolling about each other like a trio of demented acrobats. One landed on the ground, the other two on either of his shoulders.

The one on the ground started the rhyme:

"Pookas one, two, and three, we heard our name!"

The others upon his shoulders picked it up:

"Taken in vain!
It's a shame!"

The first agreed:

"But we're still game!"

The three cried together:

"No jibes or jives or we'll supply you with a frown.
We're three pookas from County Down!"

They somersaulted and scampered about the place, drinking the beer of every single leprechaun in the process.

Barney shook his head in admiration. "We love trouble, brother pookas, but you're the best."

"Never a truer word said in jest," the first pooka agreed. He reached in the pocket of his ragged pants and pulled forth what looked like a handful of golden dirt.

Yes, Mickey thought. The pixie dust would turn the trick.

The pookas jumped about the room again. They threw the pixie dust first at the fiddler, who not only woke right up, but turned from one fiddler into three. And all three immediately put their fiddles to their chins and set to work. The pookas moved on, dusting one solitary drinker after another. And once the pixie dust had settled, each drinker had turned into three, and none of the three still sat morosely at the table, for all of them had jumped up to join the dance.

And what a dance it was. The fiddlers, rather than play but a single tune, played three separate melodies, each jig intertwining with the other two, only serving to drive the dance faster and faster.

You'd have to be mad to dance to the likes of that. And so, of course, everybody did. Faster and faster. Thanks to the pookas, the room was filled with leprechauns, all clapping their hands and stomping upon the wooden beams.

"By the eyebrows of the Great Fergus!" Barney called. "This'll get the blood racing and the feet tapping over the hills of Galway!"

Leprechauns danced on the floor, on the tables, on the bar. They swung from the rafters and jigged in and out the door. There were leprechauns everywhere.

Now this was a party!

* * *

Jack didn't know if this was a good idea.

He moved his bicycle around the edges of the large village fair—one of the great events of the summer, the leprechauns had assured him. It was certainly busy enough. They passed stalls selling cheese and farm produce and others offering games of skill. Farther along, Jack could see an old fashioned hurdy-gurdy, complete with painted horses, and even a small roller coaster that had its riders screaming with delight.

Jack was surrounded by hundreds of people. All but the one woman he truly wished were here.

"So do you think she might be here?" Jack asked, not, he realized, for the first time.

"No doubt, Jack, no doubt," Seamus remarked from the bicycle basket before the handlebars, where he and his wife, Mary, rode in some comfort.

"Everyone who's anyone comes to the fair," Mary added reassuringly.

A couple of chattering women hurried by. The leprechauns vanished.

"Are you still there?" Jack called. He pushed the bicycle away from the stalls.

"And where else would we be?" Seamus's voice called back from the general vicinity of the basket. "Hello, there. Sean!"

Jack looked around. They were quite some distance from most anyone just now.

"Who were you talking to?"

"Neighbors," Seamus's voice declared.

"Will you look at what his wife's wearing!" Mary's voice added.

Jack, as usual, couldn't see anything.

"You seem very taken with young Kathleen," Muldoon remarked.

Taken with her? What nonsense.

"No, no," Jack objected strenuously. "I just don't want her going around thinking I'm some sort of creep."

It was Mary's turn to add, "That'll be the only reason you put on your best shirt then, Jack."

Well, Jack had to admit, there was that. But being nicely dressed was important for some people's opinions too. Surely the leprechauns could see— Jack stopped himself. When had Seamus and Mary's opinions become so important?

"Now to more important matters," Seamus announced. "Any sign of the beer tent?"

"Drink!" Mary's voice was very loud for a leprechaun who didn't wish to be noticed. "That's all he ever thinks about! My mother warned me. She said Seamus Muldoon would be the kind of husband who mowed the lawn in winter and shoveled snow in summer!"

Ah, there was Father Daley ahead. Jack had only had the opportunity to ask the priest's name once he was free of the Fitzpatricks. But Father Daley had saved his life the other day. The least he could do was say hello.

The priest was trying his hand at one of the games of skill, and not doing too well with it.

He was attempting, somewhat shakily, to throw a hoop over one of a series of large, round stakes. He cursed every time he missed. On the third try, he looked to the heavens.

"The Lord has abandoned me!"

Woods leaned his bike against the stall and walked over to the priest.

"How goes it, Father?"

The priest scowled at him. "The game's rigged, Mr.

Woods! I'm being cheated. This rogue is cheating the Mother Church!''

The stallholder looked suitably horrified. "Never, Father! Look!''

He took the hoop and fit it, quite carefully, over the large stake. It did indeed fit, if rather tightly. The chances of tossing one of these rings, though, to exactly fall where the stallholder had pushed it looked just about impossible.

He heard Seamus's voice whispering nearby. "The old fella's past it. Doesn't he know he can't win?''

"Give him a hand then, Seamus,'' Mary whispered back.

"Can you do that?'' Jack asked.

"What did you say?'' Father Daley asked.

"Uh—don't you do that!'' Jack said, recovering quickly. "Let me try, Father.'' He took the last ring the priest held in his hand. "Get ready, Muldoon.''

The priest shook his head. "The name's Daley. Father Fred Daley, Woods. You've got almost as bad a memory as me.''

Jack swung the ring in his hand, lining up his shot for the stake at the center. He figured so long as he got the ring in the general area Seamus could do the rest.

He saw a flash of red from the corner of his eye. He turned. Kathleen was running straight toward him!

As she crossed the space between them, she started shaking her finger right at him. She looked every bit as angry as last time.

"That's him, Father!'' she declared decisively. "That's the man!''

So Jack would be convicted without a trial? "Now please!'' he protested. "Let me explain what happened.''

Kathleen shook her head angrily. Her hair looked magnificent when she shook her head.

"I know what happened!''

"No, you don't!" Jack shot back.

But mere words would not stop her. "You were following me and—"

"Not now, woman," Father Daley insisted. "He's about to throw!"

Kathleen opened her mouth to continue.

"Silence!" the priest commanded.

Kathleen's voice started what might have become a word.

"Quiet!" Father Daley smiled beatifically. "I want to hear angels pass."

Very well. Maybe a moment's quiet would settle everyone down. Jack nodded and tossed the ring. It sailed high above the stakes, more or less on course for the center ring, but Jack might have put a bit too much energy behind it. The ring looked as if it would slightly overshoot the mark.

And then the spinning ring simply stopped in midair. Stopped and gently floated down toward the center stake, as though it was guided by an invisible hand. Well, Jack thought, it *was* being guided by an invisible hand. Good old Seamus.

The ring hovered an inch above the stake for an instant, as if the invisible hand was lining it up perfectly. Then it descended, ever so slowly, around the stake. Jack thought he heard a bit of a grunt from the leprechaun as he forced the ring home.

Jack looked up at the others. Father Daley and Kathleen gasped. The stallholder looked as if he had just witnessed the impossible.

"It's a miracle!" the priest called. "The miracle of the rings!"

Jack smiled at him. "You win, Father."

The priest shook his head. "No, my boy. You threw it."

But Jack insisted. "Your ring, your prize."

Father Daley needed no more convincing.

"Thank you, my boy." He waved at the prizes displayed along the back of the stall. "I want the big pink fella over there!"

The stallholder turned to the four-foot-long, stuffed pink elephant that the priest had indicated. For a moment, it looked as if the stallholder might object to the transaction, but then he shrugged and handed the thing over.

Jack noticed that even Kathleen was smiling.

The priest admired his prize. "He reminds me of old Father Donovan. He used to see these all the time."

Kathleen's smile abruptly vanished as she took another look at Jack. "Father, this man here is the one I've been talking about."

The priest nodded. "Talking about a whole lot, I have to say, Kathleen. From what I hear."

That seemed to startle her into silence. Jack tried to catch her eye, to maybe try another attempt at apology, but she looked away.

Father Daley continued. "And you're making a serious accusation against him, Kathleen Fitzpatrick. Now, Jack—" The priest smiled at him. "I can call you Jack, can't I?"

"I hope so," Jack answered.

The priest frowned at him. "Are you a Peeping Tom, like she says?"

"No," Jack replied.

"Straight answer to a straight question." The pink elephant bobbed up and down as the priest nodded his head briskly. "It's good enough for me. There you are, Kathleen. He's the wrong man. I'm an impeccable judge of character." He waved at the rest of the fair with his large pink prize. "Now, Jack, let's find the beer tent!"

"Just a moment, Father." He had to say something to Kathleen. He walked up to her. There was still a certain anger in her gaze, but it was mixed with something Jack couldn't quite identify.

"I'm sorry," he said softly. "It really was all a misunderstanding."

She stared at him, the anger there still. He didn't care if she was angry, as long as she kept on looking.

"That's him, Kathleen!"

Jack looked up to see the four Fitzpatrick brothers trotting quickly in their direction. They appeared a bit unsteady on their feet, as if they had already visited the beer tent. They looked eager to get their hands on Jack.

"We'll have none of that here, George Fitzpatrick!" the priest cautioned.

The four brothers paused, looking to Kathleen for what they should do next. She stared hard at Jack for a couple of heartbeats, then spun and strode away. The brothers followed.

"You should have let us have him, Kathleen!" one of the brothers said.

"Not in front of Father Daley," Kathleen snapped.

The shortest of the four joined in eagerly. "John and James could've held him and I could've hit him."

"You've a long way to go before you can do the hitting, young Harry," George chided.

The brothers and their sister disappeared into the crowd. It appeared that the priest had saved Jack from a beating at the very least.

So why wasn't he happier about it?

Mary Muldoon smiled. It was moments like this that were truly magic.

As Seamus and she were strolling about the campgrounds, they found the tent that contained the funhouse mirrors completely empty. So now they had the place all to themselves.

In one mirror the pair were ten feet tall, in the next as wide as a house. The third mirror gave them huge bodies and tiny heads; the fourth showed great heads and hardly any bodies at all.

But no matter how the images twisted and tugged their shapes, the two were always in them together.

"You look mighty handsome, Seamus Muldoon," Mary remarked to her husband.

"And you look as beautiful as a spring morning, Mary Muldoon," Seamus replied.

They hugged one another tight. When leprechauns married, it really was forever. In the mirror, their two images blended into one.

Mary Muldoon had to admit you could really see yourself in one of these.

And they called them funhouse mirrors.

What did humans know anyway?

Men! Kathleen Fitzpatrick had had just about enough of the lot of them!

First of all, that Jack Woods fellow. So what if he was sort of handsome in that awkward way, with that lopsided smile of his? He did seem to bumble into things, didn't he? And those apologies, all so sincere. Why did a devious American like that have to have such nice brown eyes?

And the priest, telling her which way was which, even though she had seen otherwise with her own eyes! And her four brothers, all muscle and no brains, trying to fight all her fights for her. Sure they all meant well, but right now, Kathleen felt as if they were all getting in her way. She decided it was for the best if she pointed them back to the beer tent and struck out on her own. A nice walk home would calm her down. She reached the edge of the fairgrounds in no time at all.

A man stood in her way. She looked up. It was him again! The American!

Well, she would just turn and walk the other way!

"No, no!" Jack called as she took a step away. "Listen, listen, please! It's not like it seems. Every time we meet I make a mess of it. I'd like to start again."

Kathleen found herself hesitating.

"Why?" she asked plainly.

Jack Woods paused an instant before replying.

"Because I want to."

"Well, perhaps I don't!" Kathleen spun about and continued her march home. That would show him. Sneaking up on her, not once but twice, and then claiming it was a mistake. Well, she supposed it could have been a mistake, a man from out of town and all, especially the first time. But the second time? And with a camera? And he had been taking a picture of her?

She hesitated, if only for an instant, and took a look back over her shoulder. Jack Woods was walking away, his head and shoulders down, looking far less than happy. He seemed a sincere sort, in his odd, American way.

No, no. Kathleen turned back toward home. She had better things to do. Whatever they might be.

Chapter Eight

Jack must have had close to a hundred photos of the countryside by now, picturesque farmhouses and cottages from all over the area, just the sort of thing Sperry, Sperry, and McGurk were looking for.

But it wasn't what Jack Woods was looking for at all.

Of all the photos spread before him, there was only one he wanted to look at: a little blurry, not quite centered, but it was still a picture of Kathleen. He hadn't even meant to take the picture. Well, at the last minute, he had.

Something had changed in the cottage room. Jack looked up.

Two leprechauns were smiling back at him.

"Please!" Jack said, clutching at his chest.

"Sorry, Jack," Mary replied.

He would never get used to this. He took a swig from the beer he had opened earlier.

Seamus Muldoon cleared his throat.

Jack glanced back at him. Seamus was staring quite fixedly at the bottle.

"Would you like some?" Jack asked.

"Ah!" Seamus said with a smile. "What a fine gesture! It had never occurred to me."

Jack passed the bottle on over, but before Seamus could bring it to his lips, Mary snatched it away.

"Ladies first, please." She took a hearty swig.

"What a magnificent woman she is," Seamus said proudly. He glanced at the photos Jack had spread across the table. "Those're some fine pictures there, Jack. Souvenirs, are they, to take back with you?"

Jack glanced over at the leprechauns. He didn't feel right, holding back a part of the truth.

"Kind of." He took a deep breath. "The fact is that I'm not just here for the rest. I've got a job to do as well."

"A job, is it? It must be a very important job to take so many photos of the valley."

"Yeah, I guess." Jack sighed. Somehow, the job didn't seem all that important anymore. He looked up at the pair.

"Is Kathleen married or anything?"

"Free as the wind!" Seamus replied.

The two leprechauns cackled and nudged each other.

"Jack here's taken quite a shine to the girl." Seamus glanced at his wife. "Can't think why."

Mary nudged her husband back. "Well, she's pretty enough in an ugly human kind of way. They'd make a fine couple."

Jack felt his ears burning. A fine couple? In an ugly human kind of way?

He wouldn't let it bother him. He had plenty to do. Maybe he'd put another log on to warm up the place.

"Okay. Yeah. Thank you," he muttered as he got up to tend to the fire.

The two leprechauns laughed all over again.

"Don't tell her brothers about us, Jack," Seamus warned. "They'll try to grab us for our pots of gold."

Jack glanced back at them with a frown. "What pots of gold?"

Mary chuckled at the thought. "It's traditional. Leprechauns are supposed to have pots of gold buried all over the place."

"When humans catch us," Seamus added, "they try to make us tell them where they're hidden."

"It's a fairy tale!" Mary exclaimed. "If we had pots of gold, do you think we'd be living in a dump like this?"

"We'd be in a palace!" Seamus agreed.

The two started laughing all over again.

The fairy palace was all aglow at the top of the hill. It was like to take your breath away, even if you were a leprechaun!

Mickey Muldoon grinned when he thought of the very special mischief that would take place tonight.

They were holding the Grand Midsummer Ball up there at the palace, and Mickey had never seen the place so busy! Fairy carriages were lined up one after another, each brought here by four of the flying creatures so that the fairies inside could arrive at the party without getting mussed. They stepped from the carriages one after another now, the women in gowns of delicate lace, the men with cloaks of shimmering silk. Some flew up to the palace proper. Others strode over to a particular spot, where a gentle jet of water carried them to softly arrive upon the platform above and the true entrance to the palace. Still others queued in front of a group of giant toads, whose job it was to blow gigantic bubbles, each bubble carrying its group of grandly dressed passengers up to the palace.

It was all so hoity-toity. Just the sort of fine-dress, extremely formal sort of thing that the trooping fairies loved. What fun it would be to throw a few leprechauns in their midst!

For the moment, Barney, Jericho, and he watched all the action from behind a bit of shrubbery.

"That's quite a party they're putting on for us up there," Barney said with a grin. "All those lucky girls just waiting for us."

"But there's no way we can get in," Jericho fretted.

"We'll find a way," Mickey replied. After all, they were leprechauns!

"We might have a bit of trouble passing ourselves off as one of them," Barney agreed.

Mickey raised a hand for silence. Right by the hedge where they hid, three young fellows, trooping fairies all, were walking and chattering and laughing to beat the band.

The leprechauns looked quickly at one another. Now this was an opportunity!

Barney stepped casually out from the bushes, looking first away from the three young troopers. He turned about and took a step back, his arms raised in horror.

"Oh, calamity!" he shrieked. Even Mickey had to admit that Barney was overacting just a bit.

Barney made sure the three trooping fairies saw him, then dove back behind the hedge. With such an over-wrought leprechaun before them, what could the fairies do but follow? The trooping trio jumped into the bushes, only to be confronted by not one leprechaun, but three.

"Hello, lads," Mickey said with a grin. "How's business?"

All three of the fairies were grabbed before they could get over their surprise. One of the three even attempted to unfairly fly away, but he was quickly disabused of that notion. Since it is common knowledge that any leprechaun is worth at least two of the troopers, Mickey and his friends made short work of the trio, leaving them tied in a bunch with handy vines.

Three finely dressed young men stepped forth from the bushes holding both masks and invitations to the party.

"My friends," Barney said to the other two, "I believe we've been invited to the ball."

Jericho scratched himself. "These clothes itch like blazes!"

Barney shook his head. "You're not used to such finery, Jericho."

On that, Jericho could agree. "It's—it's unnatural!"

Mickey studied the interesting mask in his hand. It covered the upper half of the face and had red feathers at the top. But it was the facial design that was the most striking.

Jericho frowned down at his own mask. "Do we have to put these on, Mickey?"

"Not if the guards are all blind," Mickey replied.

They put on the masks, which looked like nothing so much as slightly stylized leprechauns. Rather than the high cheekbones and the skinny noses of the uppity trooping fairies, they had the fine round cheeks and bold features of the most truly handsome of all magical creatures.

So for one night the palace fairies were all pretending to be leprechauns? At least the trooping fairies could admit who had the better parties.

Barney looked at both his fellows. "Makes us look a bit like . . . us, don't you think?"

"A bit," Mickey agreed. "But that's good." In fact he

couldn't think of a better disguise. It was almost as though they were meant to crash this particular party.

Mickey waved for the other two lads to follow. It was time for the three of them to visit the palace.

He thought it best that they took the bubble route up to the front door. The area around the toads was a bit darker than where those cascading water spouts sent fairies skyward. He didn't want any of them found out until they were good and ready.

So they stood silently in the queue and waited their turn. Not that any of the uppity fairies before them would even give them the time of day! The queue moved quickly, and they soon found themselves directly in front of a giant toad, who blew a bubble that enclosed all three of them. An instant later, they were off the ground and rising quickly.

"It's a powerful long way down there," Barney said as he looked through the clear bubble floor at his feet. "I hope this thing doesn't burst."

Jericho sniffed at the sleeve of his fairy silk. "What's that funny smell?"

"It's called 'clean,' " Mickey replied.

"Clean?" Jericho asked.

Barney nodded. "You'll not have come across it before."

The bubble had nearly risen to the palace proper. The bubble before them settled at the very edge of a long ledge, where a fairy flunky stepped forward with a long ornate pin. A single poke with this device, and the bubble burst, the fairies within using their wings to gently flutter to the ground. They then proceeded to march on into the palace, which seemed to be lit by a thousand glowworms. It was very grand indeed.

Mickey looked at his two cohorts. Now the adventure truly began.

Their bubble was next. The flunky with the pin stepped

forward. Mickey realized he was holding his breath. They had to make this look good.

The bubble burst. The floor beneath their feet was gone. Mickey launched himself forward. He saw Barney by his side. They both hit the ground running, but managed a stumbling halt.

But where was the last member of the trio? Mickey looked around.

Jericho almost hadn't made it onto solid ground. He stood balanced on the very edge of the ledge, teetering back and forth. Mickey and Barney were over there in an instant. Each grabbed a hand and dragged their friend to safety.

The flunky stared at them with a most puzzled expression. Barney reached into a pouch at his belt and picked out a handful of gold coins. He placed them in the flunky's hand.

"There you are, my good man," he said most seriously. "Don't spend it all at once."

The flunky was astonished. He bowed deeply as the three walked to the palace door. As they moved away, Barney shook his pouch. It once again seemed full to the brim with coins.

"It's a marvelous thing," Barney said with a smile, "fairy gold."

Mickey wondered what expression the flunky would have when he realized his hand was empty.

But all thoughts of flunkies and fairy gold fled when they walked into the palace proper. For there were hundreds of fairies, in clothes of a hundred fantastic colors, dancing, swirling about to the strains of a waltz, some on the floor and others waltzing through the air. All these hundreds lost in the dance.

And every male fairy was wearing a mask!

Chapter Nine

Lady Margaret thought she should be enjoying the ball more than this. Here she was, chief lady-in-waiting to Princess Jessica, a position of some importance within the royal establishment, and where did she find herself? Dancing with that self-important Count Grogan!

Well, she supposed someone had to dance with the count, and she supposed she was willing to do her part for the harmony of the palace, but did she have to look at that foolish thing on his face?

She could stand it no longer.

"Take off that stupid leprechaun mask, Grogan," she demanded.

He did as he was told, laughing as if it were the grandest joke in the world. "But these are masks of stupidity. Aren't they delicious? They're my idea, perfect for a mad midsummer ball."

"You would think of something like that." So Count

Grogan had come up with the masks, and his aunt, who just happened to be queen, let him do whatever he wanted. It was just so typical. Lady Margaret would be happier when this whole grand ball was over and she could go back to tending to the princess.

Well, now that they were here, Mickey thought, what next? He had to admit he found all these swirling fairies just the slightest bit overwhelming.

Barney poked him in the ribs.

"No point in just looking at the sweet shop. Dive in and grab a partner, lads."

He walked quickly over to a particularly beautiful fairy nearby. Ah, but they were all beautiful!

He bowed before the lady.

"As one who's been out east and seen a few things, may I say you're the most lovely. Can I have this dance?"

Before the lady could say a word, Barney had taken her arm and spun her out onto the floor.

Mickey and Jericho looked at each other. They wouldn't let anyone show them up, most of all Barney. Each of them grabbed partners and joined the dance.

But the dancing stopped abruptly as a great fanfare filled the room, the trumpeters' horns unrolling as they blew into them. Mickey looked at his partner and saw her watching the far end of the room, where three fairies entered, all wearing clothing so fine and elegant they made the rest of the partygoers appear to be wearing rags.

This, Mickey realized, must be the royal family. King Boric, dressed in enough lace and finery it was a wonder he found someplace to breathe. And Queen Morag, who wore so much jewelry it was a wonder she didn't topple over from the weight. But the third fairy was their daughter, who was so lovely she made all the others in the room look plain, with her wavy blond hair cascading to her shoulders. She wore a shimmering dress in a shade of green that might put every leaf in the forest to shame. He had heard her name. What was it? Ah, yes. Princess Jessica.

The fairies all applauded. Even Mickey joined in a bit, just to keep up the disguise.

And everybody bowed. Mickey supposed he had to do that too, just maybe not quite as deep as all those around him. The royal family were walking through the midst of all their guests, and Mickey wouldn't mind getting a better look at the princess.

She glanced at him as she passed. And she smiled.

Mickey had never seen such a smile. It was like the sun breaking through a month of clouds or those first flowers poking their way past the last bits of snow.

She walked on past. Mickey resolved that he would see that smile again.

A chamberlain's work was never done. The ball was going splendidly so far. But now was the all-important introduction of the royal family. The king waved to the orchestra and they resumed their playing. The king smiled and bobbed his head to the tune, until the queen elbowed him in the ribs.

King Boric sighed, but then bowed to his wife.

"Would you care to dance?"

"Against whom?" the queen demanded.

The king sighed again as he blew a bit of lace out of his face.

"Why do you make me feel—effeminate?"

"Oh, walnuts!" The queen grabbed him and they began to dance.

Well, at least the royal couple had joined in the festivities. Now the others could resume dancing as well. As for the chamberlain's duty, there was no helping it. The princess needed a partner.

He asked, and she accepted. If only he could remember how to waltz! Despite the fact that her feet were so small, he kept stepping on the young royal's toes.

He harrumphed in apology.

"I'm sorry, Princess Jessica. I've never danced so badly."

The young fairy replied in the most sweet and innocent voice he had ever heard.

"Oh, you've danced before?"

To the chamberlain's delight, someone tapped him upon the shoulder. He gladly gave way to the new partner.

He had done his duty. He could go back to fretting upon the sidelines. And the princess could have a wonderful evening of innocent fun.

Mickey couldn't believe it.

Here he had marched straight across the room, to where the princess was dancing with this old fuddy-duddy, and had boldly tapped the fairy upon the shoulder. The old fellow had given way without even a look back.

Mickey had stepped forward as the music played . . . and now she was in his arms.

She looked at him curiously.

"Hello. What are you staring at?"

Was he staring? He guessed he was. How could he help it? Once he had seen the princess, why would he bother looking at anything else?

But how could he put his feelings into words? A leprechaun had to try. What was he staring at indeed?

"The fairest beauty that ever stood before the eyes of

man since Helen danced her willing way along the wondering walls of Troy."

The princess blushed the slightest bit at his speech. Ah, the color made her fairer still! "It's only a gift of words you shower on me," she replied, "but I have to say they shine."

Oh, no. She had that all wrong.

"You shine, Princess mine, you shine!"

And so they danced.

Lady Margaret was nearly beside herself. Would she have to dance with this self-centered Grogan all night? He had explained in great detail the plans he had for the improvement of the palace, described at least twice his great military victories, and bragged about the way he had with women. Way he had with women? No wonder she was dancing with him. She had done it from a sense of duty after all the young ones had gone running off.

But duty could only carry you so far. Perhaps she could ask for a glass of punch. Maybe the orchestra would stop playing for a moment. Perhaps she could pretend that she was having some sort of seizure. No, it wouldn't work. Count Grogan was so busy talking she doubted that he'd notice.

A burly young man tapped Grogan upon the shoulder.

Finally, a hero to the rescue! Lady Margaret smiled at him.

The youngster grabbed Grogan and danced away.

What? He wasn't going to dance with her after all? For an instant, Lady Margaret was deeply offended.

Then she realized she was free of Grogan. In her opinion, the prankster had gotten by far the worst of the deal.

But the young dancer had deserted the count for a

young female. His sudden defection left Grogan reeling at the far end of the room.

The count took a deep breath, straightened his epaulets, and tried to catch Lady Margaret's eye.

Certainly there was something she had to check on. Immediately. At the other end of the palace.

Lady Margaret made her break for freedom.

The watershees were singing. And Mickey thought it was wonderful.

They were delicate creatures, and their voices were more delicate still. They flew up beside the orchestra as they sang in unison:

> *There are many fair things on earth as it goes,*
> *Blue skies, green grass, and the red, red rose,*
> *But fairest of all as far as we can see,*
> *Are four blushing watershees . . . .*

Then each sang in turn:

> *Like me.*
> *And me.*
> *And me.*
> *And me.*

And then they sang the chorus again. Many was the time Mickey would have thought such delicate singing much too precious. Now he found it the most marvelous noise. Everything was wonderful with the princess in his arms.

The watershees finished their song to great applause. Mickey was ready to dance again, but the princess took his arm and led him from the floor. He didn't care. He would follow her anywhere.

Together, they walked out into the palace garden. It was just the two of them now, alone.

"You look so lovely in the moonlight," he said to her.

She smiled and raised her hand so that it was only inches from his face.

"Take off your mask," she said.

Mickey's heart thudded. And so it would end.

"That's not a good idea," he managed.

She seemed surprised. "Are you frightened?"

"Yes—" he began. "No—" Nothing about her could ever be frightening.

She smiled again. "Then do it."

For that smile, he would do anything.

"For your sake only."

"I'll turn away," she said and spun away so that her back was to him.

Mickey took off his mask as she turned back.

Her mouth opened in shock.

"But—but—you're a leprechaun!" She looked down at his mask. "A real one," she added.

"I am," Mickey agreed.

She shook her head as if the very idea was beyond her. "But leprechauns are all vile, villainous, and vulgar."

Was that the way of it then? Well, Mickey had a thing or two to say about that.

"And trooping fairies are all sneering, snobbish, and selfish!" he pointed out.

She frowned. "That's not true. We're not like that."

Mickey nodded. "And we're not all vile and villainous. Now, vulgar maybe. That's fair enough—can't argue there."

She started laughing. What a wonderful sound.

"But you're still a leprechaun!"

"And you're still a trooping fairy. Does it make any difference?"

She smiled a smile the likes of which he had never seen.

"No," she said softly.

He kissed her hand.

He looked up at her face, and at that moment, he swore there was love in her eyes.

What future could a leprechaun have with a fairy princess? Well, they might not have a future, but they had this moment.

Mickey smiled broadly at her beauty, grabbed her around the waist, and kissed her full on the lips.

He let her go before she even had a chance to struggle. He laughed and ran a bit up the path.

"How dare you!" she called.

He laughed again. "Oh, I dare, Princess Jessica. I dare!"

She was doing her best to be angry, but Mickey swore he could see a smile breaking through.

"Come back here and apologize!" she demanded.

"You'll have to catch me first!" He waved a finger. "No flying!"

"And you think a princess can't run."

She hitched up her flowing robes and took off after him. Both of them were laughing as they ran about the gardens.

She should have gotten out when she could.

The burly fellow who had danced off with Count Grogan had returned to Lady Margaret's side. She had been charmed as the fellow began to dance—until he opened his mouth.

"The greatest sound I ever heard was a flamenco danced by a man with false teeth. When I was young I never wanted to dance because I thought I had two left feet. Then I found out my feet were fine. It was the two left shoes that were bothering me."

The burly fellow laughed loud and long. Lady Margaret looked to the heavens.

"I'm not stopping you getting back to someone, am I?" she asked, perhaps a bit too hopefully. "I wouldn't want to monopolize you."

Her masked partner gave her a smile worthy of a leprechaun. "No, I'm all yours."

"Oh, lucky me."

They spun about in the dance. And there was Count Grogan, frowning their way again. Was the poor man jealous? Lady Margaret didn't realize she could still have that effect on the male of the species. Perhaps she should try to catch Grogan's eye and get him to cut in.

She wanted Count Grogan to rescue her?

Now, Lady Margaret thought, she really was getting desperate.

They were dancing again, even closer than before. Princess Jessica was afraid the king and queen might start searching for her if she was too long out of sight. So Mickey had agreed to put on his mask and return to the ball.

"Meet me afterward," he whispered.

The princess looked up at him as she whispered her reply.

"I can't. It's too dangerous. You shouldn't be here."

But she couldn't take her eyes off him. And he couldn't take his eyes off her.

A leprechaun and a trooping fairy. True opposites. Sworn enemies.

Somehow, they would make it work.

Chapter Ten

Oh, dear. The chamberlain knew it had been much too quiet an evening. The way Count Grogan was purposefully striding toward the royal couple, it wouldn't be quiet for long.

The count stopped smartly before the king and queen, the expression on his face most dour.

"Sire," he said in a conspiratorial tone, "I think we've been invaded."

King Boric frowned in response. "By who?"

"Whom," Queen Morag corrected sharply. "By *whom*."

The king made a most unpleasant face, far worse than the earlier frown, but added, "By *whom*?"

Count Grogan leaned closer to dispense the awful news. "Leprechauns."

"Where? Where?" The king looked wildly about.

"They wouldn't dare!" the queen announced.

"How can you tell?" the king insisted. "With these dam-

nable masks, they all look like leprechauns." He pointed
a regal finger at the younger man. "That was your brilliant
idea, Count Grogan!"

The queen stepped between the two, her hands fluttering about as if she might be able to disperse her husband's words into the air.

"Don't blame my nephew, Boric. It was a brilliant idea!"
She smiled at Grogan. "So deliciously funny!"

But the king would not be deterred. "How do you know
there are leprechauns here?"

Count Grogan nodded knowingly. "Smell."

That only made Boric's frown deepen. "I haven't your
sensitive nostrils, Count. If you accuse them and they're
not, there will be a scandal."

Grogan only smiled. "I have a better way. At midnight,
announce that all masks are to be taken off."

"Yet another brilliant plan!" The queen clapped her
hands in approval. "Well done, Nephew!"

Midnight? The chamberlain frowned. That was only a
few moments away. The ball had been such a pleasant
affair. Now, thanks to Grogan, the festivities would be shattered.

Still, to think there might be leprechauns about, in the
royal palace of all places! What was this world coming to?

Mickey danced with Princess Jessica. He gazed into Jessica's eyes. His skin tingled where their hands met and where
her other hand rested lightly on his shoulder. Mickey could
have danced forever.

What else of value was there in the world?

The orchestra abruptly ended their waltz. All turned to
the raised platform where King Boric now stood.

"Friends, nobles, others less fortunate," the king announced. "You must all unmask at the last stroke of midnight. Off with the masks, and all will be revealed!"

His announcement was met with a smattering of applause. That was just like trooping fairies. They probably applauded anything the king said.

Jessica looked at Mickey with alarm.

"You have to go!" she insisted.

Go? How could he after he had barely found her? But this mask thing did present a bit of a problem. Mickey looked at the hundreds of fairies surrounding him. Perhaps it would be better to leave for a moment. Tonight was only the beginning. They could plan their future later.

And they *would* have a future. He looked back at his princess.

"Only if you promise to see me again," he replied.

Jessica was getting frantic. "Go before you get caught!"

But, Mickey realized, he would rather be caught than never ever be able to look into her eyes.

"Promise me!" he insisted.

She squeezed his hand. "All right, I promise. Now go!"

He supposed he had to. He looked about the room for the best exit.

Grogan had posted guards at all the doors! So this was the reason for the midnight unmasking. Grogan had found them out and was covering the common exits.

As if the doors were the only way out. Grogan had always lacked imagination. Just look at all the fine high windows around this place. Mickey strolled most casually toward a particularly promising collection of glass and wood— French windows, he believed they were called. Quite grand, really. The clock struck its first note.

He noticed that Barney and Jericho were moving that way as well. The crowd chanted as the clock struck tone after tone. The orchestra added a drumroll.

"Two . . . three . . . four . . ."

Mickey glanced across the room. Count Grogan frowned back at him. He waved to his guards, pointing to the French windows on the far side—the very windows that were Mickey's goal. This could become quite interesting.

"Five . . . six . . . seven . . ." the crowd continued.

Half a dozen guards moved quickly across the room to bar the way to the grand windows.

"Eight . . . nine . . . ten . . . eleven . . ."

Mickey and his mates kept going that way as well. They had to go somewhere, didn't they?

"Twelve!" the crowd cheered.

With the last gong of the clock, Mickey realized, everyone had doffed his mask.

So the leprechauns took their masks off too. It was worth it simply for the look on Count Grogan's face. He snarled as he waved for his troops to rush forward—as if Mickey and his friends would actually wait for them.

All three leprechauns leapt straight up into the air, executed a trio of smart somersaults, and crashed through the window glass. They landed lightly upon the other side and took off running.

Surprise would give them a moment's head start. After that, they'd have to use their wits.

They hadn't run very far before they'd reached the end of the palace grounds and the edge of a cliff. All that was before them was that suicidal drop back down to the ground.

Well, maybe using those wits would come sooner rather than later.

"What do we do now?" Jericho asked.

Barney shook his head. "Try to remember how to fly— *Mickey?*"

Mickey realized that both his friends were looking at

him in wonder. No, they weren't looking at him. They were looking at his feet—the feet that weren't even touching the ledge. Instead, he appeared to be floating a full foot above it.

Mickey shook his head. "I don't know how I'm doing it."

Barney laughed. "Sorry to be the one to tell you this, Mick lad. You're in love! That's the sign!"

"Really?" Mickey grinned. "Is that a fact?" It made perfect sense to him.

"Grab him, Jericho," Barney called, "before he comes to his senses!"

Both Barney and Jericho grabbed one of Mickey's arms. Count Grogan's shouts grew louder behind them. It was now or never.

Mickey stepped beyond the ledge, a friend clutching him on either side.

Flying for one's self and flying for three were two completely different things. Barney and Jericho, after all, managed to triple his weight. They sank quickly below the palace ledge, descending, if not gracefully, at least safely, until they reached the solid ground below.

The three began running one more time. Once beyond the glow of the palace, the trooping fairies would never find them!

Princess Jessica couldn't believe her own parents. As soon as Mickey and his friends had escaped, they dismissed all the partygoers. Nothing, apparently, was as important as talking about the leprechauns.

Count Grogan stomped angrily back into the room. That meant Mickey had escaped! Jessica had to work very hard not to smile.

"It's a vile insult to all trooping fairies!" Grogan exclaimed.

Her father turned to her then. "Jessica, did *you* spot them?"

Spot them? What could she say? Was there any way they could tell? Had someone seen her with Mickey?

It didn't matter. She couldn't possibly explain her feelings when her parents were in this sort of state. She would simply have to lie.

"No, Father," she said meekly.

It was her mother's turn to frown at Jessica. "But you danced with one of them, didn't you, child?"

"So did Count Grogan," the princess pointed out.

All eyes turned to the count.

"What?" Grogan appeared quite flustered. "I didn't know. No one knew! I deny it all—it's a foul—it's guilt by association!"

The king's frown deepened. "You mean there were female leprechauns here as well?"

"No," Grogan snapped back, "they were all *male* leprechauns."

The king and the chamberlain glanced at each other.

"Oh . . . ah . . . hmm," the king remarked.

"Yes, indeed, indeedy," the chamberlain mused.

"Lots of your guests danced with them, sire!" the count insisted. "I was the only one who spotted them behind their devilish masks!"

The chamberlain looked at him innocently. "And— obviously—you got closer than most."

The queen stepped in quickly.

"You did very well, Nephew," Queen Morag announced. "Without you, they would have gotten away with it. King Boric will give you another medal for outstanding service to the trooping community."

"Thank you, Aunt." The count did not look pleased. "But we must get revenge first!"

"Remember the Grand Banshee!" the chamberlain cautioned. "We mustn't anger her!"

The princess had to admit she was rather fond of the old fellow. While he might not be the best dancer, he was always the voice of reason.

"But they made his majesty look a fool!" Grogan insisted.

"That isn't too difficult," the queen said.

Jessica was finding this all very trying. Why were they making so much of the leprechauns? It was only an innocent jest. How could anyone be angry with someone like Mickey?

"If they get away with this, what will they do next?" the count demanded. "You must act, sire!"

The king looked at Grogan. His cheeks grew red. His breathing became shallow. His eyebrows began to tremble. Oh, dear. Jessica had seen her father get like this before. He would work himself up into a proper snit.

The king raised his fists in the air. He jumped on the nearest balloon.

"Revenge!" her father roared as the balloon exploded beneath his feet.

Another dozen explosions followed as the count and the queen joined in.

"Revenge!" they cried. And again: "Revenge!"

Revenge for what? Dancing? Jessica simply couldn't understand this.

"Revenge! Revenge!" The bursting balloons were quite dramatic.

"Revenge!" Even the chamberlain joined in.

Only Jessica stood and watched. She had always thought trooping fairies to be so noble. But the four before her jumping up and down on the balloons—including her own parents—had not one-tenth the nobility of her dear Mickey.

They stopped at last, totally out of breath, with every balloon burst. What would they do for an encore? Invade some leprechaun's lair and start shouting all over again? Jessica had had enough of her elders. She only knew one thing. If she and Mickey could be together again, everything would be perfect!

Jack swung the nine iron back and forth, whacking off the top of one weed after another at the edge of his garden. He remembered when he used to play golf to relax. Now he didn't think anything would bring him peace of mind.

"That's a mighty energetic way of doing the weeding, Jack."

Jack gasped. He almost lost his club. Seamus was at his side.

"Ah!" he replied, doing his best to remain calm. He would get used to the way these leprechauns popped in and out of existence—someday. "I'm not gardening. I'm practicing my swing!"

"Your swing?" Seamus asked.

"Golf swing," Jack explained, nodding to the surrounding countryside. "This whole area would make a fantastic course."

"No doubt about that," Seamus agreed, "though I haven't the faintest idea what you're talking about." The leprechaun waved at the golf bag. "And that's a goodly set of weapons you have there."

"They're golf clubs." Jack pointed to the golf ball he'd placed on the ground before he'd taken to the weeds. "You hit the ball with them, try to get it into a hole."

Seamus looked from the ball back to the bag of clubs. "Would it not be easier just to put it in?" He waved at the bag. "And why do you need so many? Can you not make your mind up which one to use?"

Jack shook his head and laughed. "It's a long story, Seamus. But believe me, playing golf in this setting—" He sighed. "It's all part of the Irish-American dream: the beautiful countryside, a pretty cottage on a blissful summer's day."

The small fellow grinned at that.

"With the wisest, shrewdest, wittiest leprechaun in all Ireland looking on."

"Now that was something I wasn't expecting," Jack admitted. "But all over New York, Chicago, anywhere, this is what stressed-out workers and executives dream about."

They all dreamed about this, Jack thought. But once they put a golf course here, wouldn't all this—the rustic charm, the clean country air, the feeling of being truly away from it all—start to vanish as well? That was the sort of thing they never thought of at Sperry, Sperry, and McGurk. Heck, *he'd* never thought of it when he was back in New York.

What was the way that he himself had phrased it in the business proposal? Oh, yeah. Jack remembered. He said it out loud:

"A fun-filled break away from the hustle and bustle of the city, enjoying the simple life in genuine Irish surroundings."

"That's neatly put," Seamus agreed.

Jack shrugged. "It's a living."

It was a living that would fill this lovely place with hundreds of loud American executives, with their business deals, their power lunches, their cell phones. He sighed as he sat on the chopping block behind him.

Seamus frowned. "Are you all right there, Jack? Is something bothering you?"

"I'm okay," he replied all too quickly.

But was he? He'd been taken by this corner of Ireland in a way he'd never imagined. Well, this corner of Ireland and a certain lovely young redhead.

Mickey sauntered out from the cottage. Jack was just as glad for the interruption.

"When did you get in last night?" his father called.

"Late," the youth admitted with a grin. "I went partying—to the Grand Midsummer Ball."

Seamus chuckled wryly. "You went, did you? Good boy! Stuck it to them, eh? They don't like it."

Mickey nodded as though he wasn't really listening. "I met this girl," he added. "Princess Jessica."

Seamus stopped chuckling.

"Princess Jessica?" he asked sharply. "King Boric's daughter?"

Mickey sighed. "She's an angel with a face."

"You mindless squirt!" Seamus's voice rose with every word. "Leave her be! That's an order!"

Mickey's smile faded to be replaced by that glowering look perfected by teenagers everywhere.

"Who from?" he demanded.

Seamus threw a rock at the boy. Mickey sidestepped it neatly.

"Me!" Seamus admitted. "I don't want that kind of trouble." He raised his voice as he called out to the cottage. "Mary Muldoon, this is all your fault!" He looked up to the human on the scene. "Jack, tell him to listen to his father."

Jack shook his head. "I never did."

"Neither did I," Seamus agreed, "but what's that got to do with it?"

Mary strode from the cottage. From the looks of it, she was no more happy than her husband.

"So he's told you, has he?" she called. "You're his father—speak to him!"

"I am speaking to him, woman!" He pointed his thumb at his son. "Mickey Muldoon, stay away from that girl or I'll disown you!"

"You don't own anything," Mickey pointed out, "so how can you disown me?"

"Don't speak to your father like that!" Mary said sharply.

"You do," Mickey pointed out.

Mary glared at her offspring. "It's expected. I'm his wife!"

Jack rose quietly as the argument went on. So Mickey had gotten involved with a girl from the other side of the tracks, huh? Something like that. Jack guessed he understood their situation about as well as Seamus understood golf. Oh, well. They'd work it out. They were magical creatures, after all. Jack had worries of his own. Like what he was going to do about this beautiful countryside. Not to mention a certain woman named Kathleen.

Chapter Eleven

Now this, Kathleen Fitzpatrick thought, could be the finest day of the year, if only some of the men around her would get some sense into their fool pig heads!

Here it was, the summer beach race, the premier trotting event of the season. People lined the dunes at the beach's edge—pretty much all the locals, plus a number from the surrounding towns. Bookmakers marched back and forth among the crowd, shouting the odds. Some of the other horses were gathered over at the starting line already, their drivers perched on the lightweight buggies behind them. By all rights, Kathleen should be over there with them. But would any of these men listen?

First, her brothers were impossible. She was sure, if she took her case to the judges, she could get them to see reason, but they were almost as bad. Look at them! Shifty Bert Bagnell might be the mayor, but that was mostly because nobody else wanted the job! And Father Daley had brought his pink elephant along! What kind of judges were these?

Kathleen wanted answers!

"Why aren't I allowed to race?" she demanded.

"You're a woman!" her brother George shouted back. As if that was reason enough to deny anything.

"See?" her brother James added smugly. "You can't."

"As mayor and chief race steward," Bagnell said with an insincere smile, "I have to confirm it's in the rules."

"Then change the rules!" Kathleen exclaimed.

"We will," Bagnell assured her, "next year."

"I'll see to it," Father Daley chorused.

Her youngest brother Harry grinned. "Meanwhile, Kathleen, you're out!"

She knew what this was all about. She waved at the horse she'd left by the starting line. "You're scared to face my Firefly. He'd leave your nags flat-footed at the start."

Her brother John laughed at that one. "I think not! Unless it was a race to the glue factory!"

Kathleen had had quite enough of her brothers' superior attitude. Perhaps she couldn't race, but her horse certainly could.

"I'll get someone else to ride for me," she announced.

Father Daley considered that.

"That would be fair, wouldn't it?" he turned and asked his elephant.

"Right," Kathleen replied before anyone else could object. "Will someone here ride Firefly for me?"

She looked at all of those gathered around the judges' table. Her brothers, she noticed, were doing their best to look threatening. No one moved forward.

"Come on!" she called. "There must be someone with enough guts!"

Peter Shaughnessy, a nice young fellow from the next

town over, started to push his way through the crowd.
But Kathleen's brothers formed a line. All four of them
clenched their fists. And then they growled.

Peter thought better of volunteering.

Now Kathleen was getting angry.

"I can't believe there isn't a man among you!" she
called.

But then she saw someone pushing his way through the
crowd from the corner of her eye. So there was someone
who was man enough! She'd show her brothers after all.

The smile fell from her face when she saw it was Jack
Woods.

"I'll ride for you," Jack said.

Her brothers started growling again. It didn't seem to
faze Jack in the least. What should Kathleen say to him?

What did she want to say to him?

"It's Peeping Tom!" shouted her brother George.

"Jack," the American replied. " 'Peeping Jack,' if it
makes you happy."

"Peeping Jack!" Father Daley chuckled. "That's very
good."

This was all too much for Kathleen. "Never!" she
decided. "I'm not going to let you touch my horse!"

"Why not?" Jack smiled at her. "I thought it would
make up for our little misunderstanding."

Little misunderstanding? That was what he called it?
Kathleen bit her lip. If only he didn't have such a nice
smile.

"The tide's coming in," announced her brother George.
"Let's start the race. You're too late now anyway, Kathleen."

Her brothers all grinned at that.

There was one thing Kathleen wouldn't do, and that

was to let her brothers have the last word! She looked from her smirking siblings back to the American.

Anything to show up her brothers.

"All right," she said to Jack. "You drive Firefly."

The crowd cheered as the four Fitzpatrick brothers started for their horses. Kathleen followed with Jack at her side. She looked straight ahead. He might be driving her horse for her, but that was a situation that couldn't be helped. She certainly hoped he didn't expect any favors in return.

"The name's Jack," he said after a moment. "Jack Woods."

She knew perfectly well who he was. She kept on looking straight ahead. Best not to encourage the man.

But she supposed she should say something. He was going to drive Firefly.

"I know," she replied quietly. "Kathleen Fitzpatrick."

"I know," he answered back. "Hello, Kathleen."

So they had introduced themselves again. All well and good, she supposed. But what were they supposed to talk about now?

There was always the race.

"Have you done much trotting?" she asked.

"That's what it's called, is it?"

What did he mean by that? Kathleen looked at him sharply. Surely, he must be kidding.

"You have driven a buggy before, haven't you, Mr. Woods?"

He grinned back at her. "You sit on the seat and hang on to the reins. How hard can it be?"

She didn't think he was kidding. Kathleen had entrusted Firefly to someone who had never trotted in his life! What had she gotten herself into?

They were drawing near the starting line. Her brothers had paused long enough to sneer at Mr. Woods.

"We're going to grind you into the sand!" George offered.

Jack grinned back at them. "I'll be interested to see how you do it."

"And then run over what's left!" Harry added.

"Irish hospitality," Jack agreed. "You can't beat it."

Her brothers, disappointed that Jack wasn't taking the bait, turned and walked away.

"One thing I'll say for you: You're not frightened of my brothers like everyone else."

"You kidding?" Jack answered quietly. "They scare the hell out of me."

Kathleen abruptly stopped herself from smiling. It would do no good to encourage the man.

The way he stumbled up onto the seat, Kathleen could easily believe he'd never ridden in a buggy before. Ah, well. Maybe her horse could at least beat a couple of her brothers.

"Do your best for him, Firefly." She looked up to the driver. "Mr. Woods, give her her head and she'll win the race for you."

He smiled at her. "I'll do my best."

Well, he might not know a thing about racing, but at least this American was willing to try. There was a part of her, she realized, that was quite happy with that.

Here, Jack thought, goes nothing.

He shook the horse's reins and she trotted forward, lining up next to the other starters. Firefly was obviously well trained. Perhaps she could win the race for him after all. Jack noticed there was a Fitzpatrick brother to either side of him. If they had their way, he doubted he'd even finish the race.

The mayor and the priest both stood before them.

Mayor Bagnell spoke first.

"The race is one circuit of the track"—he pointed down the beach—"to that far flag and back."

Father Daley tottered up to the mayor's side. "Try not to cheat too much," he called to the drivers. "Remember what happened last year. Get ready. Get set. Go!"

The crowd roared as the horses broke into a trot and sped across the sand toward the flag.

All the horses, that was, except Firefly. Jack was still at the starting line. He shook the reins. Firefly took off at a speedy trot. He should have thought of that before. Now he was fifty feet behind the last of the other horses. Firefly's brisk pace was shortening the distance, but Jack didn't know how they would ever take the lead.

Jack was so intent on driving Firefly forward that it took him a minute to realize he was not alone.

"What are you doing here?" he called to Seamus and Mickey Muldoon as soon as he spotted them out of the corner of his eye.

"Thought you needed a hand," Seamus replied.

Well, he couldn't argue with that. "I do!"

"Don't you worry yourself, Mr. Woods. The old leprechaun magic will see you right."

So they were going to make something happen to put him back in the middle of the race? Right now, Jack thought, a little magic was the only way he stood a chance.

"Great!" he called to the green-clad pair. "So tell me what to do."

Seamus considered for a moment before replying.

"Get nearer the others."

If Jack didn't have to pay attention to Firefly, he would

have stared at the leprechaun in disbelief. "That's it, is it? That's the advice?"

"Pretty much," Seamus agreed.

Well, then it was back to urging his own horse forward. Jack looked ahead. Actually, the Fitzpatrick brothers seemed to be helping his cause a bit. Big George had taken the lead, while the other three brothers had spread out their own rigs immediately behind him. They were busy blocking any of the other horses from getting past, occasionally swerving their own rigs to force their competitors into the sand at either side. But all that swerving back and forth was slowing down the pack, and George was taking it easy at the front, already assured of victory—at least in his own mind.

Well, Jack might have some thoughts about that. He urged Firefly forward, past a couple of stragglers. One of the brothers' wagons was just ahead, the slightly shorter youngster of the four. Harry—that was his name.

Harry looked at Jack and grinned. He yanked on his horse's reins, trying to get his cart to veer toward Jack.

Instead, Harry's horse turned the other way, taking off at a full gallop for the sea. Harry shouted, tugging at the reins, but the horse didn't slow until the cart's wheels were half lost beneath the seawater.

Harry was out of the race.

Jack glanced over at Seamus.

"Was that you?"

The leprechaun shrugged. "May have been, yes."

But Jack had come to a decision. Firefly was such a good trotter that they were now only a short distance behind the lead buggy. Jack thought this horse was good enough to do it on her own. And he didn't want anything—even magic—to get in the way.

"Well, at the risk of sounding ungrateful," he called to

the pair by his side, "this is something I'm going to do by myself."

George's horse was already rounding the flag. Jack pulled hard on the left rein and Firefly followed the first horse's lead at full speed, the right wheel lifting from the sand as they made the turn.

Mickey and Seamus went flying from their seat, landing in one of the soft dunes.

"Go on, Jack, my boy!" he thought he heard Seamus call. "Win it for the lady!"

Well, Jack planned to do just that.

He was directly behind George now. But the other two brothers, John and James, boxed him in on either side. They wanted to make sure there was no way Firefly could pass the horse in the lead.

Well, Jack thought, the Fitzpatrick brothers might be fine buggy racers, but they had never driven in California.

"Okay," he called to the brother on either side. "That's the way you want to play it. Time for a little freeway maneuver."

He pulled on Firefly's reins, causing the mare to slow ever so slightly so that his buggy fell just behind those of the two brothers. He pulled the reins slightly left, turning his horse toward the dunes. Both John and James quickly drove their horses to block him.

"This is my exit!" Jack called as he turned Firefly toward the sea, pulling his rig past the other two before either brother could recover.

Both brothers shouted in Jack's direction. They were so upset with Jack's maneuvers they weren't paying attention to their own rigs. One of James's buggy wheels connected with one of John's. The two brothers jumped free as their buggies both crashed into the dunes.

Now it was only Jack and George. He urged Firefly forward. He would win this for Kathleen.

Kathleen couldn't believe it!

When the race had begun, Jack had seemed pretty hopeless, not even knowing how to make a proper start of it. But as soon as he'd gotten Firefly started, her mare had done nothing but gain on the others. Maybe Jack was just incredibly lucky. Maybe he was just a natural horseman. Kathleen didn't care. She only wanted Firefly to win!

No one ever beat her brothers on race day. But it looked like this American just might be able to pull it off. First, he'd gotten Harry to drive his buggy into the ocean. Now, he'd gotten two of her other brothers so confused that they'd dumped themselves straight into the dunes. Now the race was down to Jack and her brother George.

"Jack . . . Jack . . . Jack!"

She realized she was chanting along with the crowd. That would never do. As her poor dead mother would have said, she must maintain some dignity.

Kathleen took a deep breath, determined to watch the race somewhat more quietly. Jack had pulled Firefly up by George's side and they were racing head to head. The crowd was cheering for both of them as the horses trotted full speed, neither one willing to give any ground.

Come on, Firefly, Kathleen thought. Come on, Jack!

Great clouds of sand rose from underneath the pounding hooves. They were in the home stretch, maybe fifty feet to go. Kathleen could see her brother grimace and Jack's solemn determination. Both men shook the reins. Both horses rocketed toward the finish.

Five feet from the ribbon, Firefly pulled ahead.

The race was hers by a nose.

The whole crowd cheered. Kathleen cheered along with the rest. Firefly had won. Jack had beaten her impossible brother!

The American slowed Firefly with a tug of the reins and jumped from the cart. Everyone pushed forward to congratulate him. Kathleen resolved to be calm. She moved to his side, meeting him just before the judges' table.

She nodded and smiled, dignified all the way. "A good race, Mr. Woods."

The American grinned back down at her.

"A good horse, Miss Fitzpatrick."

Mayor Bagnell stepped from behind the judges' table, a large silver cup in his hands.

"To the winner, Mr. Jack Woods," he announced.

Father Daley beamed at his side, pink elephant in tow.

"And without any cheating," the priest announced, "at least that I could see without my glasses."

Jack took the cup and turned, offering it to Kathleen. Hesitantly, she touched the cup's silver side. Oh, she had always wanted to win this cup!

Dignity, she reminded herself. Decorum. Her poor dead mother would be proud.

"I'd like you to have it," Jack said. "It's your horse. She did all the work. I just followed behind."

"I can't accept it," she said firmly. Dignity. Decorum. Remember her mother.

She looked up the beach and saw her brothers trudging toward the crowd. Her dirty, damp, bedraggled brothers, who not only wouldn't let her win anything, but wouldn't even let her enter the race.

Who needed dignity?

"On the other hand," she said quickly, "it would be

ungracious not to." She accepted the cup with a smile.
"Thank you."

Everyone applauded.

She smiled at her brothers stomping across the sand
and held the trophy high. It was worth it to see them scowl.

At least they were walking side by side. One thing at a
time, Jack told himself. Kathleen hugged the silver cup to
her side.

"That was a nice gesture, Mr. Woods," she said at last,
"and I never did really thank you."

"Call me Jack." He tried on his best smile.

"You're from New York—Jack," she replied.

How did she know that? Well, he supposed she could
have asked around the village; he'd had dealings with Bagnell and a couple of the others.

"How did you know?" he asked.

Kathleen hesitated. He thought she blushed a bit.

"Well, I just guessed," she said after a moment.

"Well, you're right," he agreed. "At least that's where
I live now."

"I'd like to go there," Kathleen said with a bit of a smile.
"The Statue of Liberty, all those skyscrapers."

"It's quite something," Jack added, just to answer her.
He wished he could tell her a lot of other things, like how
he couldn't get her off his mind. But he had barely gotten
the woman to talk. He didn't want to scare her off now.

Kathleen sighed. "I've never been out of Ireland."

Jack smiled at that. "I can think of a lot worse places to
be."

She looked at him sharply. "Do you like it here?"

He nodded. "I do. Maybe even more than I thought I
would."

She nodded in turn. "Well, that's good. We don't get many tourists, thank goodness."

"No." Jack felt a sudden pang of guilt. That would all change if Sperry, Sperry, and McGurk had their way. How could he do anything that might change the home life of Kathleen Fitzpatrick?

"No, you don't," he finished quietly.

He couldn't think of what to say after that. Apparently, neither could Kathleen. They walked in silence for a minute.

Kathleen looked away from the beach. "Well, I've got to get—"

Jack didn't want to lose her now.

"Kathleen, do you mind if I ask a favor?" he blurted.

"I don't know till I hear it," she replied with a smile that said she didn't mind at all.

Now he needed a favor to ask. He said the first thing that popped into his head. "Well, would you show me round the countryside? I'd like to take a few photographs of some of the beauty spots of this part of Ireland."

Kathleen was looking at him quite intently. As far as he was concerned, she was one of the beauty spots hereabouts.

"Are you married?" she asked abruptly.

Jack felt as if he had been kicked in the stomach. Where had that come from? He took a ragged breath.

"No," he admitted.

"Why not?"

Jack grinned. Kathleen certainly cut to the heart of things.

"Because—" he started. "Well—" he tried again. There had been that business with Sharon—the expectations, the broken engagement—but how could he explain that in just a few words? He didn't know what to say. Maybe if he turned it around.

"Why aren't you?" he asked.

"Never wanted to," Kathleen said with a brisk nod.

"Well," Jack agreed, "there you go."

"Meet me tomorrow morning," she replied. "Nine o'clock."

She really smiled directly at him then, maybe for the first time. The smile was gone after only a second, but it made Jack's heart beat double time. She turned and walked quickly away, the silver cup swinging at her side.

Jack watched her go. Maybe a dozen paces down the path, she turned and looked back. Their eyes met for only a second, and then she turned again. Jack thought he'd best be getting back to his cottage too. Otherwise, he'd stand here all day, just waiting for another glance.

He felt like jumping, running, singing. The air was fresh and new. The world was beautiful.

Jack had to admit it. Ireland was a most magical place indeed.

Chapter Twelve

It had been a wonderful morning. Jack never wanted it to end. Kathleen had taken him to see a dozen vistas that literally startled him with their beauty, a couple of which he had missed on his previous picture-taking jaunts by turning the wrong way down a country lane. The millhouse they'd just left, with its waterwheel and river vistas, was particularly stunning. It certainly helped to have a local around when you were doing this sort of thing. Especially if the local was someone as wonderful as Kathleen.

As they walked, she had started to quiz him about his life. First about New York, then about all the different things in America. Now she'd gotten around to his job.

"And what do you do with Sperry, Sperry, and—whatchamacallit?" she asked.

"McGurk," Jack answered. "Sperry, Sperry, and Mc-Gurk. I'm an executive vice president in charge of coordination."

"That sounds very impressive."

Jack always thought so. Still he tried to look modest, concentrating on taking a picture of the thatched hut just over yonder.

"In fact," he explained, "if I put together a particular deal I'm working on now, there's a good chance I'll make senior vice president."

"Is that good?" Kathleen asked.

Was that good? The woman obviously had no experience with American business. Jack thought to say something about it, but she had already turned away to look at something else. He followed her in silence until they crossed over a low hill and got a glimpse of the ocean through a new set of dunes. It was beautiful here, even prettier than on the stretch of beach where they'd held the race.

Still, Jack felt he should say *something*.

" 'Course, there's a lot of guys going for the same job. No guarantees. I've got to deliver."

Not that she was really listening. Jack didn't care. He'd talk about anything, just so she'd talk to him in return.

She pointed to the ground between them. "Have you seen this shell? Is it not the most beautiful thing?"

She picked it up and handed it to him. Their fingers brushed for an instant. Jack thought his heart might stop.

He took a deep breath and looked down at the object Kathleen had placed in his hand. She was right. The large shell was breathtaking, white and brown and pink. He could see a dozen colors in its spiral pattern.

"It is," he said softly, looking up at her. "It's beautiful."

There was so much that was simply beautiful here. It made Sperry, Sperry, and McGurk, even the senior vice president's job, all seem a little hollow.

Kathleen grabbed the camera from Jack's hand.

"Smile!" she called as she put the viewfinder up to her eye.

Jack did just that. It was easy to smile when he was with Kathleen.

He just wished this could go on forever.

But how could that ever be?

Kathleen decided that Jack Woods looked particularly fine when he smiled.

They had spent most of the day trooping around the countryside. It had been a long time since she herself had taken the time to really look at her surroundings. It was a most lovely place.

Now evening had come at last, and they had both retreated to the warmth of Jack's cottage to look over their day's work. It was getting late. The sky was growing dark outside. She'd have to be going soon. But not quite yet.

Jack had spread the day's photos on the table before them, and they seemed to take turns commenting on one picture or another.

Jack picked up a photo of a seagull in flight. It was supposed to be a picture of something else on the beach, but the seagull had been startled and flown in the way, surprising both Jack and Kathleen in turn.

The way the seagull spread its wings and opened its beak, it looked as if it had jumped up in surprise.

Kathleen laughed when she thought about the moment. Jack laughed at the same time.

She liked that, the two of them laughing together. She turned to look at Jack.

And Jack looked at her.

Everything stopped.

Kathleen never wanted to look anywhere else.

A log shifted on the fire, noisily sending sparks flying across the hearth.

Kathleen blinked.

Oh, she should be going. She surely should be going.

Mickey knew his mates meant well. But how could they understand? Had they ever been in love?

Here it was, a wondrous, balmy evening, and Barney was trying to argue him out of it, as if such a thing were possible!

"Jessica's the daughter of a king whose world spins on a rim of gold," he pointed out. "She'll not want to live in a dusty nook with cold hills and long roads only fit for walking."

Mickey only smiled. He did a lot of that these days. "That's in the future, Barney. This is here and now. I don't care how it goes as long as I go with Jessica."

He'd let Barney and Jericho argue to their hearts' content. After all, what were friends for? Not that it mattered. Didn't they realize love could solve anything?

Barney nodded at his last remark. "No good will come of it, but you're in love, and so you won't listen."

Another voice came out of the trees.

"Listen to him, Mickey."

He looked about and saw an oakshee step out from his tree and drift up to the forest path. These spirits looked a bit like trees themselves or perhaps like great standing logs, save that they had long faces and were ghostly white in color. They might even appear quite frightening in certain circles. But by and large they were personable folk, always good for a few minutes' chat on a summer's eve.

Besides, Mickey knew this particular oakshee.

"Hello, Jerry lad," he called up to the ghostly image. "We're talking about love."

"We oakshees know about love," the spirit replied in his moaning voice. "Don't we, lads?"

Mickey turned about and saw that other tree spirits had gathered around. It was a whole forest of oakshees!

"Of course we know," one of the others moaned back.

Well, this was a side of the oakshees Mickey had never seen. "Who do you love?" he asked.

"Trees," Jerry replied with a sigh. "We're tree spirits. We love trees."

Mickey shook his head. "That doesn't count!"

"Of course it counts," Jerry insisted.

"Just you try to do anything to our trees," added one of his mates, "and you'll see how much we love 'em!"

"But you leprechauns are decent fellas," Jerry quickly added. "You've always time to stop and 'shoot the leaves'— not like the troopers with all their measuring and blossom nonsense."

"I hate blossoms," Jericho agreed.

"They *work* too hard," moaned the second oakshee.

"Work!" Barney shuddered. "It's the death of freedom as we know it!"

Mickey looked up. Someone was coming. All the solitaries could sense that sort of thing. In an instant, the oakshees went back into their trees, and the leprechauns turned invisible.

Wait a second. Mickey knew this pair. This should prove interesting.

Who was there?

Jack swore he had heard voices in the forest, but Kathleen didn't even seem to notice. Probably just his imagina-

tion. Ever since he'd discovered leprechauns, he'd gotten
a little jumpy.

He looked back to Kathleen, who was trying her best to
explain her brothers.

"They're good souls really. It's just that they're a little
overprotective of me since our parents died. Do you have
any family, Jack?"

"A full set," Jack said with a grin. "Father who runs a
cab business, mother who runs my father, two little sisters,
an older brother, and a terrapin called Dwight."

"And they all live in New York?"

"Dwight does, and so does my brother. He's a lawyer.
But he's okay. My folks are back in Arizona, where I was
raised."

"And do you miss them?"

Did he miss them? Sometimes, he thought he was too
busy to miss anybody. But then he had come to Ireland
and met Kathleen. Yes, his family had its good points and
its bad points, but he missed them.

"I do. Yes."

"So why did you leave?"

That was easier. "Oh, I guess my career took me to the
big city."

"And are you happy there?"

That was the hardest question of all. How could he think
of New York? What could he say?

Only what he felt in his heart. He looked at Kathleen.

"I'm happy here. Right now. With you."

"Really? It doesn't take much to please you then."

She was trying to make a little joke out of all of this. But
Jack had never been more serious in his life. He touched
her cheek. She didn't move away. He looked into her eyes,
then leaned forward and gave her the gentlest of kisses.
He stepped back. Her eyes opened and they looked at

each other for the longest of moments, but neither moved away.

Jack moved forward again. Their lips met, and they kissed for a very long time.

The leprechauns and oakshees were tittering all around him to see such human romance. It only made Mickey sigh. After all, what could humans do that leprechauns couldn't do better?

He was happy for Jack, who seemed like a right fellow as far as humans went. But seeing the two of them together like that set up a longing deep in his heart and made him want to see Jessica all the more!

Well, she had promised to see him again. Mickey thought it was time to make good on that promise.

Chapter Thirteen

Lady Margaret had to admit that, in all her hundreds of years, she had never seen the likes of this. A princess of the trooping fairies in love with the likes of Mickey Muldoon! Well, Margaret was the handmaiden to the princess, and she would do just about anything to make the dear girl happy, but this might be too much!

She gazed out the palace window for perhaps the hundredth time.

"Nobody there," she repeated once again. "Not even the whiff of a leprechaun."

Jessica sighed. "He said he'd be here this evening."

Lady Margaret shook her head. The princess would have to learn a hard lesson.

"They say a lot of things, do men—especially leprechaun men. They're fond of saying things they don't mean. Words as light as gossamer and just about as serious."

But the princess would hear none of it. She sighed again, adding, "Mickey Muldoon isn't like that."

"Then where is he?" Lady Margaret demanded.

"I'm here."

Lady Margaret whirled about to see Mickey grinning at her through the window. She staggered back, gasping for breath. She couldn't stand when leprechauns did that!

Jessica laughed as Lady Margaret tried to catch her breath.

"You've made my heart go all pitta-pat, pitta-pat!" the lady exclaimed.

"Mine too," the princess agreed. She took Lady Margaret's hand and hurried her from the room.

"He's come to see me, Lady Margaret. You wait in there."

The lady frowned at that. This was all going a bit too fast for her old fairy bones. "I've been your lady-in-waiting for twenty years, so I should know how to do that by now. I'm just never sure exactly what it is I'm supposed to be waiting for."

The lady found the door slammed in her face.

Oh, dear. This was most troublesome.

Princess Jessica looked at Mickey. He was a handsome thing when he was silent, but when he opened his mouth, his words were gold.

"Jessica," he said as he took her hands, "come with me to where the rain is light and the sun is hot."

He tugged her gently to him.

"I shouldn't listen," she replied softly, "but your words are stars in my ears."

She stepped upon the window ledge and then beyond

the window ledge, using her wings to keep her aloft. She realized that Mickey was floating at her side.

"I didn't know leprechauns could fly," she said softly.

Mickey grinned at her. "We can't now. We've lost the knack ... unless we're in love." He wiggled his feet to show they touched nothing but air. "And you can't lie to gravity. Come with me!"

"I can't do it!" she said. It would hurt her parents so. And yet what he said about flying ... What clearer sign could she have of his devotion?

"We can do anything!" he insisted. He drew her toward him, away from the window, and perhaps toward a brand-new life.

"Oh, no, you don't, missy."

Princess Jessica stopped abruptly as a pair of hands grabbed her waist.

She looked over her shoulder. It was her lady-in-waiting.

"Lady Margaret!" she exclaimed.

"You're being carried to the stars on words on love," the lady chided. "Remember, most men start at the bottom and lose ground."

But how could Margaret keep her from her one true love? "I thought you were my friend!" Jessica called.

The lady nodded. "I am. Otherwise I would have called the guards."

Mickey looked down at a sudden commotion below.

"You don't have to. They're here!"

Jessica looked down from where Lady Margaret had dragged her back to the window ledge. A dozen members of the fairy guards were speeding up from below.

"I'll be back for you, my love!" the young leprechaun called as he flew off awkwardly. He obviously didn't have enough experience in the air. How could he elude the palace guard?

"Mickey!" Jessica called. "Mickey!"

But her brave leprechaun and his pursuers were soon lost in the darkness.

Mickey Muldoon ran, but his thoughts were with what he had left behind. It was tragic to be torn from Jessica like that. And because of a group of trooping fairies besides!

Well, he supposed Jessica could be considered a trooping fairy as well. But Mickey would make an exception for anyone as lovely and charming as the princess. If only he could go back and hold her in his arms. But he had other worries just now. He had only just begun learning about this flying thing for one. And those troopers behind him were armed and dangerous.

The palace guards behind him were doing everything within their power to make him a prisoner. They carried lances that shot out small round balls—strange spheres that expanded upon hitting the air, turning into great wads of webbing that would catch anything in their path. Mickey had already barely managed to avoid a couple of them. He didn't think he could escape many more. The troopers swarmed around him, using their agility to try to cut him off or to get a better shot.

It was only his growing panic that was keeping him a free leprechaun. He flew up and down, side to side, trying to keep as many obstacles as possible between himself and his pursuers. He had thought he might be able to shake them once he'd left the open air around the palace for the darkness of the close-packed trees, but the fairies stayed much too close.

He'd twisted about, doubling back behind a row of shrubs, but a couple members of the guard had flown ahead to cut him off. He turned again, flying toward a space between the trees.

A standing stone was right in his path. He somersaulted past.

The stone took the web that was meant for him. It was only a matter of time before one of those things connected with him.

Blind panic could only take him so far. He might have bitten off a bit more than he expected. He'd need some help to get free of this. And he knew just where to find it.

He flew closer to a line of familiar trees.

"Oakshees! Oakshees!" he called. "To arms! To arms! Troopers are damaging your trees with cobwebs!"

The moment he called, he saw the faces form within the bark. The spirits were waking.

He glanced behind. The troopers were closing fast.

But the oakshees were with him.

A branch had grown six feet in an instant, hitting one guardsman full in the face. Two others were grabbed by swooping tree limbs and left hanging upside down, struggling to free themselves from the maze of branches.

The troopers panicked, shooting their lances everywhere. An oakshee got a webful in the face.

Now, Mickey thought, the spirits were really riled. He found a branch he could settle down on to catch his breath. The final few troopers were quickly dispatched until only one remained.

The last one realized he was quite alone. Mickey grinned back at him. The trooper turned to flee only to be punched by a branch that somehow formed a fist. The trooper fluttered to the forest floor below.

"Thanks, lads!" Mickey called to the oakshees.

The tree spirits waved a ghostly reply.

Mickey jumped down from the branch and ran off into

the forest. As much as he liked to fly, he was surer on his feet. He wanted to get some distance from any other troopers before he considered what to do next. For this Mickey swore: Though every leprechaun and trooping fairy might stand against it, he would find a way to be with his Jessica yet.

The chamberlain sighed quietly. Not that any of the exalted fairy lords and ladies in the council chamber would have heard him. They were all too busy shouting and arguing to hear much of anything.

"A loutish leprechaun has forced his attention on a royal princess!" Grogan wailed.

His words put the queen into an even greater huff than she'd been in before.

"What are you waiting for, Boric? Christmas?" she demanded of her husband. "Our daughter's been insulted!"

The king himself was merely red in the face, working his way up toward a royal tantrum.

"I'm on the brink!" he declared.

"Topple over, sire!" Grogan insisted.

The thing of it was, trooping fairies were simply martial by nature. They loved a good fight, especially when leprechauns were involved. Even the chamberlain found himself being carried away on occasion—especially when there were balloons involved. He was a bit embarrassed about his outburst now—all that revenge business, not that anyone around here would notice that either.

But he had a job to do in the fairy court. It was once again time for the chamberlain to try to speak a bit of sense. He cleared his throat. "Remember the Grand Banshee. Listen to the voice of reason!"

"We spit on reason!" Grogan announced.

My, the chamberlain thought, how appropriate.

But the fairies around him were working themselves into a proper state. Some of them had started to glow with the power of their rage, while the king seemed to balloon to twice his usual size with anger. And puffball mushrooms were growing on the council table. That was never a good sign.

The chamberlain opened his mouth to object, but the raging, glowing, stomping fairies picked up the growing mushrooms and threw them at him en masse. The chamberlain was covered in fine brown mushroom dust.

Very well, he thought. He had done what he could.

He'd let the Grand Banshee take them all!

Mickey and a bunch of the lads were sitting about in the tavern. Somehow, for Mickey, it just wasn't the same.

Barney grinned at the others as he pushed himself away from the table. "Well, it's a balmy summer's night for a balmy summer's drink. Shall we go ram racing?"

"Count me in," replied Jericho as he rose as well. Their mates, Brian and Sean, quickly finished their beers in preparation to join the festivities.

But Mickey had other plans. "Not me. I've a date with a princess." And this time, he'd find a way to get away from meddling servants and palace guards. He led the way out of the Crock of Gold.

"You want us to come with you?" Jericho asked as he stepped through the doorway. "It could be dangerous."

Mickey shook his head. "I'm not looking for trouble."

"No need," Barney chided. "It'll be looking for you." He and Jericho turned off into the night to find a pair of racing rams. The others came out of the tavern and followed the first pair, four leprechauns off on another night's adventure. Barney waved back at his friend.

"Kiss the girl for me, Mickey lad."

Well, Mickey thought, first he'd have to kiss the dear sweet Jessica for himself. But he wasn't going to win her heart forever by merely standing around. Perhaps he'd wander back to the palace and see what developed. He turned to walk back up the hill.

A very stuffy fairy in a uniform blocked his path.

Apparently, Mickey realized, the palace had wandered back to him. Count Grogan smiled in a way that would chill a lesser leprechaun's bones.

"Ah, Muldoon," he said much too smoothly, "what a coincidence finding you here."

Mickey put up a placating hand. "I don't want any trouble, Grogan."

The count took a step forward. "You might not want it but that's what you've got."

Not if Mickey had any say in this. He'd gotten away from trooping fairies before. He jumped up, somersaulting clean over Count Grogan. With a moment's head start, he could lose himself in the forest.

He looked over his shoulder as he landed and found Count Grogan somersaulting after him.

"You won't get away that easy," the trooping fairy called as he lightly landed before him. The count pulled a stick from his belt, letting it grow to a full quarterstaff, and crouched, ready for battle.

Ah, he would love to wipe that smirk from Grogan's face. But this would never win his Jessica.

"I'm not fighting," Mickey insisted as he leapt straight up into the air. If he couldn't jump away, he'd fly.

Four more trooping fairies swooped down to block his path.

Grogan laughed. "Oh, you'll fight."

The four above flew straight down toward him, forcing Mickey to land again. As soon as the leprechaun's feet hit the ground, the four troopers came down around him, and all drew their quarterstaffs. Apparently, Grogan preferred five-to-one odds.

Mickey backed up toward the bushes. And the bushes moved. Barney, Jericho, and the other lads stepped through to join their fellow leprechaun.

Barney grinned. "I thought you might need some help, Mickey lad."

"It's all right, Barney," Mickey agreed. He wouldn't mind any help he could get.

The other leprechauns stepped forward, each one confronting one of the trooping fairies.

"Now you can go one on one with little 'Maurice' without his friends getting in the way," Barney called over his shoulder.

"Don't call me Maurice!" Grogan demanded.

Barney laughed at that. "No one cares what you like, Maurice!"

"I certainly don't, Maurice!" Jericho echoed.

Barney turned and threw Mickey his wooden staff.

"Give him a taste of leprechaun justice, Mickey lad."

Mickey caught the staff, more from reflex than anything else. But he really didn't want it. He threw the staff back to Barney.

"I'm not fighting—let them go."

Barney was astonished. "The girl has unmanned you!"

"He's a yellow belly!" Grogan jeered. "He has coward's legs like all leprechauns!"

That was too much for Barney. "I'll show you coward's

legs—and arms!" He let his stick grow into a quarterstaff as he advanced on Grogan.

Mickey only wanted to see the princess again. Why did any of them have to fight?

"Don't do it!" he called to his friend. "It's what he wants!"

Barney nodded at that. "Now there's a thing. It's what I want too!"

Mickey had to stop this. If troopers and leprechauns could do nothing but fight, what hope could there be for a life with Jessica? He stepped forward, ready to tear the quarterstaff from Barney's hands if he had to.

Someone stepped in his way. More trooping fairies?

But it was Jericho, keeping him from interfering in the fight. He tried to push past him, but his old friend grabbed him about the waist. All the other leprechauns would be against him!

Mickey watched helplessly as Barney and Grogan began their fight. And a powerful fight it was.

A skilled fighter, Count Grogan knew a dozen different maneuvers to inflict harm upon his opponent. But Barney had the leprechaun's gift for anticipating the next move, and he parried all but the weakest thrusts, then repeatedly found new ways through Grogan's guard. Grogan tried to attack Barney from above, but the leprechaun cut the trooper's legs out from under him, causing the fairy to tumble end over end. Barney somersaulted after him, neatly pushing aside the count's new attack, then smacking Grogan square on the shoulder. Mickey noticed that the leader of the trooping fairies was no longer smiling. His hair was mussed, his uniform torn, and a long bruise had appeared across one cheek. And Barney would give the self-important trooper no quarter.

Finally the quarterstaff fell from Grogan's hands as Barney smacked the other across the chest. The count called weakly as he fell.

Jericho had become so engrossed in the battle that he had forgotten to hold on. Mickey quickly ran to Barney's side. His friend had raised his quarterstaff above his head, preparing to give the fallen Grogan one final, devastating blow. Mickey placed a restraining hand on his friend's arm.

"Leave him, Barney."

Barney frowned and shook himself free of Mickey. But as he turned back to Grogan, the count regained his feet, driving his quarterstaff hard into Barney's stomach. The leprechaun doubled over as Grogan used his staff to hit his opponent in the head over and over again.

This time, Barney fell. Mickey rushed to his side.

Barney tried to smile. Some of his teeth appeared to be broken. When he spoke, it sounded more like a moan.

"I don't feel so well—"

Oh, no! Grogan had attacked him when he had been distracted. If Mickey hadn't interfered . . .

"Barney! Barney! It's my fault!"

His friend managed to truly grin at that.

"Of course it's your fault, Mickey lad." He made a small gasp. "I feel doomy somehow—feel the flame of pain in my limbs."

He looked down at his legs, except his legs weren't there anymore. Barney seemed to be disappearing: first his feet, then his legs below the knee, now his thighs and his waist.

"What is it?" Mickey cried in horror. "What's happening? We leprechauns are immortal!"

"Doesn't seem so," Barney groaned. "Where's the rest of me?"

A shadow passed over what was left of Barney, as though something had passed to block the light of the moon. Mickey looked up to the sky. A great crow circled overhead, wings spread wide. It swooped down and landed a few feet away.

In an instant, the crow had become the Grand Banshee.

She looked at Barney, but there was no pity in her eyes, only great anger. When she spoke, her voice was very quiet, but every word chilled Mickey through.

"I warned you all would pay the ultimate price." She extended a single hand toward Barney. "Now I'm taking him!"

"No!" Mickey cried. This couldn't be!

Barney shook his head, talking quickly, as if that might make some difference.

"Look . . . look . . . I'm only half the leprechaun I was." He took a ragged breath. "We meant no harm. It was simply done in the excitement of the game." His next breath held a bit of a groan. "I could do with a glass of something, so long as it's wet." His stomach was gone by now, as was half his rib cage. He turned to look at his dearest friend. "Ah, Mickey. Poor Barney brought to this by love. Kiss her for me, Mickey."

And then he was gone.

Grogan laughed, long and hard, and turned away to chat merrily with his fellow fairies.

This would not be! Mickey grabbed Barney's staff and let out a roar. He leapt toward Grogan. The count was ready, raising his staff to fend off the first blow. But there were two dozen more behind that. The count was driven back by the ferocity of the attack, and when he did manage to land a counterstrike on Mickey, the leprechaun did not even feel the blow. His mind was filled with one thought: This trooping fairy would pay for what he'd done to Barney.

Mickey fought like a man possessed. Grogan didn't have a chance. His own attacks grew weaker and farther apart. Soon, he could barely manage to defend himself against blow after punishing blow from the staff in Mickey's hands.

It had been Barney's staff.

The thought doubled Mickey's strength, filling him with a rage unlike any he had ever known. He ducked beneath a desperate swing of the count's staff; then he landed another dozen blows of his own, driving Grogan to his knees. But the count was so weakened now that he couldn't even kneel properly; his body swayed back and forth. But Mickey couldn't stop. Mickey could never stop.

The leprechaun heard a sharp crack as he hit Grogan across the back of the neck. The count fell forward and moved no more.

Mickey stared at his fallen foe.

Then Grogan began to disappear too.

Mickey threw down his staff. It was done.

The Grand Banshee said no more. She merely turned back into a crow as the last vestiges of Count Grogan vanished from the world. She flapped her wings once, twice, three times, then took flight. In an instant, she was lost in the night.

No one said a word, neither leprechaun nor trooping fairy. Instead, all stared at those places where Barney and Grogan had fallen to the earth—those places where the Grand Banshee had taken them away, perhaps forever.

Mickey realized this was no longer a simple game in which troopers and leprechauns thrashed each other for points of honor. For the first time, the battle had turned deadly, and one of their own and one of the others were gone for good.

What had they done? Mickey thought. Why had Grogan forced his hand after the Banshee's warning?

But much worse than that. What had Mickey Muldoon himself done? And to a member of the royal fairy family?

It was something, he feared, that could never be undone—ever.

Chapter Fourteen

Princess Jessica jumped up from where she had been sitting on her bed. Lady Margaret had returned at last.

"What news of Mickey?" Jessica demanded.

Margaret looked far from happy as she replied, "The worst. He's killed your cousin Grogan."

"Killed?" Jessica didn't understand. "But fairies don't die."

"They do sometimes. Let's say the Grand Banshee took him."

Jessica frowned. Surely Mickey wouldn't have meant to kill one of her family after the two of them had grown so close. Maybe the news was wrong and someone else had killed her cousin. Or maybe fussy old Grogan wasn't dead at all, and this was another one of his tricks to start a war. She would never know anything if she was trapped in her bedroom. Jessica felt more alone than she ever had before.

She knew everything would be all right if she could only see her beloved.

"I must see Mickey!" she insisted.

But the bedroom doors crashed open before Lady Margaret could even open her mouth to reply. Jessica's mother and father rushed into the room, quickly followed by the chamberlain.

Her mother rushed before her.

"Jessica, get packed," the queen demanded. "We're sending you away."

This was all moving too fast for the princess.

"Where? Why?"

"War!" the king announced with a raised fist. "Against the leprechauns!"

"They've killed our beloved Grogan!" the queen said in a voice that suggested there could be no greater crime.

"Well, I don't know about 'beloved,'" the king muttered, "but they've killed him."

The chamberlain nodded at that. "The place is much quieter, don't you think?"

But the queen's righteous fury would not be stopped. "It's Mickey Muldoon!" she declared, saying his name with such force she might have scared small children into hiding under their beds. "We're making sure you're out of the clutches of that murderous seducer!"

Murderous seducer? Her Mickey? Surely, there had to be another explanation. If only she might get her parents to calm down a bit, perhaps she could get them to see reason.

"But, Father," Jessica suggested gently, "shouldn't we hear the facts first?"

The king raised his other fist at that. "I don't want the facts. I want war!"

He was getting very red in the face.

"Careful, sire," the chamberlain cautioned. "The blood's rushing to your head."

"There's plenty of room," the queen snorted.

Jessica still wanted to find an explanation. "Cousin Grogan had a very bad temper," she suggested.

The queen turned her wrath on her daughter. "Are you defending his killer?"

Jessica shook her head. "No, but—"

The chamberlain came to her rescue. "The child has a point. Remember, if we go to war, the Grand Banshee will make it very real this time. It would be sensible to wait until all the facts are known."

"I want nothing to do with 'sensible!'" The king shook his crimson cheeks. "Jessica leaves in the morning."

So they really would send her away? How could Mickey ever find her? How would they ever be together again?

This couldn't be happening!

Jack had never had such a wonderful day.

They hadn't done much of anything really. But every moment had been spent with Kathleen.

Now they lay on a grassy hill, side by side, looking at the clouds overhead, their hands touching. Jack couldn't think of a better way to spend his time.

Kathleen pointed at a particularly large white cumulus that was ambling across the sky. "That cloud looks like a white hand waving."

"Yeah?" Jack didn't see that at all. "Looks more like a plate of linguine to me."

Kathleen laughed at that. "You have no romance in you, Jack."

Jack turned to Kathleen, his voice filled with mock outrage. "I have. More than you know. Maybe more than I know."

She turned to look at him then. They kissed. A small one this time. Jack had never known kisses came in so many varieties.

Kathleen looked back to the sky. "Is the hand waving good-bye or hello?"

"Hello," Jack replied with a smile. "Definitely hello."

She sighed. "I hope so. Is this just a holiday romance, Jack?"

"No. No, it's not." Sometimes, it even surprised Jack how strongly he felt about that.

"Then what is it? You'll soon be going back."

Where could they go from here? He hadn't thought it through. He didn't want to think about anything except what was happening right now—the two of them on a hillside watching the clouds. Why couldn't this go on forever?

But what about Sperry, Sperry, and McGurk? His apartment in New York? His whole life up until now?

"I suppose so," he admitted.

"No suppose about it."

Jack noticed an edge in her voice he hadn't heard before. But it still didn't have to end.

"You could come with me," he suggested.

"Oh, yes!" Kathleen looked back up to the sky. "Go off with a man I hardly know—and leave my brothers to look after themselves." She laughed harshly at the very thought. "If it was raining soup they'd be there with a fork."

Why was she so worried about her brothers? If nothing else, Jack thought, they could bully their way through life.

"They'd be fine," he replied.

Kathleen shivered. "It's getting cold. We'd better be getting back."

She stood and, reluctantly, Jack did too. He imagined he'd walk her back to her cottage now. And then what?

Was this the beginning of the relationship ... or the end?

Mickey had seldom seen his parents look so glum. He'd taken them to the Crock of Gold to give them the news and maybe ease the pain a bit. But there was no getting by the serious nature of the situation.

His mother shook her head. "I still can't believe Barney's gone. It's like we've known him for centuries."

"We have," his father added as he put down his beer.

"What're you going to do about it, Muldoon?" she asked.

Seamus thought for only an instant before he pounded his fist on the table. "Fight! Grand Banshee or no Grand Banshee, we'll summon all leprechauns, pookas, and other uglies to answer this vile outrage. It's a time for heroes!"

Mary shook her head at that. "Well, I have to say you're the hero of many a well-fought bottle."

That was the problem exactly, Mickey thought. Both the leprechauns and the troopers talked a good fight. But the rules had changed. Now his father was getting involved. Where would this madness end?

Maybe Mickey could make his father see a bit of reason. "Wait a minute, Da. Don't you think—"

"I never think!" his father interrupted firmly. "I act!"

And that was even more of a problem. Seamus drained his beer and rose from his seat, stomping swiftly from the tavern. Mickey's mother gave him her what-are-you-going-to-do look, honed from years of practice.

Mickey had thought that, by telling his parents of what had happened with the Grand Banshee, he might get their help in all of this. Instead, he appeared to have sent his father roaring into battle.

How could his love for one sweet maiden have led to all of this?

Jack Woods never thought he'd see this much in a seashell.

After he'd taken Kathleen home, he'd come back to the cottage and found he didn't care to go inside. Instead, he'd come out to sit on the old chopping block with a beer in hand, and he looked out at the countryside that Kathleen and he had shared together. The countryside and a certain seashell.

Something popped into existence at his side.

Oh, it was Seamus. Jack barely even flinched. Maybe he was getting used to the leprechaun's comings and goings. Or maybe he had something else on his mind. Still, he was glad the leprechaun was here. He needed someone to talk to.

"Seamus," he called to the small fellow as he passed over the beer, "I want you to be the first to know. I'm in love. For the first time in my life, I'm really in love." He thought about his words for an instant. After all, he'd almost gotten married once. But with Sharon, the engagement had come from a sense of obligation. They had dated all that time—they'd both expected it had to lead someplace. It was only after they were engaged that Sharon decided it wasn't going to lead anywhere at all.

This new relationship was totally different. Jack couldn't even think of life without Kathleen. He glanced at the leprechaun.

"It's Kathleen."

It felt good to say the words aloud. He looked back at the seashell in his hand.

Seamus studied the beer the good Jack Woods passed to him. He knew he had come out here for a good reason. Well, two good reasons, for Seamus needed to talk about the disturbing events of late.

Jack was talking about something or other himself. No doubt Seamus would pick it up as they went along.

"That's good. That's good," he replied generously. He took a pull at the bottle.

Seamus realized Jack had pushed something else under his nose.

"Isn't this shell beautiful? She gave it to me."

Seamus glanced at it ever so briefly as he handed the bottle back. "It is, yes."

She? he wondered. Who was "she?" Well, the big fellow had been saying something about Kathleen, hadn't he? As if these humans had problems.

"What's the matter?" Jack asked.

Seamus actually considered answering the man. But it was a complicated thing. Seamus wasn't exactly sure he'd understand it himself. "Best you don't know, Jack. Some things are strictly leprechaun business."

"Ah . . ." Jack said. It sounded as though he was just as glad not to know.

Best you don't know, Seamus had said. Best you don't know. Jack swore to himself. Why did there have to be so many secrets in this world? Why had he come to Ireland carrying secrets of his own?

Aloud, he said, "If she finds out why I came here, she won't understand."

"Is that right?" Seamus replied more or less automatically. He had too much on his mind just now to do any proper listening. "The Grand Banshee's taken all the fun out of it," he muttered.

"That's right," Jack answered distantly. "I was nearly married once, you know."

"Is that a fact?" No doubt whatever Jack was saying would make a great deal of sense if this other business wasn't on his mind. Seamus made a fist. "But we were born to fight and now she's trying to stop us. It's not right."

Jack shook his head. "No, the boss's daughter. It didn't work out. Turned out it was for the best but there was a lot of—you know—"

Maybe, Seamus thought, if he could explain it all to Jack, he could figure it out for himself. "There would be—" He stopped abruptly. He knew there was only one course of action. "We've no choice. We must do it for Barney."

Jack was startled at how deeply he felt these emotions. It was so different from the other relationships he'd had.

Still, it felt good to talk about it.

"Why not?" he continued. "I wasn't expecting to have it happen again. Now it has . . . in spades. Everything's changed. I feel kind of scared, you know?"

"I do, yes," Seamus agreed. "I hope we're doing the right thing. Grand Banshee or not, we are doing the right thing!"

Grand Banshee? Jack was so upset, he'd probably missed something. Ah, well, maybe Seamus could explain it to him later. Now he had to worry about how to handle both Kathleen and the folks back home.

"Sure you are," he said. "Now I can't let them change anything here. I could lose my job, but there you go."

"Yes," Seamus agreed with a curt nod.

"Yes," Jack echoed. He'd stop this whole foolish project—that was what he had to do!

He looked over to the small fellow.

"It was good talking to you, Jack," the leprechaun said with a grin.

Jack felt the same. "And you, Seamus. It cleared the air."

Seamus grimaced. Jack shook his head.

Both had the same thought.

Jack realized the true nature of his problem more clearly than ever before. But understanding didn't help. He still didn't know what to do about it.

The two of them sighed. At least it was good to have friends.

Chapter Fifteen

Mickey Muldoon looked up in the sky. It was a beautiful full moon tonight. A shame he couldn't share it with the one he loved. Instead, everyone in the world of the fairies seemed ready for battle.

"Jessica!" he called to the moon. "What are we going to do now?"

He heard a noise from behind a nearby bush.

"Psst!" the noise said. "Psst!"

A female fairy darted out from her hiding place.

"Mickey Muldoon, front and center!" she called. Mickey realized she was Lady Margaret, lady-in-waiting to his beloved. His heart raced. What could this mean?

"That's me," he announced when she said no more.

His response unleashed a torrent of words. "I must be mad coming here like this. All my years of serving as a lady-in-waiting must have made me balmy and brain loose."

She shook her head as if she might shake her brain back in place.

"A message from Princess Jessica," she added.

A message? Then perhaps there was still hope.

"She's leaving the palace tomorrow morning," Lady Margaret added.

Tomorrow morning? Then they must fly away together— before he lost her forever!

Princess Jessica was beside herself.

Her parents had worked themselves into a fine state. The king seemed to be able to do nothing but pace back and forth, and the queen's frown had grown so deep even her wrinkles appeared to have wrinkles. They only seemed to agree on one thing. Jessica had to leave.

Not of course that they could explain this decision to their daughter's satisfaction. Instead, they had hustled her out to the gate of the palace, where a coach waited to be borne away by four fairy porters who would fly both Princess Jessica and Lady Margaret to the winter palace.

"Why can't I stay with you and Mother?" she asked and not for the first time.

King Boric actually paused long enough to shake his head in her general direction. "It's too dangerous for you, child. The Grand Banshee may make you disappear too as punishment."

"We love you, my dear," the queen added in a tone that said what a problem Jessica was. "Go for our sakes."

But what of Mickey? He had promised to return. What if Mickey couldn't find her?

She looked about the landing, hoping to find some movement in the woods beyond. But she saw no one— only her parents, the four fairies assigned to fly her carriage away, and of course, Lady Margaret, who already waited within the ornately covered sedan.

Lady Margaret? But Jessica had sent her upon that very important mission. If her lady-in-waiting had returned, could that mean that Mickey wasn't faraway?

She could only hope. She kissed her parents quickly and climbed inside the carriage. The four fairies each grabbed a pole at the carriage's corner and lifted the whole carriage into the air. Jessica waved one final time as she was carried swiftly into the woods.

They were barely out of sight of the fairy palace before something flew in the window. Something tall and handsome and dressed all in green.

It was her Mickey, landing smack atop Lady Margaret.

The lady-in-waiting looked quite upset, and she might even had cried out in alarm had Mickey not already placed his hand over her mouth.

He smiled at the servant.

"I'm sorry, Lady Margaret, but I'd be obliged if you'd keep as quiet as a mouse on a blotter."

The princess nodded encouragement to her lady.

"It's all right," the princess said softly.

Lady Margaret nodded in turn. Mickey took his hand away. She glared up at where he sat in her lap.

"You snarling cur, groping a respectable woman!"

"It's just a bit cramped," Mickey said.

Lady Margaret harumphed, but without much conviction. Jessica thought the lady might actually enjoy having such a handsome fellow on her lap. The carriage only had seating for two. Until now, Jessica hadn't realized that such an arrangement might be a problem.

"What are you doing here, Mickey?" she asked, not really caring. As long as he was here, that was enough.

He replied quickly. "I wanted to see you again and tell

you about Count Grogan and Barney so your eyes won't be flashing hatred at me when we meet.''

The princess shook her head.

"Oh, they never could, Mickey."

He leaned forward then and took her hand. She leaned forward too. They kissed. Oh, how she had longed for his kiss!

"What are you two doing?" Lady Margaret demanded.

Mickey glanced back at her. "Don't you know?"

"Of course I know!" Margaret huffed. "That's why I say: Stop it at once!"

The princess looked deep into her beloved's eyes.

"Our families are going to fight each other."

Mickey nodded. "Not only our families, but every fairy and leprechaun."

Jessica frowned. This was all so overwhelming. "What are we going to do? I'm being sent to the winter palace."

Somebody knocked at the window.

"Are you all right, Princess Jessica?" one of the flying fairies outside called in.

Oh, no! she thought. They must have heard Mickey's voice—or maybe felt Mickey's weight—they suspected something was wrong!

"I'm fine!" she called to those outside. She whispered to Mickey. "You must go. They'll be looking for you. Please be careful."

Mickey grinned that wonderful grin. "I will. Then I'll find you, and we'll be together."

Jessica smiled back. "If you don't, I'll die from longing for you."

They kissed once more.

Mickey winked at her, then leapt from the carriage, flying so fast that none of her escort even caught a glimpse.

She sighed. What a wonderful, handsome young fellow he was.

Jessica already missed him.

Seamus Muldoon wondered how long it had been since the Crock of Gold had played host to a war council. All the chiefs of the solitaries were gathered here, and not just all the clans of leprechauns, but the chief of the hairy pookas, the chief of the floating and glowing sheeries, even Chief Grogoch, who seemed to be half human and half fairy and was totally covered with hair.

It was a fine turnout and a great sign of their eventual victory. But Seamus had called them all here, and it was his duty to begin.

"Chiefs," he called to all around him, "it's time we taught these arrogant, snot-nosed troopers a lesson they'll never forget. One of them killed Barney Devine. We all knew Barney and loved him." He looked about and was pleased to see those around him nodding at his words. "He was the life and soul of the party. Where's his life now? Where's the party?" Already, he could hear grumbles from the crowd about the injustice of it all. "He was open-handed to a fault. Always paid his round. You can't say fairer than that of a leprechaun." He raised his fist as he looked at all around. "We'll never have a better reason for doing down our age-old enemies!"

The others growled in agreement.

"Break open a barrel and drink to victory!" Grogoch roared.

Nobody argued with Grogoch. Nobody knew exactly what Grogoch was, but they certainly didn't argue with him.

Seamus gratefully accepted a tankard. So far, this was

going swimmingly. They'd show those trooping fairies once and for all!

The battle plans had the entire palace in an uproar. The day-to-day business of tending Mother Nature seemed to have been totally forgotten as every single fairy in the place helped the king and queen prepare for war. In all of his hundreds of years of service, the chamberlain had never seen events taken to this extreme. He feared everything—the palace, the royal family, fairydom itself—could all come tumbling down.

But the queen and king would hear none of it. Well, the king might listen, but he didn't dare to contradict his bride. And the queen? Her beloved Count Grogan was gone. She would split the Earth in two to punish those responsible.

"We've already achieved full mobilization!" the queen announced as she led the king, the chamberlain, and a military advisor toward the royal throne room. Her eyes glowed with a special fury—a fire that might only be quenched with the blood of leprechauns. Everyone followed after her, afraid to say a word.

But the chamberlain had to speak. It was his duty. He waved to the fairies flying all around them, ignoring their flower checking, their blossom production, and the hundred other tiny tasks that made the world what it was.

"What happens to our work?" he demanded. "What happens to the natural world?"

"Nature will have to take care of itself," King Boric huffed.

"We've a war to wage!" the queen agreed.

So they were totally beyond listening to reason. The chamberlain sighed. How could it possibly get any worse?

"Who's leading the army?" he asked.

"There's only one man," the queen declared. "We must bring General Bulstrode out of retirement."

Bulstrode? No, the chamberlain realized, it could get worse. Even the king blanched at the thought. Bulstrode of the million medals—so many that they weighed down his uniform, making it difficult for him to move. He was just the sort the queen would favor. Where pomp and circumstance were required, Bulstrode could be guaranteed to provide the pomp.

"Must we?" the king asked.

The queen nodded fiercely. "He has the reputation."

The chamberlain couldn't help himself. "For what?" he asked.

But the queen marched before them into the council chamber. The very chamber where Bulstrode, red of face and large of girth, awaited them.

The general leapt up as the queen entered the room. He saluted. The chair behind him fell over. The mustachioed military man staggered slightly. The entire row of chairs to either side of him collapsed.

The chamberlain sighed. This was the Bulstrode he remembered all too well.

"General Bulstrode, reporting for duty, sir!" he called out smartly. "Sorry about the chairs!"

But the queen was already fluttering over to Bulstrode, complimenting him and fawning over him the same way she used to around Grogan. As usual, the king didn't seem to mind at all. He was just glad not to be the object of the queen's attention for a moment or two.

The chamberlain realized he had been wrong about all of this. With these highborns in charge, this righteous war was not going to be a disaster. It was going to be a calamitous, ruinous, cataclysmic, and most unfortunate disaster.

He wondered if, when all of this was done, some variety of woodland creature might have an opening for a chamberlain. Because, the way things were going now, this palace, the king and queen, and all of fairyland could soon be a thing of the past.

This was the most difficult moment of Jack Woods's life. Talking to Seamus had made him realize he needed to tell Kathleen everything, especially about the business plan that had brought him here. Jack realized now that turning the local countryside into a golf course had been a very bad idea. But it had been his idea. How could he tell her what he had been planning but wasn't planning anymore? The truth was a complicated thing. Jack wondered if he'd ever told the whole truth about anything in his entire life.

Well, he'd have to start now. The two were out again, walking through the woods, the perfect place for a private conversation. He'd give anything, say anything, do anything for Kathleen.

Except, in trying to come up with just the right words to say, he realized he'd stopped speaking altogether.

"So what is it that you wanted to tell me?" Kathleen asked gently.

Jack grimaced. "It's just that I want to be honest with you, Kathleen."

That made her frown.

"Oh. When people say they want to be honest, it means they haven't been."

That wasn't how he wanted this to start. Jack decided he'd better plunge ahead.

"I have," he began. "Well, up to a point. I wanted to tell you why I was here."

She gave him a shy half smile. "So it's not to carry me off on your white horse?"

Oh, he wished he could! If only he could requisition white horses from Sperry, Sperry, and McGurk. He opened his mouth just to let something come out.

"Mr. Woods! Mr. Woods!"

Jack looked behind them. Bagnell was rushing toward them down the path. Jack and Kathleen stopped walking, waiting for the other man to catch up. He did so shortly, but it took him another moment to catch his breath.

"Hello there, Kathleen." He nodded to her and gulped some air. "Mr. Woods, I got a telephone call from New York and I was asked to give you this message. They said it was urgent." He paused to breathe again. "It's the first time we've had such a call at the post office. I thought it was one of the boys up to their tricks."

Bagnell held up an envelope. Jack took it and tore it open.

"I put it into an envelope for security," Bagnell continued. He looked to Kathleen. "It says he's to get back to America right away. For a meeting. They've heard nothing from him for days."

Kathleen frowned at Jack. "When do you have to go?"

Jack looked up from the letter. They wanted him to return at once.

He frowned. Something was wrong with the trees.

Leaves were falling off the branches—leaves that were still green. And not just a few of them. They were coming down in a torrent, swirling about like falling snow.

"Will you look at those leaves?" Bagnell called. "And it's the middle of summer! We'd best be getting shelter."

The leaves were everywhere. The three people could barely see each other. Jack grabbed Kathleen's hand and followed Bagnell down the path. Jack and Kathleen could hear the mayor crashing on up ahead, but he was soon lost from sight.

"It's like the seasons have got mixed up," Kathleen called. "What's going on?"

"I don't know," Jack replied. "But I think I know someone who does."

It was time to get back to the cottage.

Now they'd get to the bottom of this.

Jack and Kathleen shook the leaves from their clothes once he'd firmly shut his cottage door behind them. The weather was truly unnatural. Jack had an idea who was involved, one way or another. He looked around the room. It appeared completely empty. No doubt the whole family was right in front of him.

"Seamus Muldoon," Jack called.

"Who?" Kathleen asked.

"Seamus Muldoon. He'll know what's happening out there."

"Who's he?"

Jack peered into the corners for any sign of the leprechaun. "He and his family share this cottage with me."

Kathleen shook her head. "No one shares this cottage with you."

"He's a leprechaun," Jack explained.

Kathleen laughed. "Oh, yes. And I'm Queen Mab!"

Jack guessed he should have expected this kind of reaction. He tried to explain. "Seamus Muldoon is the head of the Kerry leprechauns."

Kathleen's voice was heavy with sarcasm. "Oh, *that* Seamus Muldoon. I look forward to meeting him."

Jack had a sudden doubt. He hadn't really prepared Kathleen for any of this. "You'll be all right, won't you?"

he asked. "I mean, you won't do anything stupid if they show themselves, will you?"

"Of course not," she snapped. "I'll mind my manners. I'm completely house-trained."

Well, at least he'd warned her. He turned back to the middle of the room.

"Seamus, are you there? If you could make yourself visible, I'd appreciate it. It's a bit of an emergency."

Two leprechauns popped into existence in the middle of the room in all their green-plaid finery.

"Seamus and Mary Muldoon, at your service," Seamus announced with a little bow.

Kathleen fainted dead away.

Well, Jack thought, it could have gone worse.

He rushed off to get some water.

Kathleen opened her eyes. Jack was leaning over her, a glass of water in his hands.

What a thoughtful man. Water had never tasted so good.

But they were not alone. She remembered what had startled her so in the first place. There were two . . . little people frowning over at her—little and dressed all in green. They looked just like—but they couldn't—there wasn't any such . . .

Kathleen decided she had better ask.

"You're real leprechauns?"

"You don't find any realer," the female of the pair replied. They had introduced themselves a moment before. What was her name? Mary, wasn't it?

"Of course we only show ourselves to those we like," Mary added.

"And we like you, pretty lady," added the fellow, Seamus, with a smile that seemed a bit too broad. "A fine swimmer, you are. Very nice stroke."

"That's enough of that!" Mary gave him a sharp poke in the ribs.

"What's going on out there with the leaves, Seamus?" Jack asked. "It's like fall already."

The leprechaun's face fell to a frown. "It was what I was saying, Jack. There's terrible fairy trouble ahead. I have to go. No time for distractions, however attractive." He nodded to Kathleen. "Lovely to meet you, sweet Kathleen. Jack's a fine man for a human. You could do a lot worse."

And then they were gone. Just up and disappeared.

Kathleen felt faint all over again.

Well, this was better, Kathleen thought as she made a cup of tea in her own home. Her own kitchen, with everything in place and not a leprechaun in sight.

Jack waited for her at the kitchen table. She poured him a cup of tea. He looked up at her, his face as serious as she had ever seen it.

"Kathleen, you've got to come with me."

"And why would that be?" she asked.

He spread his hands out on the table as if they might help him explain. "I've never felt this way before about anyone. I don't know what'll happen between us. I just know I can't go and leave you here."

They were wonderful words, but it didn't seem like the only way to do things.

"So why go?" she challenged him with a smile. "Stay here so you can get sick of the sight of me."

He shook his head. "I want to, but I've got no choice. If I don't go back, I'll lose my job."

"Are you so important to them they can't exist without you being there?"

Jack sighed. "No, of course not. It's to do with the reason I'm here in the first place." And that reason, she was reminded, he still hadn't gotten around to explaining. "I'll tell you all about it on the trip," he continued. "Please come with me. Please!"

Kathleen hesitated. What should she say? What should she do?

She jumped as a terrible bolt of lightning flashed and a crash of thunder exploded at the same time. They must be very near!

She and Jack both rushed to the window.

The lightning had hit the old barn! The sagging roof had collapsed completely, taking a good part of the walls with it. What wood remained standing was blackened at the tops, with smoke rising to the sky. Kathleen guessed they were lucky not to have a fire.

But what about her brothers?

Kathleen breathed a sigh of relief. All four of her brothers stared at the devastation from a good fifty feet away. That meant all four were safe!

She and Jack hurried from the house.

The biggest of her brothers, George, scowled down at Jack as he and Kathleen joined the others.

"What the devil do you want here? You've got more brass than the kings of Old Ireland."

"He's here at my invitation," Kathleen snapped back. That would shut her brothers up properly.

All of them went back to staring glumly at the charred wreckage of the barn.

"How did that happen?" Harry asked pitifully. "There's no storm."

Kathleen looked heavenward. It was stranger than that. There was hardly a cloud in the sky.

It was like the falling leaves, Kathleen realized. Something was very wrong in these parts. Her brothers wandered closer to the charred remains of the barn, as if there might be something they could salvage from the total ruin.

Jack turned to her.

"I'm sorry, but I have to catch the train tonight."

"Tonight!" she exclaimed.

"That was what was in the note." The note, she realized, he'd also never really told her about. "Please be there!"

She looked over at her poor, helpless brothers. "But . . . I can't. I want to, Jack—I do. But I just can't."

George reached down to pick up a piece of wood. It crumbled in his hands.

"I mean, look at them. They need me here. They're too old to learn new ways of being stupid. I'm sorry. It's all happening too fast. You, this, the leprechauns—I can't think straight!"

Jack took her shoulders and gently turned her to face him.

"It's your call. It has to be. But I want you to ask yourself if you're just looking for a reason to not come with me."

He glanced up at the sky.

A single snowflake hit his hand.

Jack turned and walked away.

Kathleen looked from Jack back to her brothers, then back to Jack again.

In a matter of days, everything had changed. Her safe and simple life taking care of her brothers no longer felt like enough.

And what of this man walking away? Jack Woods was no ordinary fellow. He'd shown her, in more than one way, that there was true magic in the world.

Kathleen shivered. She had always imagined that such magic would be a good thing. Instead, it might destroy them all.

Jack had vanished over the hill. Her brothers still stood there, helpless before the ruined barn. The whole world was upside down. What was she to do?

Seamus Muldoon had never seen such a magnificent sight.

Row upon row of solitary fairies marched out upon the field. There were more leprechauns than Seamus had ever seen in his long life, along with a full company of grogochs, a tremendous gaggle of dancing pookas, and a fair number of sheeries besides. Seamus wasn't actually sure how many of the glowing things had joined them. It was hard to count anyone who was that transparent. But joined them they had, along with all the other magic beings who preferred the wild world to the confines of a stuffy palace.

There were easily a thousand down there, and Seamus was in charge of them all. He stood upon the hillside, reviewing them all—whatever that meant—one of those human terms: "Reviewing the troops." Perhaps it meant he was simply looking at them a second time.

When he wasn't looking at the amassed might before him, he took a moment to admire his uniform. It was quite a sight, what with the brass buttons, the epaulets, and row after row of shiny medals. He had no idea what the medals were for, but they were medals nonetheless, and they marked him as a leprechaun of great importance.

But enough of reviewing and admiring. Seamus told Jericho to blow upon his great horn and call the troops into formation. The trooping fairies were almost here.

Leprechauns just knew that sort of thing.

* * *

Even the chamberlain, with all his doubts, could not imagine anything grander. The entire army, a thousand fairies strong, had assembled in the palace courtyard. As was customary, the chamberlain stood by King Boric, Queen Morag, and General Bulstrode to review the fairy troops. All of them, in their many colors, stood before them at attention, as disciplined a group of trooping fairies as you might ever see. How could those free-thinking solitaries even hope to confront a force like this?

King Boric, in full military regalia, stepped forward to wave the troopers into the air. Two thousand fairy wings popped into use—wings in more colors than a hundred rainbows, wings that would put a field of wildflowers to shame. Even the chamberlain felt his trooping heart stirred by such a sight. How could anyone stand against such a force?

He had to remind himself that it wasn't just a few leprechauns and other solitaries that they faced. He had to remember the Grand Banshee. They could win the battle, and the Grand Banshee might spirit every one of their warriors away.

The chamberlain felt a chill, despite the summer heat. It was a grand send-off, but it might signal the end of everything they'd ever known.

Mickey stared out at the sea.

The ocean was angry this evening, sending its waves crashing against the rocky shore. Mickey stared at the spray rising high in the air. There, in the middle of the foam, he saw an image of his love, Princess Jessica, waiting sadly for him, sitting in the window of a palace of ice, in a far-off place he didn't know. She was so beautiful, a fairy flower in the midst of winter's desolation. Somehow, he would find a way for them to be together. Somehow, he would make the whole world understand.

His daydream was interrupted by a noise, far overhead— a harsh, cawing sound. He looked above the sea spray and saw a great black crow heading inland.

It was the Grand Banshee herself, flying no doubt to fulfill her promise. For, somewhere in the hills behind him, Mickey knew a great battle was taking shape: leprechauns versus troopers; solitaries versus the might of the fairy palace. And all because one foolish leprechaun and a beautiful fairy princess had made the mistake of falling in love.

Would everything in this world conspire against them?

Not if Mickey had any say. Enough mooning. He had work to do.

It was barely evening, yet the train station, and indeed most of the village of Ballycombe, seemed strangely deserted.

Jack Woods had come to this corner of Ireland alone. Apparently, he would leave here alone as well.

He walked up onto the deserted train platform and read the sign:

BALLYCOMBE STATION

It had a wonderful sound to it. He took a deep breath of the clean air and realized he heard nothing at all. Oh, maybe a distant bird or two, but no voices, no cars, no planes overhead.

It was so quiet here sometimes. He would miss that. But he would miss other things more.

He wished Kathleen was with him now.

He could think of any number of reasons why she hadn't come. It was probably impossible for her to leave, what with her brothers and all. Kathleen and Jack really had only known each other a matter of days. They came from two completely different worlds.

Different. Jack almost laughed at the word. The rules were truly different here. He'd be going back to a world without leprechauns. And a world without Kathleen.

But he knew one thing he'd be taking with him. From this moment forward, there would be a hole, not only in his heart, but in his life, that he doubted he could ever fill again.

It started now. Seamus Muldoon could feel it in every single leprechaun bone. And then his sharp ears picked up the first inklings of the enemy's approach.

It was a sound like a thousand angry bees.

It was the trooping fairies flying high above the horizon, row after row of them appearing over the hill.

He had never seen so many troopers in his life. They kept on coming, a dozen rows, then two dozen, flying high above the battlefield. They would blot out the entire sky.

So this was it then. All of the troopers against all of the solitaries. This battle had been brewing for at least a thousand years. And it came when a certain Kerry leprechaun, one Seamus Muldoon, found himself in charge.

Well, all the solitaries would fight valiantly. Any leprechaun was worth three of those trooping dandies.

The troopers kept on coming.

Seamus did not have a good feeling about this.

* * *

Jack heard the mournful whistle at a distance, a sound that matched his mood. The train was coming, and he still saw no sign of Kathleen.

No one else had joined him on the platform. No one. Kathleen.

Part of him had been so sure they would spend the rest of their lives together.

The train stopped. A door was right before him, waiting for him to step away from Ireland and back to his old life. The steam engine disgorged a vast cloud of smoke, throwing all of the station into a fog. He couldn't see five feet in either direction. But he could still see the door.

The train was waiting for him. The steam engine chugged on idle like a living thing impatient to be started again. Jack guessed he had better get on with it.

Jack opened the door.

Seamus's army hesitated for only a moment.

The sky above was black with buzzing fairies.

They must have some strategy, Seamus thought, flying about like that. It wouldn't be much of a battle if the troopers just kept on high overhead. Perhaps they meant to intimidate the solitaries.

And Seamus had to admit he had been taken aback at first. But the way they still swooped around up there, Seamus was growing more annoyed.

He saw hundreds of small specks falling from the sky.

The trooping swine—they were dropping puffball mushrooms!

The mushrooms burst into a choking dust wherever they

hit, setting all around to coughing and wheezing, totally disorienting the troops on the ground. Seamus held his breath, doing his best to pay attention to the enemy above.

Wait a moment! A whole squadron of the fairies had detached themselves from the flying mass above and were now dive-bombing toward the ground. Apparently, the troopers were actually going to fight.

Seamus had Jericho blow the horn again. Now they'd have a proper battle. Once the solitaries had the fairies within their reach even the Grand Banshee couldn't save the troopers.

The train blew its whistle; the conductor called out to let everyone know they were leaving the station. With a squeak of its iron wheels and a huffing of its engine, the little train left Ballycombe behind.

Jack stood on the platform and watched it go. He'd opened the door, but he couldn't take that step inside, for in that instant, he'd realized one true thing: Without Kathleen, nothing else mattered.

Jack stared as the smoke cleared.

Kathleen stood on the other side of the platform, a suitcase in her hand. She had been hidden by the train, then by the smoke. She'd come to join him, but somehow hadn't gotten on the train herself.

She saw him, and her face opened up into the most beautiful smile.

Jack smiled back. He never wanted to take his eyes off of her again.

Somehow, they'd make it right.

*   *   *

It was chaos.

Seamus was in the thick of it now. He and Jericho fought off three of the troopers only to be bombarded by a new round of puffballs. By the time the two of them were done sneezing, Seamus saw a nearby grogoch overwhelmed by half a dozen of the nasty troopers. But before Seamus could lend a hand, the grogoch jumped back up, shaking every one of the fairies off. That'd teach them, Seamus thought.

The sheeries were flying now, disorienting the troopers overhead. A line of leprechauns used sharp stalks of corn as spears, knocking a half dozen troopers from the sky.

The battle was going their way for a minute. But there always seemed to be more trooping fairies flying in. Every time they knocked one down, two more took his place. This battle would get far worse before it was done.

And Seamus had another worry.

As much as he didn't want to look, he knew the Grand Banshee was up there, waiting to take both leprechaun and trooper. Sometimes, when there was a break in the enemy's formations overhead, he could see her shadow.

Over them all, a black crow flew.

The Grand Banshee would have her due.

Part Two

Chapter Sixteen

The smoke had cleared. The train was gone. And Kathleen was in his arms. They kissed.

"I missed the train," Jack said after a while.

"So did I," Kathleen said.

They kissed again. But then they looked at each other and agreed without a word; it was time to take their bags and head for home.

Jack wondered when it was he had started to think of that small cottage as home, because he did now. He belonged here with Kathleen. They left the station and turned up the road that led to both of their places.

"What are you going to do now?" Kathleen asked after a while.

Jack couldn't answer that just yet. He hadn't thought that far ahead.

One thing at a time. And right now, that one thing was Kathleen.

* * *

The battle was done for now. Seamus heard the great horns sound upon each side of the conflict as evening slid on toward night.

It had gotten properly fierce there toward the end. The troopers seemed to have a never-ending supply of those puffballs, while the leprechauns pulled out their secret weapon: sticky cobwebs that they catapulted aloft to ensnare the flying fairies midair. A great wave of troopers directly engaged an equally fearsome bunch of pookas, led by a huge dullahan swinging his head in his hand. Then Seamus had spotted King Boric through the mass of fighters, and decided he'd like a few words, personal like, with that trooping fairy king. Seamus began clubbing down anyone who got in his way, and he noticed that Boric was doing the same.

But the great horns sounded before he and Boric had closed half the distance. Just as well. Seamus realized he was exhausted. He and Boric could just as easily have their words tomorrow.

It was time to collect their wounded. Leprechauns helped their fallen comrades stagger from the battlefield as certain of the less fortunate fairies flew uncertainly away.

Seamus heard a crow cry three times above.

Now they were in for it, he thought.

The crow landed in the midst of the battlefield, halfway between Seamus and King Boric, and turned in an instant into the Grand Banshee. She said not a word, but acted instead, for Seamus could already see those troopers and solitaries still lying about the battlefield had begun to vanish. And as the fairies vanished, the Banshee grew, becoming a great and terrible thing ten feet high, with fire

lighting up her eyes and lightning dancing on her finger-
tips.

The Grand Banshee was truly angry. And hundreds who
fought would be gone forever.

Seamus decided it might be best to quietly withdraw.

Father Daley had never seen such trouble in all his many
years as a priest. Great hailstones were destroying the crops.
Hurricane rains were forcing autos and tractors from the
roads and fields. Haystacks had been catching on fire in
the noonday sun. Even the wildflowers seemed cursed,
turning from brilliant red to black overnight.

In times like this, the people of the town needed reassur-
ance, and today's Mass was filled to overflowing.

He glanced out at the stuffed pink elephant, which he
had installed in the corner of one of the pews before him.
The toy, and the miracle it represented, gave him strength.
It was time to talk to his flock.

Father Daley cleared his throat and began.

"God's in his heaven—all's right with the world. But it
isn't, is it? Now you may ask me, 'Why? Why is all this
happening? Why has the Almighty deserted us and shown
us the rocky path to eternal damnation?' " Ah. Now they
were all paying attention. One mention of damnation and
the congregation was all ears. He continued.

" 'What have we done so wrong to cause such agonizing
punishment? What can we do to stop these disasters from
getting worse and worse until our sins catch up with us
and we are dragged down into the fiery pit?' "

He paused and took a deep breath. "And I reply to you,
'I have absolutely no idea.' "

He noticed some grumbling among the congregation.
Well, perhaps they had a better idea.

"Any opinions out there?" he called.

One of the local farmers stood. "It's the little people!"

His wife chimed in. "The fairies and leprechauns have turned against us!"

The priest cleared his throat again. "Anybody with *sensible* opinions?" he added.

Another farmer stood at that, his fist raised in anger. "I blame the telephone!"

"Ah." Father Daley turned his eyes to heaven. This would be a long service indeed.

Here it was morning, Jack thought, and here they were together again. He and Kathleen had met early on and had made it just as far as the river halfway between their cottages. They'd sat down by the riverside and begun to talk. Jack wouldn't have been surprised if they sat here all day.

Kathleen was still trying to figure out just what had happened last evening.

"Did you see me," she asked, "before you decided not to catch the train? Or did you not catch the train because you saw me?"

Her questions were every bit as complicated as Jack's thoughts had been the night before. He frowned slightly as he replied.

"I think I get the drift." He smiled back at her then. "I'd decided to stay anyway."

Kathleen grinned at that.

Now it was Jack's turn. "And were you really going to come with me and not just come to see if I was going?"

Kathleen looked properly indignant. "I had my bag, didn't I?"

It was Jack's turn to smile. He didn't know if they'd ever

figure out what had happened to have them both end up like that. What did the fine points matter, as long as they were together?

They kissed. It was even better than talking. They kissed again.

Jack and Kathleen both leaned back against the river bank. If only this moment could last forever!

Jack's attention was distracted by a large fish jumping from the water. The fish hung in the air, shooting a stream of water right into Jack's face.

"What the—" Jack sputtered.

Kathleen started to laugh as Jack wiped off his face. So much for romance.

Jack jumped as a pair of leprechauns materialized on the bank before them. Seamus and Mary Muldoon grinned up at the humans.

"Ah!" he yelped. "I asked you to warn me!"

Seamus smiled sheepishly. "Sorry about that, Jack. Hello there, lovely Kathleen." He was being awfully polite. Jack wondered what the little fellow wanted.

"Was the fish your doing, Seamus?" Kathleen asked pointedly. "The fish spitting?"

Seamus looked a bit uncomfortable.

"Not directly, no."

"But indirectly—yes," Mary added.

Jack had recovered enough to ask a question of his own. "And all this crazy weather—is that you, directly or indirectly?"

"In a way," Mary interjected. "You see, there's a bit of a disagreement going on at the moment between us and the trooping fairies."

"So things aren't running as smooth as normal," Seamus added helpfully.

"Snow in summer?" Kathleen pointed out. "It must be some disagreement."

"It is quite a bit of one, yes," Seamus agreed with a shake of his head. "I mean, if you wanted to—" He paused, then started over. "I suppose you could describe it more as a—well, like—" He threw his hands up and turned to his wife. "How would you describe it, Mary?"

Mary nodded her head. "A full-out war."

"A full-out war," Seamus agreed. "Yes, that just about does it."

"A war!" Jack exclaimed. Obviously, leprechauns had a different definition of the word "disagreement."

"But it's okay," Seamus added hastily. "We're holding our own. Both sides are well matched. They've twice as many as us, but we're twice the fighters!"

"But a war?" Kathleen asked. "What's it about?"

"Oh, the usual." Seamus shrugged. "Everything and everybody. Nothing and nobody."

Kathleen shook her head at the way the leprechaun just shook this off.

"Can you not settle it peacefully? If this goes on, the farmers will lose their harvest."

"I know. It's a terrible thing," Seamus agreed. Almost too casually, he added, "So, Jack, can I ask you a question?"

"Fire away."

"Have you ever done any fighting? Been in the army, as it were?"

"I did some basic training for the infantry, but I never saw action." Mostly, Jack reflected, he sat behind a desk.

But Seamus was all smiles. "Basic training? Did you hear that, Mary? Jack's done *basic training*!"

"I heard!" Mary called back with equal enthusiasm.

It was Jack's turn to shrug. "It's no big deal."

" 'No big deal,' " Seamus said with a laugh. "Would you listen to the man!"

But Jack didn't know if he liked where this was heading. "I can't fight in your war, Seamus, if that's what you're after."

"No, no!" Seamus insisted. "You couldn't fight the fairies anyway. They'd disappear as soon as look at you. No, no. It's just we have a bit of a problem."

"The truth of it is," Mary jumped in, "we've no discipline at all, thanks to his leadership."

Seamus glared at his wife. "Thank you for that overwhelming vote of confidence!" He turned back to Jack. "What she's trying to say in her own dysfunctional way is that we leprechauns are free spirits, thinkers, and drinkers. We're not built for marching in straight lines or complicated battle plans."

"They need telling what to do," Mary added.

"And you've done"—Seamus nudged Jack's knee—"basic training!"

"And they're about as basic as it gets," Mary appended quickly. "We'd give you the power to see them all."

"You wouldn't leave empty-handed," Seamus jumped in. "We still have a few pots of gold left."

Kathleen stared hard at the small pair before them. "I thought those pots of gold were just a fairy story."

Mary grinned at that. "They are, but in case you hadn't noticed, we are fairies."

"We have a store of golden pots put away for hard times," Seamus agreed, "and these are hard times."

"What do you say, Jack?" Mary asked.

"It's a noble cause," Seamus pressed.

Jack sighed. "In a war, whichever side you're on is the noble one."

"Surely, it's not about taking sides," Kathleen insisted. "It's about getting peace again. Getting things back to normal."

"Right." Jack couldn't have put it better himself.

"That's it," Mary agreed.

"Exactly!" Seamus said with a grin. "So we need to win as quick as we can and grind those little devils into the dust!"

Jack frowned. Without Seamus, he doubted if he would have ever won the beautiful Kathleen. He wouldn't mind doing the small fellow a favor.

He just wasn't too sure this was the favor he wanted to do.

Mickey Muldoon wasn't alone anymore.

He had been cooling his heels at the seashore, hoping the whole pursuit by the trooping fairies would finally stop. But he had just spotted a fairy patrol flying above the waves, and he'd barely ducked into a cave before they saw him as well.

If they weren't going to leave him in peace, he'd come up with a real reason to upset them.

Since he'd come to this shore, he had thought a lot about the princess. Truth be told, he rarely thought of anything else. It was high time he saw her again and found a place where they could be together.

He knew he could find her. He might not know the exact location of the palace, but he had seen it in his vision. And he knew enough of the spirits of woods and swamps and meadows; out of all the magical creatures he might meet, one of them was bound to know the way.

Mickey peeked out of his hiding place. The four fairies on patrol had flown far down the beach by now, almost out of sight.

Well, Mickey had some flying of his own to do.

He would find her. After all, he was a leprechaun. How hard could it be?

Chapter Seventeen

Princess Jessica had been installed in a beautiful palace, with Lady Margaret for company and servants to see to all her needs. All her needs, that was, save one, and that one was the only thing she could think of. She turned to where her lady-in-waiting was busy stitching up a gossamer gown.

The princess sighed. "I miss him so, Maggie."

The lady made a tsking sound, not bothering to look up from her handiwork. "I miss my first husband, Randolph Goodrich III—a true gentleman. When he stepped out of the bath he always rang a small bell so I wouldn't be alarmed. In my day, you had to have impeccable manners." She nodded at the wisdom of it all. "You just couldn't make it in polite society unless you had impeccable manners."

Jessica nodded and sighed. "Mickey's like that."

The lady looked up in horror. "Never! He's a leprechaun. Totally different case. A leprechaun wouldn't recognize a gentleman if he was robbing him!"

Having made her point, Lady Margaret returned to her sewing.

Jessica paced back across her opulent sitting room—her gloriously furnished prison. She would go mad if she was trapped here any longer. How could she ever see her Mickey again?

This was more like it.

Mickey had had only to ask the oakshees, and they had pointed the way to the next stand of oak and the next group of tree spirits, who would point the way a little farther. A couple dozen oakshees later, and Mickey landed at the ice palace's front door. Now he only had to find Princess Jessica.

There were guards of course—two of them at the front door. Guarding was the sort of thing trooping fairies liked to do. In a way, Mickey was glad to see them. What fun would any of this be without the occasional challenge?

He threw a pair of rocks into some bushes across the way. Both guards went to investigate. Both guards? Could they make this any easier?

Mickey sneaked up behind them and knocked their heads together, rendering both of them properly unconscious.

But now it was on to more pressing business. Where might they be hiding a princess in this grand old building? Mickey decided he'd take a walk around the palace.

Sometimes, Princess Jessica thought, Lady Margaret did go on.

"My second husband," the lady-in-waiting continued,

"Samuel Van Pomeroy, was even more refined. He'd knock on an oyster shell before he opened it."

Jessica was speechless. She had looked out the window, and who was standing there but Mickey Muldoon. He smiled the fairest smile that the princess had ever seen, then put a finger to his lips for quiet.

Jessica glanced at Lady Margaret. The royal maid servant was much too busy with her gossamer to notice anything else. Jessica crept over to the window as Margaret continued her tale. She opened the window without a sound.

"My third husband was a little delicate," the lady prattled on. "He was the only man I ever met who was allergic to mathematics. You only had to ask him to add two and two and he'd retire to bed with a nosebleed." She sighed. "Truth be told, he was a bit of a loser."

Mickey held out his hand. Jessica took it and flew silently from the room into Mickey's arms. Without a sound, they rose out of the lady's sight, Margaret's voice slowly fading with distance.

"There are things better than love and worse than love, but it's impossible to find anything just like love." Lady Margaret sighed again. "It makes a man think almost as much of a woman as he does of himself . . . ."

Jessica waited until they had flown some distance before she asked, "Where are we going?"

Mickey grinned back at her. "Frog Bottom Swamp to see the Most High Butter Spirit, Sir Aloysius Jentee. He's an old friend of my father's. The swamp's neutral territory. They can't touch us there."

Mickey had thought of everything! Jessica squeezed his hand. At last, somewhere they could be truly together. They flew, with Mickey leading the way.

It seemed no time at all before Mickey waved, saying they were already at their destination.

The forest thinned out, giving way to meadows, which in turn were replaced by a great marsh. Vapors rose from the stagnant water, turning the sky dark overhead. The only sounds they could hear were the splash of things jumping in and out of the murk and a distant, forlorn honking.

Oh, dear, Jessica thought. It might be the only place to go, but did it have to be so swampy?

Mickey peered into the murk ahead. "I can't see anything."

"Nor me," Jessica agreed. "We'd better go the rest of the way on foot."

They landed on a grassy patch just before the cattails began. Mickey took her hand and led her forward. Fog settled over them before they had taken a dozen paces; everything around them turned to shades of gray. Water and mud were everywhere. They had to hop from one dry patch of ground to the next. They weren't alone out here either. Strange shapes moved through the mist, just close enough to startle them, never close enough to really see. Insects buzzed, birds wailed, and a weird honking rose and fell, rose and fell.

Jessica clutched Mickey's arm even tighter. The water suddenly bubbled before them, each bubble exploding with a low popping sound. It was probably marsh gas. She hoped it was marsh gas.

"Are you sure this is the right way?" she asked Mickey.

"No," he replied.

Then they would be lost as well? She grabbed his arm perhaps a bit too tightly.

"But then again, I'm not sure it isn't." Mickey did his best to smile reassuringly. At least, she supposed that his smile would have been reassuring, if they hadn't been walking through a swamp.

Mickey found a slightly larger patch of ground for them to walk on, dry land that rose a few feet above the stagnant pools to either side.

The pool on their left bubbled.

Jessica gasped.

The pool on the left splashed.

Mickey took a step away.

Something was rising from the muck.

They hugged each other tight.

The thing rose from the depths with a great sucking sound. It was covered with mud and slime; damp, brown bits of it plopped back into the water as it moved. It shambled toward them, climbing from the water onto their little patch of ground.

At least, Jessica reasoned, she and Mickey would die in each other's arms.

The muck creature stopped as soon as it was free of the water and began to shake itself.

Mud flew in every direction, quickly revealing what could only be a gnome underneath.

No, Jessica corrected herself. This was not your typical gnome. Under all that muck was a very well-dressed gnome, complete with waistcoat and spats.

"Found it!" the gnome announced. He held something in his hand: a small, dark leather ball. He turned and threw it high and hard. It disappeared into the mist.

He turned and grinned at Mickey and Jessica.

"Lost cricket ball," he explained. "Stroke of luck, what?"

"This is the Most High Butter Spirit?" Mickey seemed to be trying to make a statement, but it came out a question.

"The one and only." He bowed slightly as he examined his garments. He was the color of butter, Jessica realized, with bright yellow hair and piercing red eyes. His accent was very upper-class. His voice was so refined it made Jessica's mother sound like a commoner.

"Beastly stuff," he said as he flicked the last bits of muck away. "Sir Aloysius at your service, dear, though I don't use the 'sir.' It's a trifle nouveau, don't you think?"

She curtsied slightly in response—it seemed the thing to do—and said, "Mickey says you're an old friend."

The butter spirit grinned over at her beloved. "I've known him since he was literally knee-high to a grasshopper. Isn't much taller now, are you, laddie? His father and I were close. We've done wonderful mischief in our time." He shook his head at the thought. "You must be Princess Jessica."

"Can you do anything for us, Uncle Aloysius?" Mickey asked.

Aloysius Jentee patted the leprechaun on the back. "Bust my gaiters, laddie. I can offer you sanctuary. This swamp is a little safe haven from the menacing tides sweeping fairyland." He turned to the surrounding swamp. "Honk! Honk!" he called. "Honk! Honk!"

And the swamp answered back.

"Honk! Honk!"

Large frogs rose out of the mud to every side.

"Honk! Honk!"

And as the frogs honked, they turned into butter spirits, much the same size as Jentee, but with large eyes and flat noses, so they resembled nothing so much as butter-colored crickets. Dozens of them approached, casually walking across both patches of dry land and the surfaces of the surrounding ponds.

"These are the chaps," Jentee called. "Good souls. Not a decent cricketer among them, I'm afraid, but they try." He waved for the pair to follow him.

"You're not Irish, Mr. Jentee?" Jessica asked.

"Call me Aloysius. How can you tell?" His chest swelled with pride. "I was educated in England. We butter spirits are all Anglophiles." His smile fell as he looked about suspiciously. "That's why they had us exiled to the swamp." He grinned again. "I once said to an English friend, 'Breeding is everything, isn't it?' And he said, 'No, but it's a lot of fun.' "

Jentee honked so hard with laughter that he almost fell over.

"Honk! I'm wasted in this swamp. I really am. Honk!"

While Jentee was lost to his merriment, the other butter spirits joined in.

"We used to live in Sligo," one explained.

"Dairy country—famous for it," another added.

"We're particularly fond of butter, you see," a third said with a winsome smile.

"Honk!" a number of the others agreed.

Jentee had stopped laughing at the very mention of butter. He fussed at the lapels of his elegant vest.

"You haven't got any butter about, have you?" he asked most casually. "Irish, Danish, English—we're not particular." He half closed his eyes at the very thought. "Spread thick. Gad. What delights! What decadence! Honk! Honk!"

It would have been nice to have brought some sort of gift, but the princess hadn't had time to think of such niceties. If only they hadn't been running from both sets of parents.

"I'm sorry," Jessica replied.

Jentee took a deep breath, the anticipation evaporating from his expression, as if he was prepared to rise above all that.

"No matter." He brushed at his vest. "We've adapted. This is our domain and I think we've done pretty well.

Transformed it into a little patch of England. It's all warm beer and cricket on the green!"

Jentee waved at the way ahead. Through the mist, Jessica could see the faint outlines of some large white building. Not that she had much experience in this sort of thing, but a member of the royal family did receive an education. So it was that she recognized what appeared to be an English cricket pavilion, complete with a terrace and a large clock set above the veranda. Even more unusual, there was not simply one but three flagpoles, all flying the British flag.

"Why so many Union Jacks?" Mickey asked.

Jentee's chest puffed out again. "Just so everyone knows, this is Little England. We'll get you settled, and then you must join me for tiffin."

This was even beyond Jessica. "What's 'tiffin?' "

"Tea and cucumber sandwiches." He sighed. "No butter, I'm afraid."

Jentee instructed a pair of butter spirits to show the visitors to their rooms.

Very well. They would make the best of it. At least they could be together here.

But how long could they stay in a swamp?

Lady Margaret wrung her hands. She had gotten herself back to the royal summer palace as soon as she realized what had happened. Surely, they had to understand!

King Boric, wearing a uniform that seemed to sport half the medals in the kingdom, stood by his grieving queen. Even the chamberlain looked more distraught than usual. If only Lady Margaret could properly explain the situation!

"He spirited the child away, your majesty. It's the devil's work!"

The queen looked at her quite pointedly. "Are you sure you were watching, Lady Margaret?"

What was the queen implying? When Lady Margaret watched, she watched! "My eyes were open twenty-four hours a day. I never slept. I hardly ate, and when I did, I didn't look at my food!"

"Lady Margaret's right," the king interjected. "It's the devil's work. Leprechauns have special powers we don't know about."

Queen Morag began to cry.

"I'm sure Muldoon won't harm her," the chamberlain interjected. "He needs her as a hostage."

That didn't seem to comfort anyone.

General Bulstrode burst into the room, huffing and puffing up to the royal family. His uniform had nearly as many medals as the king's. As he hurried, they tended to clank.

"I've just had word from our intelligent officers!" he cried.

The queen stopped crying abruptly. "*Intelligence* officers!" She laughed bitterly. "The only thing that stays in the heads of those dolts for more than five minutes is a cold!"

"Mickey Muldoon's taken Princess Jessica to the butter spirits in the swamp!" Bulstrode blustered.

The queen got to her feet. "We must rescue her!"

The king frowned. "It's neutral territory. We can't go in there."

"Don't worry," Bulstrode announced between huffs. "It's in hand. Everything's under control. Being organized like clockwork. Nothing left to chance."

The guard shouted outside as three sheeries flew into the room. Lady Margaret got a chill just seeing the phosphorescent beasties. They swooped low overhead, buzzing the king and queen, the chamberlain, even General Bulstrode. Everyone was leaping about to get out of the way.

One of the glowing ickees headed straight for Lady Margaret! She dove under a table.

When she looked out, they were gone. Guards and servants and royalty were all picking themselves up and dusting themselves off.

And the queen was glaring at General Bulstrode.

"Everything's under control, is it?" she demanded.

Chapter Eighteen

Kathleen had never seen such weather. Here it was, the middle of summer, and a raging snowstorm had sprung out of nowhere. She thought she saw a rainbow at the same time. It felt as if all the different weather the world had to offer was trying to happen at the same time.

At least she had made it through the wind and snow to Jack's cottage. She knocked on the door, but no one answered. She hoped Jack was all right in this storm. The door was open. She was sure Jack wouldn't mind if she got herself in out of the elements.

She stepped inside.

It was like the middle of night in this place. Even though it was only three in the afternoon, the storm outside was that dark. She went over to an oil lamp and lit it with the last match in a box nearby. At least she had some light. Kathleen shivered. Now she might do with a little warmth.

She walked over to the fireplace, but there were no

matches anyplace about here either. Well, Jack had to keep matches somewhere. She'd just start an orderly search. Perhaps there might be some in the drawers beneath the oil lamp.

She found two full boxes in the first drawer she opened. The drawer also held two separate piles of photographs. One of the ones on top showed Jack and Kathleen together.

Well, she'd just look at the photos for a moment to pass the time. She smiled as she glanced through the first pile, pictures of Jack that she had taken, pictures of her that Jack had taken, and a few pictures of the both of them that they'd talked other people into taking. It was a lovely record of their last few days together.

The second pile, however, showed no people at all. It was instead a record of all the local homes and sights of interest. Now why would he have these?

Oh, well. She could ask Jack about them when he returned. She went to put the second pile back in the drawer when she noticed a piece of paper that had been right below the photos, but that she hadn't seen before. It was a typed letter, with the letterhead of Jack's company, Sperry, Sperry, and McGurk.

Well, maybe this would explain all the photographs. She took out the letter and read.

Kathleen couldn't believe her eyes. *This* was what Jack had come here for?

She read the letter a second time.

Now she felt cold inside as well.

Jack had never seen such a storm. The snow was blowing with such ferocity that the very road itself seemed to want to close over him. He jumped out of the way of a sliding snowbank and trudged over the final hill. He could barely see his cottage ahead. He saw a light in one of the windows. Kathleen must be waiting for him, safe inside.

Jack stepped inside, stomping his feet to get the snow off his shoes. Kathleen sat very quietly at the table.

He smiled at her. "Hi. You got here okay."

She did not smile back. Instead, she looked down at Jack's photographs, which she had spread across the table. She held a letter in her hand. It was the proposal letter he'd done for Sperry, Sperry, and McGurk.

"You're not on vacation!" she said angrily. "You're here to buy up all our property, aren't you? To turn this place into another Disneyland!"

Oh, no, Jack thought. He never did explain it fully, and now it had come to this. Well, he thought, better late than never.

"It's my job," he began, "and it wasn't going to be Disneyland. I was going to buy some vacation houses for Americans. Give them the chance to live out their dreams. I tried to tell you."

"When?"

Jack paused. He guessed he hadn't really ever tried to explain. He had almost brought it up any number of times, but it had always seemed simpler to talk about something else.

Besides, that letter had been written before he'd ever set foot in Ireland. He had to tell her how everything had changed.

"But then it didn't matter," he insisted, "because I'm not going to do it!"

Kathleen waved at the photographs. "You were stealing our homes!"

"I wasn't!" How could he make her see? Buying up property in a rural corner of Ireland made sense on paper. It was only after he'd gotten here and realized how his

project would affect the locals' whole way of life that he
had had second thoughts. "Look, I've just rung New York
and told them this place is no good for them. I've just
been phoning from the post office."

But Kathleen was too angry to listen to anything. "That's
a lie!" she shot back.

She was so beautiful when she was angry. "The locals'
way of life"—who was he kidding? It was Kathleen's life
he couldn't bear to change. Didn't she realize she was the
whole reason he had changed his mind?

"It's not a lie!" he insisted. "I love you!"

"And that's a lie too!"

She threw the photographs at him and grabbed her coat.
Before he could stop her, she was out the door.

Kathleen.

The door slammed back, blown open by the wind. He
looked down at the photos flung across the floor. This
wasn't supposed to end this way.

How could he make her understand?

The chamberlain did not care for the swamp.

Oh, certainly, he and the squad of fairies who accompanied him could fly high enough above it to escape all but
the occasional noxious whiff of the marsh gases below.
And if they flew fast enough they could avoid most of the
buzzing, biting insects, some of them almost as large as
fairies themselves. Bulstrode had managed to give them a
very detailed map, so they could fly straight to Sir Aloysius
Jentee's home without getting lost trying to follow the
twisting waterways below.

Gases. Insects. Twisting waterways. The chamberlain's
shudder reached all the way to his wings. But he hated the
swamp most because he knew they were being watched.

Below them, at strategic intervals, sat any number of large frogs, who honked to their fellows as they passed. The chamberlain might know the way to Jentee's estate, but Jentee, and anyone under his protection, would know of their approach well in advance of their arrival.

The chamberlain glanced about at his elite guard, half a dozen of the best troopers in the king's service.

All seven of them would not be enough, should anything go wrong.

Jessica and Mickey sat out upon Jentee's veranda, watching the butter spirits' cricket game. Not that it was much of a game. Every time the bowler splashed through the marsh and tossed the ball, the ball refused to bounce on the swampy ground; instead it disappeared in the mud before it got anywhere near the batsman. Then the spirits would spend a quarter of an hour looking for the ball and start all over again. Jessica decided she didn't understand this sport at all. According to Mickey, this made the whole proceedings more fast paced than the usual cricket game.

Unfortunately, the whole thing gave Jessica too much time to think. She missed seeing her parents—even though they could be impossible. She missed having a clean change of clothes. She missed being someplace that actually had large stretches of dry land.

She sighed.

"I hope we've done the right thing, running away like this."

"Running away's against all my principles," Mickey replied with a smile, "but I'd give them all up for a smile from your shining eyes and lips."

Oh. His honeyed tongue always made her feel better.

She smiled back at him. They kissed, long and slow. It almost let her forget the swamp.

She heard Aloysius Jentee clearing his throat. She gently broke away from Mickey and saw that the butter spirit had joined them on the veranda.

He nodded approvingly. "Gad, I can see it's love between you two. Though I once danced the tango all night at the Savoy with Lady Astor, I've never loved anyone or anything—except butter, of course." He waved at the never-ending cricket game. The players had once again lost the ball. "Do you think I've missed anything?"

But before either Jessica or Mickey could speak, a frog hopped in their direction, honking most insistently.

Jentee nodded as if he understood every honk. He frowned at his guests.

"Ah, they've found you."

They had found them already? She should have known her parents would call on all the resources of fairyland. She looked to Mickey.

"We'd better move on."

"No, no, dear girl," Jentee assured them. "I wouldn't hear of it. I'll deal with them." He honked jovially. "Never fear, Jentee's here. But meanwhile, while I entertain them, might I suggest a stroll in the garden for you?"

He waved toward a patch of dank, misty bogland directly behind the house. That, Jessica thought, was a garden?

"The bulrushes are magnificent this time of year," Jentee added.

Mickey took her hand and led her away. She noticed he looked most troubled as well.

As the chamberlain suspected, Jentee was waiting for their arrival. The chamberlain and two of his party landed and were immediately shown to the steps of Jentee's pavilion, where the leader of the butter spirits waited with two of his fellows. The chamberlain immediately demanded the whereabouts of the fugitive pair.

"Yes, indeed, dear friends," Jentee replied most heartily. "Princess Jessica and Mickey Muldoon are here under my protection."

"We want them!" demanded one of the two fairies in the chamberlain's escort.

Oh, dear. He should have insisted on doing all the talking, the chamberlain thought.

Jentee was properly taken aback. "Your tone, sir, is offensive. You can't have them."

"Then we'll send troops to take them!" the second fairy added.

That started Jentee laughing.

"Try it, gents. Honk! Honk!"

With that, the two other butter spirits turned into frogs, their long tongues lashing out to grab the two offending fairies, who were then instantly whipped back into the two frogs' mouths. The frogs swallowed.

The chamberlain was alone.

Jentee shook his head. "Oh, dear. Oh, dear. That was unfortunate."

The frogs had become butter spirits again, both licking their lips.

"But scrumptious," one of the spirits added. "Almost as good as butter."

"Nothing's as good as butter," the second objected.

The chamberlain decided he'd better do something before he became the third meal.

"We came here under a white flag of peace," he began.

"Curses!" Jentee exclaimed. "Someone should have told you I'm color-blind! Except for the red, white, and blue of Old England, God bless her one and all. There's nothing more to say."

"There's always something more to say," the chamberlain replied. "May I speak plainly?"

Jentee looked a tad disappointed. "I'd prefer it devious, but be plain if you must."

He'd be as plain as possible.

"I'd like to bribe you."

All three butter spirits stepped back in horror.

"Bribe?" Jentee exclaimed. "Never, sir! The idea is offensive to my ears. We're English to the bone—word given, word kept. An *Englishman's* word! Enough said! Besides, what could you possibly bribe us with?"

The chamberlain smiled. "Butter."

The look on Jentee's face told the chamberlain they would soon be doing business.

Mickey Muldoon didn't like the feel of what had been going on back there. Jentee, though friendly enough, seemed a bit too ready to talk to all concerned. It made alarm bells ring in the back of his leprechaun skull. Mickey didn't exactly understand it himself. The butter spirits had just seemed a bit too slippery. So as soon as they'd gotten out of sight of Jentee's pavilion, he'd told Jessica they weren't going back.

"Mickey," Jessica protested, "we didn't even say good-bye to Aloysius."

Mickey shook his head. "I don't trust him. We're better off away from here."

"He's been very good to us."

"Maybe it's his pear-shaped vowels or the way he cocks his little finger when he spreads mud on his bread. I could be wrong."

He heard a sound overhead and pulled Jessica down to hide behind a clump of high reeds.

An entire troop of fairies flew overhead, carrying two large churns in their midst. On the side of each churn, Mickey could read a single word: "Butter."

Jessica's grip tightened on his arm.

"You weren't wrong."

As soon as the fairies had passed them, the two started to run.

Chapter Nineteen

The storm was gone. It was summer again.

Jack could care less. All he wanted to do was sit on this log and think about what he could possibly say to Kathleen.

"Well, what's the verdict?"

Jack looked up. It was Seamus again, this time in some sort of military uniform. Jack could barely get together the strength to nod to the leprechaun.

"Verdict?" he asked.

"About helping the cause," Seamus reminded him.

"Oh, that. Sorry. I haven't thought."

Jack sighed.

"We're engaged in a war that will determine the fate of civilization as we know it, and you haven't *thought!*" Seamus peered up at Jack. "What's troubling you?"

Jack shook his head. "I had a terrible row with Kathleen last night."

"Oh, is that it?" The leprechaun laughed. "Woman

trouble. I have that twenty-four hours a day. Was it when she found out you were here to buy up the cottages?''

Jack stared at Seamus. "How did you know that?"

"We're leprechauns. We know when any mischief is afoot. I looked into your heart''—he waved back at the cottage—''and then I looked into your drawer over there.''

Ah, yes, Jack thought. That drawer. He glanced at the leprechaun.

"You aren't angry with me too?"

"No, no. I knew you wouldn't go through with it. Besides, we would have scared off anyone who wasn't right.''

Jack shook his head in amazement. Seamus had known what was happening all along.

"Mind you," the leprechaun continued, "those people you work for—Sperry, Sperry, and McGurk—they sound like three villains after my own heart. They're not American leprechauns, are they?''

"No, just property men." Jack could see their frowning faces in his head. "A very unforgiving trio.''

Seamus nodded knowingly. "They sound like trouble, so they must have a touch of the leprechaun in them.''

Jack stared hard at the little person. If Seamus understood just what Jack was about, maybe he could . . .

"Maybe you could explain things to Kathleen," Jack blurted.

"Maybe I could," Seamus considered. "Of course it would be in return for some little favor you do me.''

"Like helping you out?"

"You scratch my back, I'll scratch yours. It's the way the world turns. It'll take your mind off your troubles.''

Jack nodded. "All right. But you've got to square things with Kathleen.''

Seamus grinned broadly. "She's as good as back in your arms, Jack." He whistled.

Jack jumped as another fifty leprechauns materialized directly behind Seamus. He took a ragged breath, trying to calm his heart. Maybe he was getting used to Seamus, but he wasn't used to fifty more.

"I want you to turn this hairy rabble into a fighting machine," Seamus instructed.

"By myself?" Jack asked. He didn't think he could organize one leprechaun, much less fifty.

"Oh, I'm sure you'll do fine," Seamus answered easily. "And you have all day."

All day? Jack was about to object when he realized Seamus and the others had disappeared. He looked up and saw the reason why. He was about to have visitors.

It was the Fitzpatrick brothers. The four of them barreled down the path, pointing at Jack and mumbling among themselves.

What could they possibly want? It was about Kathleen, no doubt. Certainly, they'd listen to reason.

Jack took a couple steps forward to meet them at the edge of the path.

As soon as George was in striking distance, he took a swing. Jack barely managed to duck the blow.

"Wait!" he called. "Hear me out!"

"Let me hit him," pleaded Harry, the youngest of the four. "Let me hit him. You promised!"

Jack retreated a bit, putting the chopping block between himself and the four.

"What did you do to our sister?" George demanded.

"She's been crying her eyes out all night!" James added.

The four brothers all started to walk to one side of the chopping block. Jack quickly moved to the other side, keeping the block between them.

"Stand still so I can hit you!" Harry demanded.

"I've been trying to talk to her, but—" Jack began.

"You hold his arms and I'll hit him," James instructed his brothers.

"No," his brother George replied. "You hold his arms and *I'll* hit him."

"It's my turn. I never get to hit anyone." Harry was beginning to whine.

"You're too young," George replied. "You have to learn how to clench your fists first." He made a very large fist from his very large hand by way of demonstration.

"You can't expect to go straight to the hitting," brother John agreed.

Jack had had enough of this. "Can't we discuss this over a drink?" he suggested. "Then if you still want to get physical, well—"

All four brothers paused and exchanged looks among themselves.

George rubbed at his neck. "Why not? My throat's as dry as the Sahara."

James grinned. "Remember, my favorite drink is my next one."

Harry only stared sullenly at Jack. "I want to hit him now."

Jack decided to ignore that and led the way into the cottage. All four brothers followed. He stepped aside as the brothers headed for the kitchen cupboards.

"The beer's in the—" Jack saw that the cupboard was already open. "Ah, I see you've found it."

He walked over to the cupboard and discovered the Fitzpatrick brothers had taken all the beer. Every single one.

"That's fine," Jack insisted, swallowing despite the dryness in his throat. "I wasn't thirsty."

Harry put down his bottle long enough to ask, "Do you have any snacks at all?"

"No." Jack shook his head. "No, I don't." Now that he had the brothers' hands occupied, he had an important question. "Is Kathleen bad? I must see her."

George glared up at him. "She says you wanted to turn our farm into a casino."

"That's not true," Jack replied.

James rose halfway from his seat. "Are you calling our sister a liar?"

All four of the brothers seemed to growl.

"Of course not," Jack added hastily.

George put down his bottle for a moment, his tone gentler than before.

"Er, I suppose you'd pay a fair fee for the properties?"

"It doesn't matter," Jack answered. "I'm not going to do it. Not since I got to know the place."

George nodded, a half smile on his face. "But the money would've been good, wouldn't it?"

"If it's money you're after," came a voice out of thin air, "how do you feel about getting some gold?"

George raised his eyebrows. "Some gold? Well, I— Who said that?"

All four of the brothers looked around the room with great suspicion.

Jack wasn't at all sure of the wisdom of this course of action.

"Are you sure you want to do this, Seamus?" he whispered.

"Who you talking to?" Harry demanded.

"You need help, don't you?" Seamus replied. "See if they've done any soldiering."

John looked a little frightened. "What's going on?"

Jack tried to smile reassuringly. "You boys know anything about drilling? Army-type drilling?"

"Sure," George replied a bit uncertainly, "we were in the school cadet corps."

"We liked the shouting," James added.

"Giving orders," John agreed.

"Really?" Jack said. "You surprise me. But you might like to help out our leprechaun friends. Commander Muldoon, front and center!"

Seamus popped into existence on the table right in front of all four brothers.

"Jaysus—" George said.

"Mary—" John added.

"Mother—" Harry amended.

"Of God!" James concluded.

Jack nodded to the leprechaun.

"Commander Muldoon, these are the Fitzpatrick brothers."

But before Seamus could say a word, George had grabbed him by the coattails.

"Got you!" George grinned. "Now, leprechaun, tell us where you've hidden your pots of gold!"

"What are you doing, Fitzpatrick?" Jack demanded.

But Seamus was the very picture of calm. "Pay no heed, Jack. It's traditional. It's what these flat-footed peasants do when they stumble on poor defenseless leprechauns."

"We're *rich!*" Harry chortled.

But Seamus Muldoon had already vanished, leaving George holding nothing but an empty jacket.

Jack heard laughter coming from all around the room. Leprechaun laughter.

Jack shook his head sadly.

"I thought you might be able to behave like gentlemen, Fitzpatrick, so we can stop all the disasters you farmers are having before it's too late."

"And maybe get your hands on some of the gold for

your troubles," Seamus's disembodied voice added, "*after* we win."

George considered that.

"Oh, right." He nodded. "That sounds fair enough."

Seamus popped back into existence. George handed him back the jacket with a sheepish smile.

"Sorry about that, Commander. Matter of instinct."

Seamus accepted the jacket with the best of grace. After all, it was time to drill.

The leprechaun led them all to the back of the cottage. He turned to the four brothers, waving his arms at the yard behind him.

"Now can you drill some discipline into this fine army of layabouts?"

The brothers all looked around.

"What army of layabouts?" James asked.

A whole troop of laughing leprechauns materialized right in front of them.

All four dropped their beer bottles. And Harry fainted dead away.

Well, Jack didn't know what he expected out of Ireland, but it was nothing like this.

He sat next to Seamus, watching all four Fitzpatrick brothers drill fifty leprechauns. Or attempt to drill them.

"Left! Right! Left! Right!" the brothers called.

The squad, led by a two-foot-high fellow with the name of Jericho, did their best to follow orders. They weren't too bad at marching in a straight line; they only occasionally bumped into each other.

"Quick march!" the brothers called. "About-face!"

Some of the leprechauns sped up; some didn't. Some of the leprechauns turned; some didn't. Jack winced. Once the orders became more complex, the leprechauns did nothing *but* bump into each other.

Seamus sighed where he sat by Jack's side. Seamus had been doing a lot of sighing of late.

One thing that could be said for the Fitzpatrick brothers: They were so stubborn they wouldn't give up. They kept on shouting. And the leprechauns kept on bumping.

But Jack had looked beyond the leprechauns and seen Kathleen striding toward the lot of them in a most determined fashion. He rushed over to greet her.

"Kathleen!" he called, opening his arms to embrace her. "Am I glad—"

She pushed him aside. "No, that's over!"

If anything, she seemed angrier than before. How could he make it right?

"But I want to explain," he began.

She barely looked at him. "I want nothing more to do with you. But something has to be done about this war. It's getting worse. The milk's turned sour and we've already lost a whole field of wheat. Any more and we're ruined." She frowned over at her brothers.

"What are they doing?"

"Helping me help the leprechauns," Jack explained.

That got her to look at him at last.

"But you have to stop the war, not fight in it."

He nodded.

"I know. I'm doing what I can."

"Just great. The city boy turns up to save us poor country folk from doom and destruction!"

Jack looked at Kathleen. He'd had just about enough of her sarcasm. He opened his mouth and the words poured out.

"Now hold on just a minute here! I pulled someone out of the river, okay? That's all I did. Suddenly, I'm military advisor to an army of invisible people two feet high. That was not in the travel brochure, and I'm having a hard time handling it. On top of that, I fall in love with the most beautiful girl I've ever seen, even though she drives me crazy, and so as not to upset her, I lie to my bosses and lose them a fortune and so blow my job and no doubt my apartment as well. She now hates me because she thinks I'm still lying to her. Meanwhile the world is probably coming to an end, and frankly this city boy has just about had it!"

He turned and stomped away.

Kathleen looked after the retreating Jack.

On occasion, the American could speak his mind. She was surprised to realize she'd like it if he did so more often.

But, no. This whole business had been a sad mistake. She had responsibilities if she was going to save the farm.

She looked down to see Seamus Muldoon strolling in her direction.

"Ah, Kathleen," the leprechaun said with a smile. "Your brothers are doing a fine job. A fine job."

"Keep drilling," George was shouting at the other leprechauns. "Drilling is what war is all about. Drilling and killing!"

"We're tired!" one of the leprechauns called back. "Our little legs aren't used to it. We'll have to become invisible. It's less tiring for us."

The other leprechauns shouted their agreement.

"All right then," George said after a moment's consideration.

The leprechauns promptly vanished. The brothers tried shouting a few orders, but there was a certain doubt in their voices.

"It's all right," Seamus shouted. "They're still there. Keep going."

"Yes!" one of the invisible leprechauns added. "We're still here waiting for your orders!"

George and the others went back at it with renewed enthusiasm.

"Left! Right! Left! Right!"

"Pick up those invisible feet!"

Seamus looked back up at Kathleen.

"Well, Kathleen, I hear you and Jack have had a falling out. Now if you want my advice—"

"I don't!" she snapped. Now even leprechaun men would run her life!

Seamus's grin only grew broader. "Sure, but I'll give it anyway. It's no skin off my nose. Forget all the troubles in your head. Listen to the joy in your heart. He's a fine man, and you're as beautiful a flower as ever graced the valley. And if I was two hundred years younger and three feet taller I'd show you what— Hello there, Mary Muldoon!"

Seamus's wife only glared at her husband for an instant before she looked up at Kathleen.

"Mistress Kathleen, what are your four idiot brothers doing talking to themselves in an empty field?"

"They're drilling the troops," Kathleen replied. "They've all gone invisible."

Mary shook her head. "No, they've all gone for a drink." She pointed to the next field over, where fifty laughing leprechauns were strolling off into the distance. Her four brothers were too busy shouting orders to notice.

This might have been funny, Kathleen realized, if she wasn't so angry. And why did she suddenly feel as if she wanted to cry?

* * *

Jack sat forlornly on the hillside by his cottage. Nothing he did ever turned out right. He looked up and saw that Mary Muldoon was sitting next to him.

"Anything wrong, Jack?" she asked.

He sighed. "Not much, except it seems I've got to stop a war, save the world, and win back the only woman I've ever loved."

Mary smiled. "Is that all?"

"Yeah, that's about it." He stared down at the ground. "I'm just an ordinary guy, Mary."

"You're the first human in years to actually see us leprechauns and make friends. You can't be *that* ordinary."

Jack shrugged. "It was just luck—maybe good, maybe bad."

But Mary still wouldn't let it go. "It still makes you extraordinary."

He looked over at her again. "So what do I do?"

She smiled at him and said, "Your best."

Jack considered that. All right. Okay. That was exactly what he would do. His best. And it would make everything work out.

He turned back to thank Mary for the advice. But she had already disappeared.

Chapter Twenty

Now Seamus Muldoon had a real army. Sure, they still had a bit of trouble following orders. But thanks to the Fitzpatrick brothers, they at least knew what the orders were. Seamus would shout a few of them next time they faced the troopers. That would put fear into the enemy!

"See them marching properly now," he said with a bit of pride. "I don't know if they'll scare the enemy, but they scare the bejaysus out of me!"

He stood on a hillside and watched them go by: leprechauns, pookas, and all the rest marching toward the fairy palace. They'd finish this war for good. And now that the leprechauns had tasted a bit of discipline, how could they lose?

The chamberlain had returned to the royal palace to discover that even the throne room had been converted into a war room, complete with a giant table full of maps of the surrounding countryside. At least he assumed it was the surrounding countryside. Everyone seemed to be too busy giving orders to have much time for explanations, even the king and queen, who took turns jumping from their thrones to demand the latest information.

General Bulstrode, the chief order shouter, marched into the room. "Bearer of bad news, sire."

King Boric looked up, totally confused by the interruption. "Who? What?"

"Mickey Muldoon's escaped our patrols and still has your daughter. The leprechauns will probably try to use her for blackmail."

The chamberlain sighed. So his whole mission to the swamp had been in vain. "Damn it! We're beaten!"

The king looked askance. "Don't know the meaning of the word."

Bulstrode nodded helpfully. " 'Beaten' means we're finished. Done for. Kaput, sire."

That certainly managed to stop the conversation. The chamberlain cleared his throat. Somebody had to do the thinking around here.

"We could try the same plan," he ventured. "The princess is important to us, so we have to snatch someone who is important to them."

Bulstrode actually picked up on the idea. "Like Muldoon himself! I'll put the commando team together right now."

The king was not convinced. "That's all very fine and good, but they'll have to find him first. Where is he?"

"Outside!" Bulstrode pointed toward the balcony.

Outside? the chamberlain thought. Here? Now?

King Boric led the rush out to the balcony. There, in the fading light of evening, were dozens of lights posted at regular intervals, showing Muldoon's entire army camped outside. The chamberlain didn't even have to look around to know that they surrounded the palace. All this must have happened while Bulstrode and the troopers' high command were inside, exchanging orders.

An officer rushed to Bulstrode's side. He saluted smartly and handed him a brown envelope marked "top secret." The officer turned and marched away as Bulstrode tore open the envelope and pulled out a single sheet of bright white paper.

"What is it, General?" King Boric asked.

"White paper," Bulstrode replied with a wave of the sheet. "Top, top, top secret."

The king took a step closer to the document. "What does it say?"

Bulstrode frowned as he waved the paper again. "Don't know. Blank. Invisible ink. Safer that way."

Queen Morag pointed out at Muldoon's camp. "What about *that*?"

The general stiffened a bit. "Nothing to worry about, ma'am. I fought alongside the great Finnigan himself at the Battle of Bonger's Reach." His great eyebrows rose as he remembered the fateful day. "Intelligence had discovered that the devils attacking us were the enemy!" He nodded at the wisdom of it all. "In the end, we defeated the queen and her ugly sisters, but it was a close-run thing. Now I'll find a second glory!"

The queen, the king, and the chamberlain exchanged very worried glances. Their general's condition was far worse than they thought.

"I'm coming with you in that raid, Bulstrode," the king announced.

"No, no, sire," Bulstrode blustered. "I'm in charge."

"That's what I'm afraid of," the king said.

* * *

Ah, Muldoon thought, he had a grand army and an even grander army camp. He and his wife had taken a tour of the whole place, which had hundreds of tents, many of them properly set up. As to the others—well, the lads had promised to get around to them shortly. And here, at the camp's very center, they'd put up a great searchlight full of glowworms, which one of the pookas turned about so that the light swept the whole campsite.

But now they had reached the command tent, and Seamus had other plans.

"I'm going for a drink with the pookas," he told his wife. "It keeps up morale."

"Yours or theirs?" she replied sharply. She looked about the camp with a frown. "Have you posted sentries?"

"Of course. And I've ordered them to stay sharp."

Mary shook her head. "They're as sharp as billiard balls!"

"Nothing will happen here tonight, woman!" Seamus Muldoon had prepared for everything. And now Seamus was prepared for a drink.

He marched smartly off toward the waiting pookas.

The king realized he had not quite thought this through. Oh, he was quite certain that Bulstrode couldn't be left on his own. The fellow seemed to wander in and out of sanity. But perhaps the king was not the best person to accompany him.

King Boric first had his doubts when he met the fairy commandos, all dressed in black, their faces darkened by charcoal, and each sporting half a dozen weapons about his person. Should a man in Bulstrode's condition be that close to so many sharp objects? And then, as soon as the commandos had provided Bulstrode and him with similar attire, they had jumped into action. And he meant jumped—straight over the side of the cliff by the palace.

The commandos landed lightly. Bulstrode and the king were not so lucky. Boric thought he had already pulled at least three muscles, including one in his wing. Perhaps all that sitting around on the throne had made him a little soft. Perhaps he should have gotten, say, the chamberlain to keep tabs on Bulstrode. What did the chamberlain do all day anyway?

But it was too late for regrets. The king was here, in the middle of the action, although he trusted that most of the action would be handled by those three commandos.

The three commandos waved them forward to creep along the base of the palace wall.

"You shouldn't be here, sire," Bulstrode whispered. "It's too dangerous."

"I'm your king," Boric whispered back. "I have to lead."

And perhaps he should do just that. He moved to the front of the line.

A sound came from overhead.

What? Where? The king jumped at the horrible noise, the low moan of the devil himself.

"What was that?"

"An owl, sire," Bulstrode reassured him. "Would you like me to take over?"

"No, no," the king hastily replied. The general would be dangerous with too much authority. That was why he had come. There must be some reason why he'd come.

He waved Bulstrode forward. "But you can go at the front. I'll be right behind you, leading the way!"

They crept onward, into the enemy camp.

* * *

King Boric was at his wit's end. Not only was this mission dangerous, but it was taking forever. That damned glow-worm searchlight the leprechauns kept shining meant that the king's party had to keep doubling back upon them-selves. On occasion, they had even been forced to go invisi-ble. But that meant they couldn't see where the others were going! Bulstrode had already trod on the king's invisi-ble feet—twice! Boric never knew this sort of mission could have so many problems.

It was lucky that the leprechauns didn't have many sent-ries, and those they did have weren't paying much atten-tion. Still, the commandos had almost run straight into a crowd of rowdy pookas, and in getting away from them, Bulstrode had nearly stumbled over the sleeping head of a dullahan. Boric noticed something else as well. No matter where they zigged or zagged, they always ended up sneak-ing deeper into the enemy camp. It seemed to make no sense.

Until now.

This tent, at the very center of the leprechaun camp, with its bright green banner flying overhead, looked important. It was larger than anything else they'd seen for one, and besides, it had a guard! Anything with a guard was worth investigating, Boric thought. And General Bulstrode actually agreed!

Bulstrode waved for the others to hide as a messenger approached the guard.

The messenger handed something over, no doubt a dis-patch of great importance.

"It's for Commander Muldoon."

Yes! Boric's spirits flew. They had found their quarry at

last. The messenger left as the guard disappeared inside the tent.

Bulstrode waved for the others to follow him to the back of the tent. Boric noticed that the commandos had come up with a blanket and a wooden club.

Bulstrode grinned and pointed. They could see a well-formed shadow on the wall of the tent, as if the occupant stood almost against the wall itself. Commander Muldoon was being most obliging.

One of the commandos whacked the shadow with the club. The figure inside fell unconscious without a sound. The other commandos reached under the canvas and drew out the body, covering it with a blanket as they did so to protect themselves from the curious looks of passersby. Two of the commandos lifted the still form between them and prepared to hurry away.

"Let's go invisible again," Boric said.

"Can't," Bulstrode replied. "Not carrying Muldoon's body. It wouldn't disappear." He tugged at the corner of his great mustache. "Gad, what a chapter this'll make in my memoirs!"

They hurried out of the camp in a straight line. Boric was having a bit of difficulty keeping up. Perhaps, he considered, he should cut down on that third helping of dessert. If only those fairy pastries weren't so enchanting!

Bulstrode waved at Boric to hurry up. The nerve! Boric was the king. He'd escape in a kingly manner.

Bulstrode and the commandos looked quite alarmed. What? Who? Boric looked around quickly and saw the beam of the searchlight was heading right for them!

He turned back to the others, but they had already taken flight, lifting the still body as they flapped their wings to gain altitude. They were flying? Why hadn't anybody told him? He was the king!

Boric blinked. The searchlight was shining right in his eyes. And if he squinted, he could see dozens of leprechauns running from all over the camp to surround him.

They stared at him in silence for a long moment. What could he do? He was the king, after all.

Exactly, Boric thought.

He cleared his throat and pointed to himself.

"And this is what King Boric looks like. All right? I've made myself up to look like him? So you won't miss him at the castle . . . ." He stood at attention, trying to look as royal as possible.

"He's the most powerful fairy in the land," he continued, "a magnificent fighter, leader of men, and frightener of sheep."

"We heard he was an ineffectual old windbag who was bullied by his wife!" somebody in the crowd called back.

The other leprechauns started to laugh.

"How dare y—" Boric caught himself. "Old Windbag! Ha ha! Very good! Demonstration over!"

The leprechauns applauded and started talking among themselves. This would be as good a time as any.

Boric leapt into the air, his wings extended, flying for all he was worth.

It seemed they were hunted by everyone.

Mickey and Jessica flew from the swamp, back toward the fields they knew. But a squad of fairy troopers made them hide in the bushes below, and they decided to travel on foot so they could be closer to cover. But the paths here were filled with marching leprechauns, and they had to hide from them as well. Neither side would understand. Both troopers and leprechauns would try to separate them.

Mickey could think of only one place that might be safe.

He brought his princess back to the cottage the Muldoons called home.

They entered quietly after dark, careful not to be seen by prying fairy eyes, either trooper or solitary. If only Mickey could have a few quiet words with his parents about the situation. But both his mother and his father were gone. The only one around was that human, Jack Woods.

Mickey sighed. There was no helping it.

He'd have to bring Jack Woods into the whole mess.

Chapter Twenty-One

The leaf fell very slowly.

It was an oak leaf, Jack could tell. At first, he could see the tree, perhaps the most magnificent oak he had ever seen, but now he saw nothing but the leaf, falling, falling, falling.

It hit the ground with a crash louder than thunder.

And he was watching another leaf drop from the tree. Falling. Falling.

The crash was even louder.

Jack's eyes snapped open. A dream. It had to be a dream.

He swallowed hard. He blinked. Mickey Muldoon stood at the foot of the bed.

Maybe Jack was still dreaming.

"Mr. Woods! Mr. Woods! Wake up!"

No. That was the leprechaun's voice. Jack sat up.

"Mickey!" he called.

The leprechaun waved to a small blond girl just about

his size who was curled up and asleep on a chair cushion in the corner.

"That's Princess Jessica," he explained. "Where's my da?"

Jack stretched and yawned. "Off with the army. They're besieging the royal palace." Princess Jessica? Princess of the fairies? But that was why Muldoon and the fairies were fighting in the first place. "Maybe you can get to him, try to make him see sense and make peace."

He got out of bed and walked over to the washbowl to splash some water on his face.

"It won't happen unless the two sides both want it," he continued, "so maybe the princess here could talk to her— Mickey? Mickey?"

He turned around. Mickey was fast asleep at the foot of the bed.

Maybe, Jack thought, it would be better for all of them if this waited until morning.

The situation was no less confusing, but at least they were all awake. Jack sat patiently while the two small folk told their story.

"My father won't listen," the princess explained. "Not even to me. He'll think I'm under a spell."

Mickey nodded at that. "Mine'll think the same."

Jessica sighed. "Evil thoughts sit on their shoulders. A saint would shudder if he passed both of them now on a dark night. It's our fault."

"If we hadn't run away together," Mickey agreed.

Jack thought they were being far too hard on themselves. "I know I'm the new guy round here, but my guess is that you're just an excuse for them to fight."

"But it's not just a fight!" Mickey insisted. "The Grand

Banshee's taking the lives of the soldiers. We're not immortal anymore.''

This was new. "Who's the Grand Banshee?" Jack asked.

"The head, the chief, the great arbiter of all things fairy and leprechauny," Mickey explained.

Really, Jack thought. There was the solution, staring him in the face.

"Let's talk to her."

Jessica frowned. "Talk to the Grand Banshee?"

"Where does she live?" Jack asked.

"Top of Moonstone Mountain." Mickey nodded his head as he thought it over for himself. "Yes, I think you're right. It might work. She has the power."

So everything would be made right again. Well, almost everything. Jack remembered how Kathleen had made so much sense when she'd talked to the leprechauns about the war. He wished he could ask her to help explain things to the Grand Banshee.

Well, why couldn't he?

Jack looked seriously at the small couple. "I'd like Kathleen—Kathleen Fitzpatrick—to come with us."

"Why?" Mickey asked.

Why? It had made sense to Jack when he'd thought of it a moment ago. But he had some difficulty putting his thoughts into words.

"Another human," he began. "She's from these parts," he added. That *was* important, after all. "She's a woman." And what a woman! No, he couldn't think of that. "It'll show everyone's concerned." Yeah. That made sense. "That we're all in it together."

Both Mickey and Jessica were looking at him with knowing smiles.

"What?" Jack demanded.

* * *

This was far better, Kathleen thought. Just her and her pony on a country lane, her sitting in her trap, letting Firefly trot for all she was worth.

The simple things were the best. Out here in the fresh air, she didn't have to think about any men whatsoever— not about her brothers prattling on about leprechauns and certainly not about anyone from America who was so charming that when she was around him she couldn't think straight. Oh, Jack. Kathleen sighed.

No. She wasn't going there. She and Firefly were out for a little exercise, nothing more, and she'd let nothing else enter her head.

They were coming to the fork in the road. Kathleen decided to take the left-hand side and wind her way back toward her cottage. She tugged on the reins.

Firefly trotted toward the right-hand path.

Kathleen tugged harder.

"No, no, Firefly! To the left! The left!"

But the pony took the right-hand way. What was the matter here? Firefly was much better trained than that. Kathleen pulled back the reins to get her pony to stop.

Firefly ignored that too. The pony just kept on trotting.

King Boric had to admit it had been a magnificent adventure.

Not that he hadn't had his doubts. And the rough moment or two, like the point when he'd been left behind with the leprechauns. And those owls! The king had never liked owls. But now that the royal palace had come into view, he could put the whole thing into perspective. They had executed their plan flawlessly. Their captive was still

thoroughly wrapped in that blanket and carried by a pair
of commandos. Now they returned to the open arms of a
grateful palace.

Some days, it was good to be the king.

The king led the way through the great French windows,
settling at the very middle of the throne room as Bulstrode
and the others landed around him.

The palace guard cried out a greeting. His queen and
the chamberlain rushed into the room. Oh, the excitement
was electric!

"What is it, Boric?" Queen Morag asked.

Bulstrode answered for him. "Victory!"

"Glorious!" Boric agreed. "There will be songs sung
and statues raised commemorating this victory!"

Bulstrode considered that. "I want my statue to be of
me on a horse. I look so good on a horse. Copper or
bronze. I don't mind."

"What happened?" the chamberlain chimed in.

Boric thought they'd never ask. "We kidnapped the
leader of the leprechauns. Seamus Muldoon!" He waved
for the commandos to unroll the blanket.

They did so, depositing their prize upon the marble
floor.

A very annoyed female leprechaun stared up at them.

Female? Not Seamus Muldoon at all then?

The queen cleared her throat.

Oh, dear, Boric thought.

Some days, being the king was greatly overrated.

Kathleen should have known they would end up here.

Firefly stopped abruptly in front of Jack's cottage. No
matter what she did, she couldn't rid herself of the man.
Jack came running out of the house, carrying a heavy

pack upon his shoulder, and jumped into the trap next to her. The nerve of the man! Kathleen was almost speechless.

"What's going on?" was all she could manage.

"No time," Jack answered. "We're off to see the Grand Banshee. Moonstone Mountain."

Kathleen's anger flared the minute he spoke. "You've no right! How did you get the pony to come here?"

One of the leprechauns materialized, sitting atop her pony! It was the young one—Mickey!

"That was me, I'm afraid." He patted the side of the pony. "Moonstone Mountain, Firefly."

She realized there was something else flying about her: a small blond creature with a pale green gown and matching wings. Was this a fairy?

Firefly flew forward as if she were enchanted. Kathleen barely had time to grab on for dear life.

In moments, they had reached the mountainside. Kathleen swore the place was some miles away. But it was enchantment that had gotten them here, one way or another.

Apparently, enchantment only took them so far. The way grew too steep. Firefly could no longer manage the load. Mickey announced that, from here, they'd have to go under their own power.

Now she was supposed to get out and walk? For a moment, Kathleen considered letting the others go on without her. Still, the Grand Banshee herself?

Kathleen climbed down from the trap. Since she'd gone this far, she might as well see it through. Besides, she still hadn't given Jack a proper piece of her mind.

The chamberlain knew it would come to something like this. It was the sort of thing one would expect with Bulstrode in command. The general was an expert in snatching defeat from the jaws of victory. Now, instead of capturing the head of the leprechaun army, they'd managed to capture his wife.

Bulstrode acted as though nothing had gone wrong. Instead, he led the royal party into a large, empty room. Well, it was not precisely empty. In the very center of the room was a single chair.

A pair of guards brought Mary Muldoon in behind them.

"What are you going to do now?" the queen demanded.

Bulstrode brushed at his epaulets. "Interrogate her. This is an interrogation room, ma'am. I took the trouble of turning it into one myself personally."

The queen frowned at the place.

"There's nothing in it except a chair."

"That's what makes it a proper interrogation room!" Bulstrode insisted.

Their prisoner laughed at that. "You're going to interrogate me? About what? Seamus never tells me a thing. He just grunts when I ask him anything."

The queen nodded. "It's the same with Boric."

"That's a husband for you," Mary Muldoon agreed.

The queen made a face very like the king's, creasing her brow with confusion. In a surprisingly deep voice, she uttered a single grunting sound.

"Huh."

The chamberlain had to admit it was rather good. That was a royal grunt if he had ever heard one.

Mary Muldoon nodded to the queen and grunted in turn.

"Huh."

No doubt that was an equally accurate representation of Seamus Muldoon. Oh, dear. At that moment, the chamberlain was very happy that he had never married.

"You've got it in one," the queen agreed.

Mary sighed. "Disappointing, aren't they?"

The queen shook her head. "Very."

"Excuse me," the king remarked rather pointedly. "Could we get back to the matter in hand?"

Mary stared back at him.

"So? What *are* you going to do with me now that you've got me?"

No one seemed to have an answer for that.

"It's dishonorable!" Jericho shouted.

Well, yes, Seamus supposed, it was that. If only so many people hadn't crowded into his tent so early in the morning. He winced when they made the slightest noise. And when they shouted . . .

He realized they all expected him to say something.

"Yes, yes, dishonorable. That's the word."

"Revenge!" cried the pooka captain far too loudly. "We must have revenge! Or something like it."

"Tear out their livers!" the grogoch agreed in the most grating voice the leprechaun had ever heard.

Seamus grimaced. If only he hadn't drunk quite so much the night before.

"What are you going to do, Muldoon?" the pooka demanded.

So now they wanted him to talk again? Sometimes, life wasn't fair at all.

"Do?" Seamus managed. It only hurt a bit to speak.

"They've kidnapped your wife!" the pooka reminded him. If only the hairy fellow wouldn't get so excited. Or so loud.

"Have they?" Seamus had to gather his thoughts. "Oh yes. To be sure. It's a dastardly piece of work."

"Fiendish!" the grogoch captain agreed.

Seamus sighed. That only hurt a little. "I still can't believe it." Mary gone away. A day or two without Mary. Or maybe a week. "Oh, dear." He had started to smile. He shouldn't have done that.

"You must get her back!" the pooka demanded.

"Get her back, you say? Get her back." Mary back from being kidnapped. Mary giving him a piece of her mind. *And you said you posted sentries!*

He tried hard not to shudder.

"Attack the palace now!" Jericho urged. "It's the only way."

The others cheered at that. Muldoon's head pounded twice as much as before.

He took a deep breath. He had to get a handle on this, no matter what he had done the night before.

"I'd like to," he began, forcing his brain to work in complete sentences. "My blood's up and racing and all that. But at this time I can't just think of myself, but the good of all solitary fairies." He took a cautious breath. His brain seemed to be working now almost as fast as his tongue. "The best thing would be to have a counterhostage, like Princess Jessica. I've heard my son has her at this very moment at Woods's cottage!"

Jericho gaped at him. "You mean we could exchange Princess Jessica for your wife, sir?"

Seamus thought about that for an instant before answering. "Exchange her? Are you mad? I'm not going to waste a prize like Jessica in order to get back Mary Muldoon." He thought again of how angry his wife would be. "Anyway, if they spend any time with her, they'll be paying *us* to have her back."

"So what are you going to do with Jessica?" Jericho asked.

"Win the war!" He waved his fist in the air—it only hurt a little bit. "I'm sure King Boric wants to see his daughter a damn sight more than I want to see my wife!"

Everybody cheered at that too.

Jack never thought he'd be so glad for physical exercise. But here he was, next to Kathleen once more, and the long climb up the mountain gave him a chance to explain.

"Sperry, Sperry, and McGurk asked me to look into prospects," he continued. Kathleen hadn't looked at him much since he'd begun, but at least she wasn't trying to stop him.

"Well, to tell the truth," he added, "it wasn't Sperry, Sperry. It was McGurk who asked me."

"Do I care?" Kathleen replied all too lightly. "McGurk! With a name like that, you'd know him to be a man who'd ruin peace and beauty."

"I haven't seen much peace since I've been here," Jack replied.

That gave her pause. Her voice was softer as she added, "Usually, it's very quiet."

"I don't know about that, Mistress Kathleen!" Mickey called back from where he and the princess flew on ahead. "We try too hard to be up to our necks in trouble."

"But this is the worst we've ever been," Jessica pointed out.

"*The* worst!" Mickey agreed.

Kathleen frowned at the wee folk. "You should be on my side, not his! Besides, it's about other things too."

Jack knew it would come to this.

"Like I didn't tell you."

"Yes." Kathleen nodded her head curtly.

"I guess I was hiding it," Jack admitted. "I didn't want anything to spoil what we had."

Kathleen looked up at Jack then. Their eyes met. If only . . .

"Problem!" Mickey called. Kathleen looked away.

Jack turned to see what was the matter.

It was a problem indeed. Sometime in the past, a rock slide had covered the path, completely blocking their way. Above the rubble blocking their way was a sheer cliff face rising twenty feet or more. Below it was another sheer drop, maybe twice as high as the cliff above.

Jack frowned. He wouldn't let a few rocks get in his way. "We'll have to swing around it."

Kathleen frowned back at him. "Just like that?"

"Unless you've got a better idea."

He'd brought a length of rope in his pack. He pulled it out.

"Are you a climber?" Kathleen asked.

" 'Social' or 'mountain?' " Jack replied.

Nobody seemed to find that funny.

"Give me the rope there, Mr. Woods," Mickey said, "and I'll tie it on somewhere."

Jack handed over one end of the rope. Mickey and Jessica flew upward, looking for a place to tie it. Jack looked at the sheer drop again and had a moment of doubt.

"It will be a human-size knot, won't it, Mickey?"

The fairies tied the rope to an exposed tree root a few feet overhead.

They had a plan. Kathleen would go first, climbing out over the rocks to a point where the path was clear again while she kept a grip on the rope so she wouldn't fall. Jack would follow.

Kathleen grabbed the rope and started climbing over the rubble. Jack stayed close behind her. A loose rock slipped from beneath one of Jack's feet, but he managed to grab on to a ledge with his free hand.

He looked down. Big mistake.

"Ah! Don't look down!"

Kathleen did just that.

"Ah!" she replied.

Mickey and Jessica flew close by their sides.

"You're doing fine there!" Mickey encouraged.

Jack wasn't fooled for an instant. "Oh, yeah, thanks. Easy for you flyboys to say."

"Will you stop shaking the rope?" Kathleen demanded.

"That's me shaking, not the rope," Jack replied. He did his best not to turn his head. He wouldn't look down again. He'd only pull up. Wouldn't look down. Wouldn't.

The picture of the drop was firmly stuck in his mind.

Well, at least it couldn't get much worse than this.

He heard a clap of thunder.

Hailstones started pelting down. They were the size of golf balls! Mickey and Jessica flew under a protected overhang, but Jack and Kathleen were left hanging out in the open.

Ow! Jack felt as if he was being pelted with rocks.

Kathleen yelled. A large hailstone had hit her on the forehead. She lost her grip on the rope.

Jack grabbed her wrist as she almost fell past him. She almost jerked him free of the rope as she fell, but he managed to hold on. She dangled in space beneath him, a killing drop below.

"Hold on!" Jack called.

The hail kept on coming. Jack felt as if Kathleen's weight was going to wrench his arm from his socket. His grip started to slip.

Mickey and Jessica flew past him, right into the hailstorm, and each gripped one of Kathleen's shoulders. A large stone hit Mickey in the back, almost sending him reeling. He shook it off, and he and Jessica tugged Kathleen upward.

Yes! With the little people's help, Kathleen's weight was no longer dragging down Jack's arm. He found he was slowly able to draw her toward him and toward the end of the rope dangling below.

"Grab the rope, Kathleen!"

She managed to clutch at the rope with first one hand, then the other.

"Got it!" she called triumphantly.

Jack released the grip on her wrist so he could grab the rope with both hands too.

Now all they had to do was get back on the path.

Jack concentrated on working his way across the rocks. And he resolved that he was never going to look down again.

Chapter Twenty-Two

Jack was totally exhausted. At least the hailstorm had stopped. And they'd made it past the landslide to a spot on the path wide enough so that all four of them could lie back and try to catch their breath.

Right this minute, Jack never wanted to climb another hill or see another scenic vista. When he'd thought of Ireland as picturesque, this wasn't exactly what he'd had in mind.

Kathleen propped herself up on her elbows and looked to the two little people.

"Thanks, Mickey and Jessica, for your help."

Mickey grinned a bit sheepishly. "That's fine."

Jessica squeezed his arm. "See what happens when fairies and leprechauns work together?"

Mickey and Jessica kissed. Jack sat up and looked at Kathleen. She sat up and looked away.

"That's okay, Kathleen," he called out to her. "No thanks necessary."

She looked a little flustered at that and maybe just a tad peeved. "I was just about to thank you," she insisted.

Jack nodded. "Oh, well, okay then."

"Thank you," she said hurriedly.

"That's it, is it? Thank you. Nothing more? No small gift or offer of adoption?"

He thought he saw the beginnings of a smile on Kathleen's face.

"Thank you . . . very much."

Jack smiled for both of them. "Very much? Okay, that's good. I'll take very much for a start."

Kathleen leaned forward and kissed him on the cheek so fast that he had no time to react.

"And don't think there's anything to that!" she warned. She stood and moved on up the path.

Mickey grinned at Jack. "Nothing gets to a lady's heart quicker than saving her from falling to her death."

Jack smiled back and got to his feet. It was time to finish what they'd started. It was colder up here, as if the hailstones had changed the season to winter. They had to push against a chill and steady wind as they drew near the top of the mountain.

Mickey turned abruptly off the path, walking between two huge boulders. Jack and Kathleen followed, barely managing to squeeze between them. Mickey led them into a sheltered clearing protected from the wind.

Jessica flew before them. "That's the entrance there." At the far end of the clearing was a cave.

Cautiously, all four walked inside.

The first tunnel opened into a decent-size room, but the only other exit from the room was barely two feet high.

"It's tiny," Kathleen said. "We'll never get in."

Mickey stepped forward. "I'll go by myself. I'll deal with the Grand Banshee."

"And me," Jessica insisted.

Mickey shook his head. "No, it might be dangerous."

But Jessica was just as stubborn. "We do this together so she can see both sides want peace."

Jack nodded at that. "Makes sense, Mickey."

Mickey frowned, overwhelmed by the logic of it all. "I know, but leprechauns have no sense." He marched toward the opening.

"I'm coming whether you like it or not," Jessica announced firmly as she marched as well.

Before they could take another step, the rocks about the smaller opening started to flicker with bits of flame, a fire that grew from one second to the next until the flames shot eight feet high. Both Mickey and Jessica flew back to Jack and Kathleen as the flames resolved themselves into a figure who stood eight feet tall.

Mickey swallowed hard.

"It's a changeling!"

The fire creature bowed ever so slightly. "Fergus Flynn, Esquire, the Fiery Changeling of Moonstone Mountain, if you please! The one and only guardian of the cave of the High Council. Malignant spirit of the dead. Killer of cattle, goats, and anything that moves. Destroyer of towns and all-around good fellow!"

He chuckled in a way that was not at all pleasant.

Well, Jack had already dealt with his fair share of fantastic creatures. What difference would one more make?

"We're here to see the Grand Banshee," he announced.

Flynn's fiery face looked down disapprovingly. "Have you an appointment?"

"No," Mickey admitted.

"We didn't know we needed one," Jessica added.

"You do." Flynn smiled, and his expression was every bit as unpleasant as his chuckle. "And if you don't have one I can dispose of you any way I please. It's a little known changeling law."

"How do we get an appointment?" Kathleen asked.

"From the Grand Banshee," Flynn replied.

Wait a moment, Jack thought. "But we can't see the Grand Banshee unless we have an appointment."

"Not easy, is it?" Flynn agreed.

No, Jack wasn't going to be defeated this easily. Not after almost getting killed on the mountainside and maybe just beginning to win back the woman he loved, not to mention probably losing his job over that same woman and a bunch of little people he probably shouldn't even believe in! Jack would find a way around this blowhard. He talked regularly with leprechauns. That should be good for something.

"Hmm," Jack remarked skeptically.

Flynn lifted his fiery head. " 'Hmm?' What does that mean?"

"It means," Jack replied, "I know a bag of hot air when I see one."

"Bag of hot air?" Flynn demanded. The flames in his face turned from yellow to red. "Are you talking about me? I'll squash you flat!"

Good, Jack thought. The fellow was taking the bait. "Rubbish. You're not big enough!"

The changeling responded by growing another foot or two. "You still think I can't?" His fire was so intense it made the whole chamber as bright as day.

Jack scowled up at the towering fire creature.

"You're big, Flynn, but you're still nothing!"

He glanced about at the others. He was doing all the work here. He made a small waving motion with his hands for the rest of them to join in.

Kathleen started it for them. "He's the kind of man I'd ask to stay with me when I want to be alone."

"An answer to a maiden's prayer," Jessica agreed lightly. "No wonder so few girls are praying nowadays."

The changeling roared and grew even taller.

"You've got size, but you don't dominate, Flynn!" Mickey added with a laugh. "Lad, you could get lost in a crowd of two!"

The changeling roared even louder and grew to nearly twice his original size, his fiery form taking up one whole side of the cavern.

Jack turned to Mickey. "Now! Go!"

Mickey and Jessica darted between the incredibly large changeling's legs.

"Stop!" Flynn called. "You can't do that! It's cheating!"

He lifted one of his great flaming legs in an attempt to stomp the pair. But by growing so large, he'd become rather slow. The two wee folks easily avoided him.

He snarled, bending down to shoot a fireball down the small tunnel. Jack hoped the two of them were fast enough to avoid it.

Speaking of fast enough, maybe the humans should get out of here too.

The changeling looked back to them, an expression of pure fury upon his flaming face.

Kathleen and Jack ran.

Seamus had sent some of his boys on ahead to roust out his son. Now the leprechaun captain and two of his soldiers scoured the cottage Seamus had called home for the last hundred years.

"Mickey!" the captain called. "Mickey Muldoon! Where are you?"

Apparently, there were problems here. Seamus thought he'd best materialize and lend a hand.

"Where are they?" he demanded as soon as he'd made himself visible.

His captain saluted. "No sign of them, sir!"

Seamus shook his head. "The boy's totally unreliable. I thought he had Jessica."

"Maybe they've gone straight to your camp," the captain suggested.

Well, it was obvious no one was here. "Good thinking," Seamus told the captain. Had to keep up the old morale. "Let's go!"

But before they could step out the door, who should burst in but the Fitzpatrick brothers? Seamus groaned inwardly. This was not a time for humans.

Worse, though, was that the Fitzpatrick brothers saw them.

"Kathleen's missing!" the biggest of them called accusingly.

"She's been kidnapped!" added the smallest.

"It's you lot!" cried one of the brothers in-between.

This is what Seamus got for showing himself to humans in the first place. He shook his head.

"I've no time to argue with you idiots. I've got a war to run!"

Of course, the brothers were not about to see reason. Instead, they all growled and jumped forward to grab Seamus and his cronies.

Well, they couldn't have that, could they?

Seamus and the other three vanished from sight. This would make it a bit more interesting. The Fitzpatrick boys all looked about in confusion. Of course, their consternation only got worse once they started tripping over invisible leprechauns. The four humans roared, angrier than ever before.

Well, leprechauns could handle that as well. Seamus and his cronies picked up whatever jugs, bottles, saucepans, and the like that they found handy, smashing them atop the Fitzpatricks until the four ceased to move.

Ah, it was more peaceful already. Now the leprechauns would just toss the four out of the cottage and leave them in a pile in the front yard.

Too bad there was a war going on, Seamus thought. Otherwise, they'd have taught the Fitzpatricks a proper lesson!

Mickey had to admit caves were not his favorite places. Jessica and he had managed to dodge the changeling's fireball, and they were fortunate he hadn't sent another. The narrow passage had opened up a bit as they walked, and the walls themselves seemed to glow with an eerie light. He was glad that Jessica was by his side. Not that he wanted to put her in any danger! But without her walking with him, Mickey doubted he'd be able to walk at all.

Eventually, the passage came to a set of stairs leading down. They took them silently, holding hands. The stairs seemed to go down forever; the staircase below was lost in the shadows. Bats flew overhead, squeaking with alarm. Mickey realized they were crying out a warning.

"Go back!" the first bat called. "Go back!"

"Go back!" the second bat agreed.

But they didn't go back. They had to see this through. Mickey squeezed Jessica's hand. They descended the stairs. They stepped into the shadows.

The stairs ended just below.

They found themselves in a huge cavern. A great wind

pushed against them. They had to struggle to move even a step forward.

Two trolls walked by, struggling against the wind in an entirely different direction. They carried a mirror between them—a mirror that didn't reflect the cave, but rather showed a sunny field with singing birds, bright flowers, and a glittering stream.

But Mickey forgot all about the mirror when he saw what waited for them at the far end of the cavern.

It appeared to be a hotel called the Hotel Splendide.

Not that it was in the best repair. Indeed, its sign was crooked, with a couple of the neon letters flickering badly. The walls were cracked and the windows broken. The place didn't look as if it had been used in years.

But where else could they go?

Mickey and Jessica pushed their way against the wind, step after slow-motion step, until they reached the door.

It opened easily. They walked inside.

They were in a hotel lobby. And a very nice hotel lobby it was. They were confronted by fine curtains, overstuffed furniture, and pillars painted in gold leaf. Huge chandeliers illuminated the hustle and bustle as a whole staff of trolls, in crisp uniforms that covered everything from their heads to their hairy feet, tended to the clientele.

At the main desk, two long-faced trolls in tuxedos appeared to be waiting for them. Their gold-embossed name tags denoted them as the manager and an assistant.

"Can we help you?" the troll manager called as they approached.

"I hope so," Mickey replied.

"I hope so too," the manager agreed. "We are here to serve."

"Guests come first," the assistant agreed.

"Mind you," the manager said, "we don't often get leprechauns here."

His assistant frowned in thought. "The last one was . . . let me think—" He looked at Mickey, then at his manager. "Must have been"—he brightened suddenly and raised a finger in the air—"never."

The manager shook his head at Mickey and Jessica. "They're ugly, aren't they?"

"Uglier than whales," his assistant agreed.

The manager stared at his assistant. "How do I know how ugly whales are? Whales usually stay at the Excelsior."

Mickey decided it was time to move the conversation along. "We've come to see the Grand Banshee."

"Have you an appointment?" the manager inquired.

"Do we need one?" Jessica asked back.

"No," the assistant added, "but you can't see her without one."

"How do we get one?" Jessica asked.

This was all sounding too familiar to Mickey. "Ask the Grand Banshee?" he added.

The manager looked mildly surprised. "Oh, you know that routine?"

"From that big purple idiot at the entrance," Mickey answered. At least, he had looked purple under all that flame.

The manager made a disappointed clucking sound. "You just can't get the staff nowadays."

Jessica stepped forward. "Call her please!"

This seemed to surprise the manager even more. "Oh, the 'p' word. We don't hear it very often around here, do we?"

"No, we don't." The assistant nodded to both Mickey and Jessica. "In which case, let's see what we can do."

The troll manager opened a great book on the desk before him. He smiled.

"Ah, look! You're in luck. We've had a cancellation. The Grand Banshee can see you now."

The assistant waved them toward a curtain to their right.

That was it? Mickey thought. A simple please and they were on their way. This was why Princess Jessica had to be a part of this.

Leprechauns, after all, hardly ever said "please."

Seamus was not in the best of moods as he returned to camp. He was especially in no mood to talk to Jericho or anyone else for that matter. Jericho joined him anyway.

"Where're Mickey and Princess Jessica?" the young leprechaun asked.

"I don't know!" he snapped. "They're still missing."

Jericho took half a step away. "What are your orders, sir?"

Seamus sighed. There was no helping it now. He looked at Jericho for a long moment before he replied.

"I suppose there's nothing else for it. I'll have to do the honorable thing and rescue my wife." He sighed again. It was his fate. "Otherwise, morale will fall. Not *my* morale, but the rest of the men's." One had to accept one's fate. "But no more of that. We attack!"

"They might torture her if we attack," Jericho pointed out.

Torture? Hmm. He hadn't considered torture.

Seamus sighed one more time. "You're a good lad, Jericho, but you can't cheer me up that easily."

* * *

The chamberlain found this all too familiar.

They had made a hash of things as usual. And now King Boric, Queen Morag, General Bulstrode, and he had to figure some way out of the mess. Oh, Mary Muldoon was in the war room with them. He supposed that was out of the usual. But then, Mary Muldoon was a part of the mess.

King Boric was doing his best to sound authoritative. "Send a messenger to Muldoon. Tell him we'll give him his wife back on conditions."

"Such as he gives Jessica back," the queen added.

"If he has her," the chamberlain added in turn. After all, they really didn't know just where Jessica and Mickey had gotten themselves.

The king considered this. "If he hasn't . . . we'll get him to pull out."

Mary Muldoon started to laugh. "Because of me? Ha! You don't know Seamus Muldoon. He'll be glad I'm gone." She waved her index finger at the king. "Now he'll be able to booze all night and sleep all day. And chase every love-shaken girl he can pick up from the hedges and byways. It's paradise for him!"

Oh, dear, the chamberlain thought.

It sounded all too plausible. From the expressions of the others in the room, they thought so as well.

It was not a happy war room.

Mickey and Jessica were ushered through the curtains. And there she was. The Grand Banshee. Her mane of hair or feathers or whatever it was had been plastered fashionably close to her skull, and she wore a silver lounging outfit rather than her usual black robes.

Mickey still found her a trifle frightening.

"Welcome to the Hotel Splendide." She waved at them, a glass in her hand. "Have a drink."

"No, thank you," Jessica replied politely.

"We're here to—" Mickey began.

The Grand Banshee cut him off. "I know why you're here."

Jessica looked around the room, a lovely, well-appointed salon. "This is beautiful."

Mickey decided he couldn't be any more frightened if he asked a question. "Why are you living in a hotel?"

The Grand Banshee smiled. "I just love room service."

Very well. Apparently, her grandness would be civil and not strike them dead where they stood. It was time for Mickey to get to business.

"Grand Banshee, we came to ask you to stop this war."

"We started it," Jessica quickly added. "Mickey and I. We're in love and our families don't approve."

The Grand Banshee shook her head. "It's good of you to take all the blame, but I know that wasn't the only reason."

"Well, perhaps," Jessica said a bit doubtfully. "But everyone's being hurt. Everything's being destroyed."

"Can you stop it, Grand Banshee?" Mickey asked.

She looked sad as she replied, "No, I can't."

Jessica frowned. "Why not?"

"We can't stop them doing what they really want to do. I warned them." She looked straight at Mickey with her fearsome eyes.

"I warned you!"

And she had, Mickey realized. And he hadn't listened, choosing instead to attack Count Grogan.

"But no one listened," her grandness continued, "so I took away their immortality. But still they didn't take any notice."

Jessica was getting even more upset. "But if the war carries on, there'll be no fairies left in Ireland!"

"Not only that," the woman agreed, "if they don't get back to looking after nature, there will be no Ireland or anywhere else, come to that." The Grand Banshee waved for Mickey and Jessica to follow her over to a large glass sphere in the corner of the room.

"Look at this."

Mickey looked inside and saw an image of a magnificent oak tree. He could swear he'd seen the tree somewhere before. But the tree did not look healthy. Most of its leaves were brown, and many had already fallen as if it were the last few days of autumn.

"From here I can see Mother Nature herself," the Banshee said.

"Beautiful," Mickey agreed.

"Except that her leaves are always green and growing and have been for thousands of years."

"But now they're brown and falling!" Jessica cried.

The Grand Banshee shook her head. "Because she's being neglected and ignored. Once the last leaf falls from the tree, then all growth in all things will end."

Jessica looked at her grandness. "Can we stop it from happening?"

"I don't know." She shook her feathered head. "I've never seen her like this before. Perhaps if the fighting stopped. But it might be too late already."

"How long do you think we've got?" Jessica asked.

Mickey didn't think he'd ever heard such sadness as was now in the Grand Banshee's voice.

"A few days. No more."

Chapter Twenty-Three

Mickey had never seen it so quiet before. The whole field before the fairy castle was utterly still.

On the way here, Jessica had talked of her hope that his father and hers might have come to their senses and settled their differences. Seeing this peaceful scene, he could almost imagine such a thing had happened.

The leprechaun camp appeared totally empty. No guard peered out from behind the gates of the fairy palace. It was beyond peaceful. The whole place looked totally deserted.

Mickey noticed the slightest movement in the grass. Bits of the grass were being flattened, more or less in a straight line. Mickey recognized it for what it was. An invisible leprechaun was walking across the field.

But he was wrong. It wasn't just a single line. Grass was being stamped down along the whole expanse before them. Great patches of the field were being battered down under the weight of leprechaun feet, hundreds of feet, a whole leprechaun army.

Mickey and Jessica both gasped as the army became visible all at once, as though by some silent signal. There were not just leprechauns before them, but pookas, grogochs, dullahans, and sheeries. But the leprechauns and their allies were silent no more, for they all screamed as they rushed toward the palace.

The front ranks of the leprechaun forces were all armed with axes and saws. Mickey saw no sense in this until he realized they were attacking the foundation of the palace itself. Although many were hacking away at it, the task still seemed hopeless. The foundation was a mass of twisted roots and dirt as hard as iron. Maybe, Mickey considered, they were trying to carve a path of attack to the palace above.

But this, apparently, was only one small part of the leprechaun battle plan. Another group of grogochs, pookas, and leprechauns was led across the field by Jericho. Mickey's own father, Seamus Muldoon, appeared before the charging throng to cheer them on.

Then the trooping fairies finally appeared, toting cobweb fireballs, choking puffballs, and even whole wasp nests, which they proceeded to drop upon the leprechaun army below. It was not a pretty sight.

Seamus led his forces into the trees. The Grand Banshee had been right. This was a battle far fiercer than any Mickey had ever seen.

And if it kept on like this, both leprechauns and trooping fairies were done for.

So far, Seamus thought, everything had gone according to his master plan. The first wave of troops was attacking the base of the palace. It was purely a diversionary measure, of course—something to worry the troopers while Seamus and the rest got on with the true attack.

For that, Seamus had arranged the cooperation of the tree spirits.

Everyone was in place. Leprechauns hung from every conceivable branch and leaf. The oaks groaned a bit under the weight. Oh, well. In battle, everyone had to make sacrifices.

Seamus nodded to those around him and called out, just as he had arranged, "Right now, my oakshee friends, do your best!"

The oakshees began to shake their branches back and forth.

"Hang on, lads!" Seamus called to the others.

The branches became more agitated still, whipping to and fro with the strength of a great wind storm.

"We're ready enough," Seamus called. "Fire!"

The oakshees thrust all their branches forward.

And just as they'd arranged, every single leprechaun let go.

Oh, my.

This was the first time the chamberlain had really been able to see General Bulstrode in action. The chamberlain was not impressed.

Mostly, the general marched up and down along the top of the palace wall, huffing and puffing, hemming and hawing. He seemed astonished when the leprechauns finally launched their attack.

"The fools are trying to break in!" He spoke as if the very idea were unthinkable. "Impossible! And I've got the medals to prove it!'' He waved to a special aide he kept nearby at all times. "Strike up a rousing tune, boy!"

The aide, a young fairy who came outfitted as a virtual one-sprite band, started in on playing pipes, a tin whistle, and a bhodran all at once. Out came a jaunty martial tune.

Bulstrode laughed and clapped his hands in time, shouting to the leprechauns below, "You'd better learn to fly if you want to take me on!"

As if they were merely waiting for Bulstrode's voice, the trees just beyond the palace walls began to whip wildly back and forth. Those were the same trees, the chamberlain noted, upon which were lined hundreds of leprechauns.

The great oaks snapped their branches forward. And the leprechauns let go, screaming bloody murder as they came flying from the trees!

Apparently, Bulstrode had been giving them ideas.

But there was no more time for blame. Leprechauns were landing all over the palace grounds. A few smacked into the walls and lost consciousness, but most landed nimbly on their feet, ready for a fight.

"Gad," cried Bulstrode, totally aghast, "more fiendish tricks. Ahhhh!"

The chamberlain wondered what startled Bulstrode now. But it was Seamus Muldoon himself, landing right in front of the general. The general felt about his person, searching for a weapon, any weapon.

Muldoon took Bulstrode out with a single punch.

The chamberlain had mixed emotions about that. He turned his attention elsewhere. The leprechauns might have had the element of surprise, but it would take far more than that to carry the day. The fairy army had gathered just outside the gates, waiting for the general's orders. But now they followed no orders at all, rushing forward to meet the leprechaun attack.

Now the true fight began.

Leprechauns were everywhere. But trooping fairies countered their every advance. The chamberlain managed to knock down a pair of leprechauns still woozy from their recent flight. He looked about and noticed even Queen Morag and Lady Margaret whacking any leprechaun who wandered too close to where they were watching the action.

But Muldoon and his cohorts had not run out of tricks. Sneaky leprechauns were lowering ropes to their comrades below. Courageous fairies intervened, pushing the rope climbers away with long poles.

And what of their leaders?

As usual, the chamberlain noted, Muldoon and King Boric fought through the crowds, eager to get a chance at each other.

But more fairies arrived from within the palace gates. The leprechaun forces were badly outnumbered, and the troopers beat them back at last. Some of the leprechauns escaped by sliding down the ropes.

Muldoon must have given a signal, for two ghostly sheer-ies rose above the battlefield, blowing on flower trumpets.

The battle was done for the day. Troopers rushed forward to collect the wounded, while the leprechauns carried off many of their own.

Many, but not all.

What the chamberlain saw next chilled his blood.

Those left behind, leprechauns and fairies both, were disappearing where they lay from the field of conflict. Just vanishing. Gone forever.

The Grand Banshee had fulfilled her promise.

How long could this go on?

* * *

Mickey and Jessica looked on in horror. So many, both troopers and solitaries, gone for good.

They could take no more. They looked at each other and, without a word, walked away through a field that had been covered by snow. They didn't stop until they could no longer hear a single sound from the two camps behind them.

They paused before a small, still pool of water.

There, in the pool, as if reflected from above, stood the mighty oak the Grand Banshee had shown them, the most magnificent oak in all the world. But the oak of nature didn't look so mighty anymore. There were even fewer leaves upon its branches than before. Time truly was running out.

"All we did was fall in love," Jessica whispered.

"It was enough to set them at each other's throats," Mickey agreed.

The fighting was the fiercest he'd ever seen. And it was quite apparent that neither side wanted it to end.

If none of their parents were willing to change things, then it was up to them.

Chapter Twenty-Four

Nature was dying. Mickey had a sad, sinking feeling as he and Jessica stared at the horrible image before them.

"There are hardly any leaves left," Jessica whispered.

It was no mistake that they'd come to this pond. Here, in this world, another tree waited for them.

Mickey pointed to the thorn tree on the far side of the pond. Its blackened, gnarled branches seemed alive with small dark insects. As the tiny creatures crawled about the thorns, the bark appeared to ripple, almost as if the tree itself could not stay still.

"Evil things sit in those twisted branches," Mickey said. He knew of the legends. He took Jessica's hand and looked deep into her eyes. "Lovers who lean against the thorn tree lose their love forever."

Jessica looked very afraid. "I don't want to lose my love!"

"Nor do I," Mickey agreed sadly. "But if we stopped

caring so much about each other, maybe we could return to our families and they'd make peace.''

He saw the same resignation in Jessica's face that he felt in his own heart. There was nothing but to do it then.

They walked slowly to the tree. They kissed a final time, then closed their eyes and leaned against its blackened, thorny trunk.

Mickey could feel the tree moving at his back. He saw flashes of light through his closed eyelids and felt a series of quick electric shocks. The whole world seemed to be on fire. Mickey wanted to pull away, but trapped in the spell of the malevolent tree, he couldn't move.

The spell flared a final time. Mickey fell to the ground. His whole body felt numb.

Was this what happened when you lost your love?

He opened his eyes. Jessica had fallen beside him, but was already getting back on her feet. He scrambled to do likewise.

"How do you feel?" he asked cautiously.

"All right," Jessica answered after a moment's consideration.

Now for the painful part. Mickey added, "And how do you feel . . . about me?"

Jessica shrugged. Mickey's heart sank. The thorn tree had done its evil work!

"All right," she admitted. She frowned at Mickey. "What about you? How do you feel about me?"

Mickey hadn't thought about that. "All right," he replied as he shrugged too.

"Good," Jessica replied tentatively. "Well, that's all right then."

"Yes, it is," Mickey replied. But how could they be sure? Mickey looked at the blond curls he used to hold so dear and those lips that were so sweet to kiss. But that was the way he used to feel. Now the thorn tree had changed everything . . . hadn't it?

Mickey had to find out.

He looked Jessica deep in the eyes. "So to test it, to make sure it's finished, all over between us. If I was to give you a little kiss like this—"

He leaned over and kissed her quickly.

"You'd feel?" he prompted.

Jessica considered the question for a moment.

"Nothing," she replied.

"Ah . . . good . . . nothing." Well, that was the way it was supposed to be.

Jessica turned back to him. "And if I was to kiss you back—like this?"

This time they kissed a little longer. Well, it did remind Mickey of the past. Somewhat. What they used to mean to each other and all.

But Jessica needed a reply to her question.

"Not a thing," Mickey answered.

"Same for me," Jessica agreed.

But that still wasn't enough of a test. Mickey took her in his arms.

"And if I was to hold onto you like this—"

Jessica put her arms around Mickey as well.

"And I was to put my arms around you," she replied.

They kissed again—a real kiss, a kiss that felt as if it should never end.

"Maybe just a little tremor there?" Mickey said softly.

"Just a small one," Jessica whispered back.

Mickey knew they would have to test their feelings for a long, long time.

* * *

In recent days, Kathleen had not lacked for adventures. Now she'd helped a young leprechaun and a fairy princess to reach the cave of the Grand Banshee and come back to her own farm to tell about it.

But the adventure was over. Black storm clouds swirled overhead. And Jack Woods still walked at her side.

He looked at her as they walked to her cottage.

"What about us?" he asked.

Oh, no. She wasn't falling into that trap.

"What about us?" she replied.

"You know what I mean," Jack said.

Kathleen shook her head. "I can't trust you anymore. It's as simple as that."

"It isn't as simple as that," Jack insisted. "You know I'm in love with you."

Now why did her heart skip a beat?

She bit her lip. Her mind was made up.

"So you say."

"I've given up everything because I want to find happiness here."

Kathleen looked away from him. "I'm not stopping you."

"As it happens, you are."

With that, Jack turned away and walked farther down the path.

Kathleen didn't want the man to go. But Jack had lied to her, hidden all the real reasons he'd come to this place. Why didn't that feel important anymore?

No, no, she told herself. Kathleen Fitzpatrick, you have your pride.

But was that all she was going to have?

* * *

Mary Muldoon would show them. No one could keep a leprechaun captive for long! Especially the wife of Seamus Muldoon!

So she'd tied her sheets and bedclothes together and made a ladder on which she could slide down to safety. Now, while they were involved making their trooping fairy plans, she'd toss the ladder from the window and make good her escape.

She waited in silence for a minute to make sure no guards—or worse, any busybodies like Lady Margaret— were about. But all was still in her corner of the palace. She secured her makeshift rope to a bedpost and tossed the other end out the window.

She looked out at the courtyard below. Oh, dear, that was a long way down. But her bedclothes rope nearly touched the ground. She'd best make use of the opportunity.

Mary felt better as she got closer to the ground. She chuckled.

"You can't keep a good Muldoon down. We leprechauns know a trick or two!"

When she had reached the end of her rope at last, Mary dropped into the courtyard below. Now which way was it to the gate?

Someone coughed behind her.

She spun about. General Bulstrode stood there with half a dozen of his fairy guard. And the general did not look happy.

"Going somewhere, Mrs. Muldoon?"

Mary was truly startled. Here was a fellow who had trouble telling which end of a sword was which, and he was waiting for her? Had she been that obvious?

Mary sighed. "The final insult: recaptured by a complete idiot!"

The guards led her back to the upper room that served as her cell. Mary realized that, for the rest of her stay, she'd probably be sleeping without bedclothes.

At least Jack was gentleman enough to see Kathleen to her door.

She stepped inside and gasped. All four of her brothers were in there, sprawled on various chairs, and all four looked as if they'd been in a proper fight. All of them were sporting cuts and bruises, and a couple of them were winding bandages around an arm or a leg.

George frowned up at her. "Where've you been?"

"We went to see the Grand Banshee," Kathleen replied.

"The Grand Banshee!" John exclaimed.

Harry looked to his brother. "Who's the Grand Banshee?"

"I don't know," John admitted. "I was just repeating what she said."

"She's in charge of all the fairies," Jack explained. "We asked her to stop the war."

Kathleen shook her head. "She couldn't. Or wouldn't." But enough of her explanations. She wanted to know about her brothers. "What happened to you?"

George stared at the floor. "We slipped."

"All of you?" Kathleen demanded.

"Yes," James agreed.

"On some slippery stuff," John added.

"Powerful slippery stuff, it was," Harry concluded.

"Hello there, lads!"

Seamus Muldoon popped into sight in the middle of the room.

All four brothers leaned away from the leprechaun. Kathleen wondered what mischief they'd all been up to now.

Seamus scratched at his beard and grinned. "Sorry about the trouble earlier."

"Oh," George said. "Trouble? I don't recall any trouble. Do you boys?"

All the brothers shook their heads to a resounding chorus of "No."

"I aim to make it up to you," Seamus continued.

"How?" George asked. "Not that there's anything to make up, mind."

"I'll show you where we buried our pots of gold!"

All four brothers cheered at that and jumped to their feet. Apparently, Kathleen thought, their aches and pains weren't quite as bad as they first appeared.

Seamus led them all outside, and George instructed each of his three younger siblings to grab a shovel and start digging.

The brothers gasped as they unearthed a black kettle. They could barely contain their glee when they pulled off the top and discovered the pot was filled with gold.

"There's more," Seamus added with a grin as he pointed to various places about the yard. "There's one buried there. And one there. And there."

Each of the three brothers with a shovel began to dig a brand-new hole.

Seamus waved for Jack and Kathleen to take a few steps away.

"Where're Mickey and the princess?" he asked.

"We don't know," Jack replied.

Seamus scowled at that. "My son should've been with us when we attacked the palace."

"Did you win?" Kathleen asked.

That brought a grin back to the leprechaun's face. "It was a glorious draw."

"Does it mean peace?" Jack asked.

Seamus shook his head. "Never. Total victory or nothing!"

Kathleen had had just about enough of this.

"Time's running out, Seamus! The Grand Banshee showed Mickey and Jessica there will be nothing left for anyone if nature dies!"

Seamus paused, actually considering this. "But the trooping fools have to agree to peace as well. And they'll never do that while they think Mickey has spirited Jessica away."

"Then we have to get them to explain," Kathleen insisted. "Where would they have gone?"

Seamus nodded after a moment's thought. "Probably to the swamp. It's neutral territory."

Kathleen looked at Jack. They had work to do.

Her brothers would be occupied for hours.

"We'll be rich, rich, rich!" they chanted together.

Kathleen looked at the first kettle they had unearthed and saw that it was empty. The gold had disappeared. Kathleen didn't have the heart to tell them. Right now, she had more important things to do.

The troopers had taken Mary Muldoon back to the interrogation room and put her under full-time guard. If that wasn't bad enough, King Boric, Queen Morag, and Lady Margaret kept pestering her with questions!

"Will you give us your word you won't try to escape again?" Boric asked sharply.

"Of course I won't," Mary replied as sharply back. "And even if I did, would you believe me?"

Lady Margaret frowned at the expanse around the single chair. "This is a terribly bare-looking room, your majesty. You could do wonders with a few flowers and some cushions. Maybe a small sofa."

Bulstrode marched in before anyone could say another word.

"Sire, I think you should come and see what progress we've made."

The king seemed relieved to have something to do that didn't involve Mary Muldoon. "Excellent, Bulstrode."

Both of them left quite quickly.

Mary shook her head. "What is that idiot Bulstrode doing now?"

The queen shook her head right back. "They're digging a tunnel to get out of the palace."

Mary didn't believe her ears. "Digging a tunnel to get *out*? That's not right. We're besieging *you*. We should be digging a tunnel to get *in!*"

The queen sighed. "I've tried to tell them, but they won't listen."

"They never do," Mary agreed.

"They've already forgotten about my daughter," the queen added sadly.

Lady Margaret started to sob.

"Poor sweet Jessica! Under that leprechaun's spell!"

What? Mary couldn't let that statement go unchallenged. She cleared her throat. "I think you'll find it's the other way round. Mickey has been bewitched by a chit of a girl. He's stopped listening to his mother."

The queen sniffed at the very thought. "Of course, that's what you would say. It's typical double-dealing leprechaun behavior."

"Double-dealing, is it? Now you listen to me . . ."

But the queen had already turned away. "I have no

intention of listening to someone whose idea of washing is to stand outside and wait for rain."

Oh, now Mary was really going to give them a piece of her mind. Escape? How could she possibly escape when she needed to put these fancy fairies in their place!

The chamberlain had been waiting for this moment.

The ballroom was in a total shambles, with great piles of dirt all around the gaping hole in the middle of the once elegant floor. And when Bulstrode led Boric in for an inspection, a look of great pride and accomplishment covered the general's mustached face. As for the king's expression? The chamberlain thought "shock" was a good way of putting it.

"Our engineers are working on the tunnel night and day!" Bulstrode exclaimed.

The king cleared his throat. "And it had to be in the middle of the ballroom, did it?"

"Yes, sire." The general pointed out the window. "It's a direct line between here and there."

"Has the queen seen what you've done to her floor?" Boric asked gently.

Bulstrode shook his head. "Not yet."

"When she does, make sure I'm here to watch."

"Certainly. Come, sire." Bulstrode took a step toward the hole.

The king looked down in horror. "I'm not going down there!"

"No, outside to see the rebel camp." The general walked around the hole and between piles of dirt to reach the balcony. The chamberlain followed the pair outside.

Bulstrode was pointing again, waving his fingers above

the length of the enemy encampment. "We're digging the tunnel under that field and under their camp."

The king smiled. "They'll get quite a surprise when we pop up."

From a tunnel that long? The chamberlain didn't like it.

"If the tunnel doesn't collapse first," he muttered.

"Good point," the king said.

The chamberlain blinked in surprise. "That's a first. I made a good point."

"Bulstrode!" Boric announced. "See that it doesn't!"

"That's already taken care of, sire," the general assured him. "I've given strict orders to it that it's not to collapse."

Strict orders? To a tunnel?

"Oh, that'll work then," the chamberlain muttered. "We'll all sleep easy in our beds tonight."

Both the king and the general were too pleased with their plan to really hear his words. Maybe, the chamberlain thought, it was time for another line of work.

There was nothing else to do then, Mickey thought, but to return to the swamp. But this time, they had come prepared. Mickey and Jessica landed in front of the pavilion, a package between them.

Jentee should be expecting them. A line of frogs had honked at the pair as they approached, and now the amphibians continued to honk all around. Mickey looked at Jessica. Perhaps it would be better if they took their business inside.

They climbed the pavilion stairs and walked straight to Jentee's room, then knocked on the door.

Jentee opened it himself and asked the two to come inside. His room looked quite comfortable, with big leather chairs and flowers preserved under glass jars. The walls were covered with photos of famous cricket teams and other memorabilia. Mickey and the princess walked into the room. Jentee closed the door behind them.

Mickey had to admire the butter fairy. No matter what he'd done to them, Sir Aloysius Jentee was still all smiles.

"Gad, life is full of surprises. I never expected to see you two back here. Don't you know I sold you out to the trooping fairies?"

"Why did you do that, Uncle Jentee?" Jessica asked.

Jentee shook his head regretfully. "I'm sorry, child, but it was either you or butter. And butter always wins." He sighed, the very picture of regret. "I'm sorry. I'll have to turn you over as promised."

"Can't you break that promise?" Mickey asked.

Jentee sniffed at that. "No, no, no. I gave my word, the word of an English officer and gentleman. Sorry, laddies. I can't break it."

Mickey leaned close to him and said a single word: "Butter."

Jentee blinked, wide-eyed. "What's that? What's that?"

"Not even for butter?" Jessica asked innocently.

They lifted the package they had brought with them onto a table at the room's center and tore it open. It was filled with packs of English butter.

Jentee couldn't take his eyes off it.

"Ahh. And English butter to boot. This puts a whole different complexion on the matter. Butter changes everything." He smiled at them both. "After all, you're the son of one of my best friends, and you're his fair lady." His gaze drifted back to the butter. "I would've given you up then, but this is now."

"I thought it would make a difference, Uncle," Mickey

replied with a smile of his own. "But we didn't come here for sanctuary. We want your advice."

"Really? Why me, lad?"

"This situation needs someone who's clever, devious, slippery, and crooked."

"Someone who can see round corners," Jessica added.

Jentee smiled broadly at that. "Flattery will get you everything. Yes, indeed, you've come to the right chappie. I've been that way all my life, I'm glad to say. What's the problem?"

"We want to stop this war and bring the families together," Jessica replied.

"It'll have to be something really spectacular and shocking," Mickey added.

Jentee rubbed at his yellow chin. "Hmm, have you thought of suicide at all?"

Jessica frowned. "Well, if you think it might really help."

"No, no," Jentee said quickly, "I don't mean real suicide. It might succeed, but you wouldn't be there to enjoy it, and that would defeat the whole point of the exercise. No, if your families thought you'd ended your lives rather than be separated, that would do the trick just as well."

Mickey and Jessica looked at each other.

"It might," Jessica admitted.

"How could we do it?" Mickey asked.

"Follow Uncle Jentee."

The butter spirit headed for the door. He led them out of the pavilion and into the swamp. They stopped in a glade filled with a wild assortment of plants and flowers. Jentee looked about until he spotted a plant filled with heavy red pods. He picked a few and squeezed their juice into a glass vial.

"This is poison," he explained. "Well, let us say it acts like poison. Drink it and the blood stops and you go into a coma." He sighed. "Of course, a lot of people I know are in a coma without drinking this. No names, no pack drill. What? What?" He held the vial up for all to see. "Anyway, to all intents and purposes, you're dead."

Jentee looked about again until he spotted a yellow plant. He picked a few pods from this in turn, squeezing their juice into a second vial.

"This is the antidote. Drink it and you come back to life, provided you drink it within ten minutes of taking the poison. If you don't, I'm afraid you really do die." He got a faraway look in his deep red eyes. "No more cricket on the green, no more warm beer, no more butter!"

He handed the two vials to Mickey.

So their plan had begun.

Kathleen and Jack were once again riding in the pony cart behind Firefly, urging her this time toward the swamp. Jack was a good man, Kathleen thought, at least in this. Whenever there was action, she could forget about their troubles. But then, as soon as things grew calm again . . .

"Mickey! Jessica!" Jack's shout brought Kathleen out of her thoughts. She looked up and saw the two little people flying straight toward them.

The two landed on the edge of the trap.

"Mr. Woods!" Mickey greeted them.

But Kathleen knew they had no time to waste. "Thank goodness you're safe. You have to come back and explain. They all think you're under some magic spell."

"We are," Jessica said with a smile. "We're in love."

Love? Kathleen thought. Yes, it could be magic.

Mickey's voice brought her back to reality.

"We have a plan! Listen, listen!"

He quickly described how he and Jessica would fake their deaths to bring both camps to their senses.

"It sounds good," Jack said when they were done.

"I can't think of anything better," Kathleen agreed.

"I'll need a fifteen-minute start," Jack added. "It'll give me a chance to prepare them."

He got down from the trap and started to walk toward the fairy palace.

"Good luck, Mr. Woods," Jessica called.

"Good luck," Mickey added.

Kathleen looked at him too "Good luck, Jack."

She wanted to say more. But what?

Jack nodded back as he hurried away.

"Look!" Jessica cried.

She pointed to a puddle in the road.

Reflected in the water was the image of a nearly barren tree.

Jack marched across what must have been a wheatfield before the crop had all been scorched by the strangeness of the weather.

And speaking of strangeness, the clouds looked particularly ominous today. Lightning streaked across the sky, and the wind seemed to whip from every direction.

Well, he didn't have time for the weather. He put his head down and doubled his pace.

The wind was howling now, a terrible sound, like the cries of damned souls.

He looked up. A small funnel-shaped cloud was moving across the barren field. If he hurried, he could get out of the way.

The funnel swept closer with alarming speed. He was a

full-grown man, over six feet, close to two hundred pounds. Surely he could push his way through . . .

The funnel rushed to meet him. The winds surrounded him, lifting his feet from the ground. He was caught in the whirlwind! It was lifting him higher and higher.

And then two great hands appeared from nowhere to pluck him free of the wind.

Chapter Twenty-Five

It was a woman who had saved Jack. A woman who he would have sworn was ten times his size. But then she was only five feet something, though her skin was the color of night and her great mane of hair, which sometimes looked a bit like a crown of feathers, might set her apart from the locals.

Jack found himself on a country path with the woman before him. He didn't understand how she'd done it, but he knew without her he would have been a goner.

"Thanks for the help," he said.

"You should always look where you're going, Mr. Woods," she replied.

"You know who I am?"

She nodded and smiled. "I'm the Grand Banshee."

Jack couldn't hide his surprise. "*You're* the Grand Banshee!"

"Why? Did you think I'd have two heads and breathe fire? 'Cause I can do that too."

"No, no, no." He didn't want to give her the wrong idea, after all. "Thanks for saving me there."

She nodded again. "I was keeping an eye on you. I want this war to end as much as you do."

"We've got a plan," Woods said.

"I know."

Well, of course she would. She was the Grand Banshee.

"Will it succeed?"

The woman sighed. "I'm all seeing, not a fortune-teller."

"So you wouldn't know whether Kathleen and I—" Jack began.

The woman waved her hands for silence. "Absolutely not. Totally unprofessional. But I can tell you one thing: This plan of yours had better succeed. It's everybody's last chance!"

With that, she turned into a crow and flew away.

Their last chance.

Somehow, even as the black bird grew smaller in the distance, its cawing seemed to grow louder and louder.

He had to find Seamus . . . now.

It took Jack another ten minutes to find the camp. It looked deserted. But looks could be deceiving, especially where leprechauns were concerned.

"Seamus!" he called. "Seamus!"

Seamus Muldoon materialized directly in front of Jack. An instant later, his entire army materialized behind him.

"Good to see you've joined the side of right and justice, Jack," the leprechaun called.

Jack frowned. "I want to talk to you alone, Seamus!"

The leprechaun waved for Jack to follow him to a far

corner of the camp. There, Jack quickly related what he and Mickey had decided were just the right words to say to the senior Muldoon.

"You have to call a peace conference here now!" Jack concluded.

"What?" Seamus demanded.

"Otherwise, your son Mickey and Princess Jessica are going to commit suicide."

The leprechaun looked even more startled. "He wouldn't do that to his own da!"

Jack shook his head. "He would, and will, unless you get in touch with King Boric and at least talk. Mickey and the girl are coming here within the hour."

Seamus shook his head fiercely. "I can't do it. I can't. I have my pride. A Muldoon's pride."

"What's that against your son's life? Besides, once you have Mickey and Jessica here, alive and well, Boric will see you have his daughter."

"Of course he will!" Seamus laughed. "Good thinking, Jack! It's sneaky. I knew you wouldn't let us down!" He jumped up, calling out as he ran, "Jericho! Jericho!"

Well, Jack thought, he'd started the plan in motion. He hoped the others could pull off their parts as well.

Now he just had to wait.

This could be most interesting.

The chamberlain, King Boric, and General Bulstrode stood outside the palace gates looking down at the field below. Instead of an army, a single leprechaun approached, a leprechaun festooned with white flags.

"What the devil does he want?" the king demanded.

"The white flags!" Bulstrode exclaimed. "They've surrendered!"

The chamberlain sighed. Trust the general to jump to conclusions.

"It's another glorious victory for yours truly," the general beamed. "Perhaps we could name a street after me. 'Bulstrode Boulevard' has a nice ring to it, don't you think?"

The chamberlain had had enough of this.

"Shut up, Bulstrode," he remarked.

He'd been wanting to say that for a long time.

It was very satisfying.

This became more interesting still.

The chamberlain ordered a couple of their soldiers to bring up the leprechaun who had come under a flag of truce. Once in front of the palace, the leprechaun had said his name was Jericho and asked to talk to the royal family. Over Bulstrode's objections, the chamberlain had brought the emissary into the throne room, where the queen waited with Lady Margaret and Mary Muldoon.

There Jericho had told a most distressing tale.

"Jessica will kill herself?" the queen asked when he was done.

"No!" Lady Margaret wailed. "No!"

"And my Mickey?" Mary asked quietly.

"Together," Jericho replied with a nod, "unless both sides meet and talk."

King Boric stomped his feet. "I don't believe it! It's another leprechaun trick!"

"I believe it," the queen said simply.

"She wouldn't do it!" Boric insisted.

"She would." Lady Margaret sighed. "She's in love."

The king paused, his eyebrows raised in thought. "I would have done it when I was in love." He glanced suddenly at his queen, hurriedly adding, "Obviously, I still am, but . . ." His voice trailed away.

Mary nodded solemnly. "Muldoon isn't clever enough to think up a trick like that just to get you talking."

And there was sense to this proposal too. The chamberlain chimed in, "After all, he just wants to talk. If we don't talk and the two—"

The queen cut him off. "Of course we'll talk. Boric!"

She would see that things got done.

The chamberlain knew it. With the queen in control, the arrangements had only taken a matter of minutes.

The warring parties were meeting on the battlefield before the royal palace, halfway between the palace itself and the leprechaun camp. Both sides had gotten their flags and banners waving, their drums beating. They were ready to meet. The chamberlain accompanied his king and queen, and they brought Mary Muldoon along under heavy guard.

Now they could see the leprechauns approach. Seamus Muldoon was in the lead, with his emissary Jericho close behind. But they also brought someone considerably taller.

"Aarrk!" the king quailed. "They have a human to fight for them!"

"Don't worry," the chamberlain replied. "They're docile as long as you don't make any sudden movements. Don't catch his eye."

At least that was what he had heard.

The trooping fairy delegation marched forward to meet the leprechauns.

"Where's Bulstrode?" the king whispered.

"Underground," the chamberlain whispered back. "Still digging."

The king nodded. "Perhaps it's for the best."

He looked at the human and cleared his throat.

"Who's this?" he said to Muldoon.

"A neutral to act as observer," the leprechaun replied.

"I'm not fighting," the human added. My, but he had a loud voice.

"It wouldn't matter to us if you did," the king replied brusquely, almost keeping the quaver out of his voice. "Chamberlain?"

The chamberlain stepped forward, escorting Mary Muldoon.

"On behalf of King Boric and his trooping fairies," he announced, "we thought you might like to say hello to your wife."

Seamus nodded to Mary. "Hello." He turned back to the king. "Now let's get on with it!"

"Is that all you have to say, you half-gutted mackerel?" Mary demanded.

Muldoon sighed. "He said I might like to say hello, and that's what I've said. Hello! Now let's get to the important stuff." He pounded his chest. "I'm Seamus Muldoon, of the clan that were lords of Offalay before his ancient majesty here was a thousand years from being born."

The leprechauns applauded.

King Boric rose up to his full two feet. "My family stretches back to before a leprechaun thought of building a mud hut. The one I believe you still live in!"

All the trooping fairies cheered.

"We're not here to discover whose family is the oldest," the human put in, "but to try to work out a peace settlement for your children's sake."

"Peace?" Seamus Muldoon cried. "What peace? These trooping fairies killed Barney Devine and others and drove my son into exile."

That was too much for the king. "You've kidnapped my daughter, Jessica, put a spell on her, and killed my nephew, Count Grogan."

Muldoon blinked in surprise. "Grogan was your nephew?"

"Only on my wife's side of the family," Boric added hastily.

But this was all going too slowly for the queen. She strode forward, demanding, "Where's my daughter? What have you done with her?"

"I don't know where she is," Seamus replied. "She enticed my son away from his duty with her female magic. He should be standing here by my side."

"Not downwind," Mary remarked.

The human apparently had had enough of this. "You're here to talk peace!" he cried.

As loud as he was, nobody wanted to listen to him.

Kathleen could hear the voices rising and falling on the other side of the field: faint cheers from the little people and Jack's somewhat louder protests. As they expected, the talks did not seem to be going well.

It was time to finish the plan.

Mickey and Jessica jumped down from the pony cart. Kathleen handed them the red vial.

The two wee folk kissed. Then Mickey drank half the potion, and Jessica drank the rest.

Mickey looked at Kathleen. "It must be within ten minutes."

"Don't worry," Kathleen reassured them.

But the poison acted quickly. Both Mickey and Jessica sank to the ground. They lay side by side, totally still.

Kathleen cupped her hands around her face, calling to the nearest leprechauns and fairies.

"Quick! Over here! Jessica and Mickey!"

The wee folk, too busy until now to even notice her, turned about. A few brave ones flew and ran in her direction.

"Quick!" she called. "Carry them to their parents!"

The troopers lifted the princess from the ground, while leprechauns hoisted Mickey upon their shoulders.

Quick! Kathleen thought, hoping to hurry them along. The plan had less than ten minutes.

Everyone was yelling.

Mary Muldoon sighed. She supposed it had to come to this. Seamus and the king kept getting louder and louder until at last they started exchanging blows. Now it looked as if those on both sides wanted to join in.

"Can you believe this?" she asked.

"With our husbands in charge, *yes!*" the queen replied.

At least *they* could agree on something.

The fighters paused as a deep, mournful drumming approached the delegations. The group parted to show two bodies being borne by four leprechauns and four fairies.

"Jessica!" the queen cried as she recognized her daughter.

"Mickey!" Mary wailed as she saw the still form of her son.

"What happened?" Seamus demanded.

Kathleen Fitzpatrick pulled her pony cart into view.

"They took poison," she called.

"No!" The word escaped from Mary's lips.

"It can't be!" the queen agreed.

Both broke into tears.

"Why?" Seamus demanded.

"I warned you," Jack said. "They thought they were responsible for the war. They thought if they died it would end."

Now even the king and Seamus were driven to tears.

"My poor lonesome boy," Seamus moaned.

"Child, child, my lovely child," King Boric wailed.

"You can't let it end like this!" Jack continued. "You must make sure their sacrifice wasn't in vain. End the war. Now!"

Of course he was right. How could they have been so blind?

"Yes, yes," the king said. "How do we do it?"

"There must be a peace treaty!" the chamberlain replied.

"Later," Jack said. "Right now all you have to do is shake hands over the bodies of your children."

"Shake hands?" Seamus was still having a little difficulty.

Jack nodded. "A handshake between gentlemen is more binding than all the contracts and treaties in the world."

"That's true," Jericho agreed. "Do it!"

Yes, Mary thought. It was the least they could do for Mickey.

"Shake hands!" she told her husband.

"Now, Boric!" the queen demanded.

Seamus and Boric reached out their hands over the still bodies of their children.

They shook. The war was done.

Both sides cheered.

But why was Jack waving to Kathleen?

Kathleen took a deep breath. It was up to her now. She had the yellow vial in her hands, and a couple minutes left to administer the antidote before it was too late. She'd use Firefly to get her there on time. She shook the reins. Firefly broke into a trot.

They were only halfway across the field when she heard a great rumbling sound. The ground in front of Firefly split apart into a great hole. The middle of the field before her sank into a yawning pit. She pulled back on the reins. She wasn't sure she could stop her pony in time.

Jack was running toward her. Firefly reared on her hind legs. Kathleen was tossed from the cart, but as she fell, she saw Jack reaching for her, only to be struck by the pony's flashing hooves. Jack fell backward into the hole.

And Kathleen was falling herself. She hit the ground, and the yellow vial flew from her hand. She looked up and saw it smash on a rock, the precious antidote splattered on the ground!

What would happen to Mickey and Jessica?

Kathleen struggled to her feet.

And what about Jack?

"Jack!" she called. "Where's Jack? Jack!"

She gasped when she reached the edge of the cave-in. Jack lay, crumpled and still, at the bottom of the hole.

"Quick! Quick!" she called to all those around her. "Someone help!"

Leprechauns and fairies jumped or flew into the hole. Between them, they lifted Jack's still body and laid it upon the grass.

Kathleen couldn't stop the tears.

"Jack! Jack! I didn't mean any of it, Jack! I love you, Jack!"

Why did she only realize that now?

Chapter Twenty-Six

The chamberlain had never seen such a disaster. The son and daughter of the rival leaders and a well-meaning human besides—all brought to this. And three fine women reduced to tears.

"Come on, men. We're there!"

The chamberlain looked down into the hole to see Bulstrode pop his head from the dirt, a mining helmet perched atop his head.

"You're nowhere, you blundering fool!" the king shot back.

"It's happening!" Mary Muldoon called.

"No!" Queen Morag shrieked.

But the Grand Banshee fulfilled her promise once again. She would take all those felled by the conflict. And this time, that meant Mickey Muldoon and Princess Jessica. The chamberlain could see their bodies begin to disappear: first the toes, then the feet, then the ankles . . .

The queen and Mary looked overhead as a black shadow fell across them. The chamberlain peered up to see a great crow circling in the sky.

The crow landed and turned into the Grand Banshee herself.

The chamberlain noticed that the bodies had stopped disappearing. Only Mickey's and Jessica's legs had vanished. Had the Grand Banshee had a change of heart?

"Grand Banshee," the queen called, "save our children."

"Save them," Mary agreed.

"Bring them back to us," Seamus pleaded.

"You must!" King Boric added.

"And Jack," the human named Kathleen called from beside the poor man's still form. "Save Jack!"

The Grand Banshee shook her head. "I can't save Jack."

Kathleen screamed. "No!"

"He doesn't need it," the Grand Banshee added. "He's just winded."

At that instant, the human named Jack groaned and sat up.

"Jack!" Kathleen cried. "Jack, you idiot! You did that on purpose!" And she proceeded to cover him with kisses.

Poor Jack didn't seem to know what was happening. But he also didn't seem to mind it one bit.

"But Jessica and Mickey aren't so easily saved," the Grand Banshee chided. "It's the price you pay for this stupid war."

Jack shook his head. "But it's over."

Kathleen helped him to his feet. Somewhat gingerly, Jack walked over to address the Grand Banshee.

"They've shaken hands over the bodies of their dead children."

"It's out of my hands," the Grand Banshee replied. She

looked to all of those around her. "I can do nothing unless you really want peace in your hearts. Then you'll do it for yourselves."

"Gentleman's agreement," Seamus Muldoon shouted. "No more war!"

"Never again!" King Boric agreed.

"Don't say that, sire!" Bulstrode blustered as he climbed from the hole. "I'll be out of work!"

Both Boric and Muldoon whopped him one so that he fell right back into the hole.

"It only works if everyone wants it," the Grand Banshee cautioned.

Cries of "We do! We do!" came from both sides. There was only one voice not heard from.

Boric and Seamus both glared down into the hole.

"Oh, all right!" Bulstrode's voice shouted from the pit.

With that, the Grand Banshee smiled, and the dark clouds that had been hanging overhead rolled away. And in the sky, they could see the great oak tree of Mother Nature herself.

The tree was bare, with one last leaf, falling, falling away. The chamberlain remembered the warnings. Had they come this far only to be too late?

The chamberlain gasped. A green shoot appeared where the last leaf had fallen. In an instant, another dozen green shoots followed, then another dozen, and a dozen more.

The tree was growing again. Nature was saved.

"Look!" Mary Muldoon called.

The chamberlain turned back to the bodies of Jessica and Mickey. As he watched, their legs and feet magically appeared where they belonged.

The whole crowd gasped as both opened their eyes and sat up.

"What happened, Da?" Mickey asked.

"Where are we?" Jessica asked.

"Home!" Queen Morag answered with the biggest grin the chamberlain had ever seen.

Everyone cheered.

But the Grand Banshee wasn't done. She waved her hands in the air, and one after another, those who had died and vanished, leprechauns and trooping fairies both, reappeared, each one looking as if he had just woken from a long sleep.

"Barney!" Mickey called.

Barney stretched and smiled. "I must have gone to sleep. I'd had a few and was dead tired."

Jericho laughed. "You were dead all right!"

"What's been happening?" Barney asked.

"Not much," Jericho replied.

"This and that," Seamus added. "We'll tell you later."

"What's going on, Grand Banshee?" Jack asked.

The Grand Banshee smiled. "It's a surprise."

Jack shook his head. "I didn't know you could bring them back like that."

Her grandness laughed. "If you'd known, it wouldn't have been a surprise, would it?"

The field was full of fairies who had just reappeared. Just about everyone seemed to have come back to them. No, now that he thought of it, not quite everyone.

"Where's Count Grogan?" the queen asked.

"I'll be keeping him for a hundred years or so more," the Grand Banshee replied. "Just to be on the safe side. No need to overdo the happy ending."

"Good thinking, Grand Banshee," the king said quietly. "Wife's side of the family."

"My work's done," the Grand Banshee announced. "See you all stick to your word."

"What about a drink before you go?" Seamus Muldoon called.

The Grand Banshee paused. "Well, just this once."

"Drinks all round," the king announced, "on me!"

"Those are the happiest words in the English language!" Seamus Muldoon agreed.

A great cheer arose as barrels of beer were rolled out into the field.

So for the rest of the day and into the night, they had music and laughter and drinking and dancing beyond belief.

This had worked out rather better than the chamberlain had expected.

Jack Woods was quite busy tossing the photos into the roaring bonfire Kathleen and he had built before his cottage. All these photos of the picturesque countryside—gone for good.

"Good-bye," he called, "Sperry, Sperry—"

"And McGurk!" Kathleen added for him as she tossed in a few photos of her own.

"No, we musn't forget old McGurk!" Jack agreed.

He looked at the roaring fire for an instant, then turned to kiss Kathleen.

The part of his life that the photos represented—that part was done. But now he had a whole new life to plan.

Kathleen couldn't believe it.

By the time she and Jack had returned to her farm, her four brothers had dug holes all over their yard. There were hundreds of holes in every conceivable spot, as if her four siblings had been digging every minute she was gone.

Her brothers weren't happy. And she could tell they blamed Jack.

"You scurvy nicknocker!" George exclaimed. "No pots!"

"No gold!" Harry added accusingly.

"You cheated us!" James continued. "You and that toddling tripe hound Muldoon!"

Seamus appeared at that instant, as if he had just been waiting to hear his name.

"Somebody call?" he asked with a grin.

"Get him, lads!"

All four brothers dropped their shovels, ready to charge at the leprechaun. Jack stepped between Seamus and the angry four, trying to calm things down. But Seamus himself did not seem fazed in the least. He held up his hand.

"The gold is there. You haven't dug in the right place."

Harry looked around. "We've dug in every place!"

"You haven't dug there!" Seamus pointed. There, in the middle of a hundred holes, was a tiny patch of undisturbed earth.

"That looks good!" Jack agreed.

"Good, is it?" George grumbled. "There's nothing here!" He grabbed his spade and walked over to the patch, then plunged the shovel into the soil.

A great rumbling filled the yard. George took a step away. The brothers looked at each other uneasily.

The rumbling turned to a roar as a great gusher of deep black oil shot high in the air.

"Oil!" John called.

"Oil!" George agreed.

"We're rich!" James spoke for all of them.

Seamus turned to Jack and Kathleen.

"It'll only gush a couple of days," he whispered, "then flush out, but it'll keep them happy."

So the leprechaun was tricking her brothers again? Ah, well. They deserved it. And it would give Jack and Kathleen time to make their plans.

She smiled up at Jack. "I'd like to be married here in Ireland."

Jack looked surprised. "I haven't asked you yet."

"Were you going to?" she demanded.

"Maybe," he replied with a smile. He was teasing her now. Well, she supposed she deserved that too.

They turned to kiss again. Kathleen slipped a bit on the oil covering the ground around them. Jack tried to steady her, but he slipped as well. They grabbed each other and fell to the ground.

Seamus tried to walk over and give them a hand. He fell as well. All three of them tried to hold on to each other and get up, but it was no use. The ground was too slippery. They fell and fell again.

Really, what could all of them do but laugh?

Now this, Mary Muldoon thought, was a day that would be long remembered!

The wedding march played as Jack and Kathleen came down the aisle. Kathleen's four brothers all looked a bit stuffed into their best suits, but they were beaming at Kathleen all the same. Father Daley waited behind the altar to begin the ceremony.

Mary Muldoon waved. It was time for the other guests to arrive.

Leprechauns and fairies swarmed into the church, filling every nook and cranny not occupied by a human. Of course, the little folks would be invisible to all but Jack and Kathleen. But Mary could tell by the smiles on their faces that the marrying couple were very pleased at the turnout.

Barney Devine went and sat by the stuffed pink elephant that the priest had installed in a corner pew. He grabbed the elephant's head and nodded it toward Father Daley, as if encouraging the priest to begin.

Father Daley smiled and nodded back.

"Dearly beloved," he said.

And this, Mary thought, was only the beginning of the festivities.

Epilogue

Now this was a fine stretch of countryside—a beautiful dell covered with a carpet of wildflowers. Not, of course, that you could see most of the flowers at this moment. The dell was packed with trooping fairies and leprechauns, not to mention pookas, grogochs, sheeries, dullahans, all those oakshees watching from the surrounding woods, and dozens of other magical creatures. And of course Jack and Kathleen, who sat back on a slight hillock that overlooked the scene.

Everyone watched, silent, enraptured, as the Grand Banshee herself placed floral garlands on the heads of Princess Jessica and Mickey Muldoon. Most everyone was dabbing at their eyes, while Mary, the queen, and Lady Margaret had a good cry.

The Grand Banshee looked at the pair as she cautioned, "All the words in the world don't make a marriage binding. It's what you do!"

She placed Jessica's hand in Mickey's.

"I pronounce you man and wife."

And all the magical creatures gathered about cheered as the two bands, one leprechaun, one fairy, struck up a jaunty tune. It was a glorious noise.

"Beer!" Seamus Muldoon called. "More beer!"

"Listen to the man!" King Boric agreed. "Listen to the man! The first sensible thing I've heard him say!"

Tankards found their way to both of their hands, and Seamus and Boric drank to the day.

Mary Muldoon shook her head. "He's turning your husband into as big a sot as he is."

Lady Margaret paused in her sniffling long enough to ask, "What are we going to do?"

Mary and Queen Morag looked at each other.

"Dance!" they chorused.

Each grabbed a partner and did just that.

Out of all the revelers, only General Bulstrode looked distraught. Barney Devine handed him a tankard of beer.

"Drink up, Bulstrode," Barney urged. "What's the matter?"

Bulstrode looked down at the tankard and shook his head. "No more fighting."

Barney laughed. "Write your memoirs. 'How I Saved the World and Other Fairy Stories.' "

Bulstrode looked up. He smiled. "Wonderful idea, sir!"

He grabbed Barney Devine and led both of them into the dance as well.

Everyone was dancing! Jack and Kathleen swayed together upon the hill while a pair of delighted watershees perched on Kathleen's shoulders. Seamus and Boric turned about and saw a new crowd of leprechauns trooping into the dell.

"What is it, Seamus?" the king asked.

Muldoon smiled. "A touring troop of Irish dancers!"

"Aaahhh!" Boric cried in horror.

"Too late!" Seamus answered. He called to the newcomers. "Go for it, lads!"

The bands struck up an Irish jig.

Then there was dancing beyond any ever seen before and a clapping of hands and stomping of feet so great that the very foundations of the Earth might shake and the wondrous tree of nature flutter her limbs in time.

The dancing troop began as the others watched and clapped along, but the joy was too great, the moment too wondrous. Soon everyone was dancing, and the great joy seemed to rise from the dell to fill the entire sky.

Such moments as this couldn't last forever. It had been a wondrous day. The grand party drew to a close. The bands played a final waltz.

Kathleen and Jack, winded from what they'd done before, sat and watched upon the hillside.

Groups of guests waved good-bye and vanished.

The bands disappeared, though the music played on. Leprechauns and fairies both were vanishing now, Barney and Jericho, the chamberlain and Lady Margaret. Seamus Muldoon and King Boric waved their beer tankards in a gesture of thanks toward the couple on the hill. Then both Seamus and Boric were gone as well. Only Jessica and Mickey were left, dancing in each other's arms in the center of the deserted dell.

The music faded. The two looked up and waved. Jack and Kathleen waved in return. Then Mickey and the princess were gone as well.

Jack put his arm around Kathleen.

He pulled a seashell from his pocket, the same shell Kathleen had given him not so long ago.

They looked at it together.

"It is beautiful," Jack said softly. "I can see it now. I can. It is the second most beautiful thing I have ever seen."

Kathleen looked at him. She had tears in her eyes. They kissed again, then turned to leave.

And all that remained in the dell was two floral garlands, Mickey's and Jessica's, left on the ground amid a riot of wildflowers.

It was a fine beginning.

And in January 2000, Hallmark Entertainment Books will present . . .

THE 10th KINGDOM
by Kathryn Wesley

The 10th Kingdom is a contemporary drama set in a fantasy world where magic and fairy tale characters come to life. A young woman and her father are transported into a magical world, which is both frightening and funny. There they race to save the 9 Kingdoms, governed by trolls and goblins and the descendants of Snow White, Cinderella, Red Riding Hood and other members of the fairy tale nobility, from The Evil Queen.

A major ten hour television event on NBC. And coming soon on video from Hallmark Home Entertainment.